I0733364

THE NOOSE OF A NEW MOON

By Helen Harper

BOOK ONE OF THE WOLFBRAND SERIES

BOOK COVER DESIGN BY YOCLA DESIGNS

BOOK COVER DESIGN BY YOCLA DESIGNS

Prologue

She didn't feel very well. Her skin was cold and clammy, and her whole body was shaking. It was like that time last year when she'd had the flu, except something about this felt worse. No, not something. *Everything* about this felt worse.

She curled into a ball on the hard floor, wishing she had a blanket or something to hold for comfort. This wasn't right. It didn't take an adult to work that out.

She could dimly hear footsteps approaching from the other end of the corridor. She felt herself stiffen. And then *he* was there, gazing at her from the other side of the metal bars with a smile on his face.

'Angelica.' He said the word as if it were a caress and it made her skin crawl. Every time he said her name, another part of her shrivelled up. The worst part was that he knew it. That was why he kept saying it.

'Angelica. My angel.' His eyes crinkled at the edges as he continued to smile. 'You are my angel now, aren't you?' He pointed at her arm. It still hurt. 'You have my mark on you. It proves you're mine.'

She didn't move. All she could do was stare at him like a dumb animal.

He turned away, gesturing to someone out of sight. A plate appeared, which he held up in front of her. She could smell it before she could see what was on it. Steak. Raw, thick bloody steak. Her mouth watered. God, she could probably eat a horse, let alone a single steak.

'Angelica,' he purred. 'Are you hungry?' He picked up a corner of the steak between his finger and thumb. A single drop of blood trickled onto the white plate. 'I will feed you, Angelica. If you're good.'

She managed to unfurl her body and stand up on trembling legs. She reached one thin arm out through the bars. He jerked the meat away, dangling it just out of reach. 'First,' he said, 'I want to see. Change. For me.'

She shook her head. No.

From the other side of her cell, someone shouted out, 'Don't do it! You don't have to do it! You don't—' He didn't get to finish his last sentence. His words were twisted into a high-pitched scream. A

—

moment later he fell silent once more.

The man in front of her continued to smile pleasantly. 'You see, Angelica? You have to obey. If you don't, it won't be nice for you.'

A sudden wash of crystal-clear understanding hit her. He could hurt her as much as he wanted, but she wasn't his to command. He couldn't do this to her. She wouldn't let him. She raised her chin, defiance flickering in her eyes, and she uttered a single word. 'No.'

He wasn't dismayed by her answer; if anything, it seemed to please him. He dropped the steak and ground it into the floor with his heel. He gestured again. 'Bring him,' he said.

She tensed and tilted her head, listening. Oh no. She shook her head. 'Don't,' she whispered. 'Please.'

The man's smile widened.

The two men carrying her father dragged him into view. He had several bruises on his face and she could smell his blood, both from old wounds and new. When he saw her, he jerked free from his captors and flung himself against the bars. 'Sweetheart! Are you alright? What have they done to you?'

From behind her father's back, the man raised a gun and pointed it at his head. 'Angelica,' he said. 'What's it to be?'

He didn't have to ask. The burning rage and bone-shaking fear had already taken over. She was no longer in control – *it* was. She snarled and her body twisted, then she snapped towards the bars that confined her, slamming into them again and again and again. There was only one thought in her mind. Kill.

The man smiled down proudly at her tiny, quivering, werewolf body. 'Good girl. Good girl, Angelica.'

—

Chapter One

When it comes to werewolves, the one thing nobody talks about is how itchy their balls become when they're covered in a layer of soft, fuzzy fur. Devereau Webb reflected on this small matter as he padded through the small copse of trees planted artfully around the children's play park.

He wasn't far from the entrance of the building he called home. He could, of course, hunker down and perform lupine yoga to use his tongue to deal with the offending itch. He knew it was possible because he'd already tried it, but this was the mouth with which he kissed his niece on the cheek. Once he'd satisfied his curiosity that the feat was physically possible, the niggling part of his brain that remained human wouldn't allow him to do it again. More's the pity.

He did his best to put the mild discomfort out of his mind and paused underneath a small oak tree. Dawn wasn't far off, and he fancied he could already see the sun rising over the top of the buildings to the east of the city. Dew covered the ground causing an earthy smell to rise and permeate the air, masking the usual city scents of petrol, rubbish and people.

A flicker of movement to the far right caught his attention and his body quivered involuntarily. Rat. He resisted the urge to bound after it. He was a predator and he was hungry, but he had standards.

A solitary taxi appeared from round the corner about three hundred metres away. It trundled along the road before pulling up at the curb just beyond the line of trees where he was waiting. He watched, sinking back on his haunches, as a dishevelled couple reeking of alcohol and sex and the optimism of youth staggered out from the back seats.

As the taxi pulled away, the woman bent down, unbuckled the straps on her shoes and slid the offending articles from her feet. Devereau tilted his head and focused on her. Vodka and cranberry – that's what she'd been drinking. Her perfume was light and floral, clashing with the pungent smell of her companion's aftershave which was still eye-wateringly strong even after a night on the town. She wobbled slightly as she straightened up, her shoes in her hand.

Less than three seconds, Devereau decided. He'd be on her in less than three seconds, even if she ran. He shivered, his golden fur rippling down the length of his body.

The man was wearing a patterned shirt and skinny jeans. They didn't suit him. He had broad shoulders and thin legs, so the tight denim made his torso look as if it were balancing on toothpicks like a canapé at a party. A juicy morsel of pink flesh ready for the eating… A sliver of drool escaped from the corner of Devereau's mouth. He licked his lips.

'Babes.' The woman had a thick accent, London through and through. 'Babes.' She waved at her boyfriend to get his attention. 'Take my shoes, babes.'

The man did as he was told. From the trees, Devereau Webb snorted. The couple froze.

'Do you think that's…?' the woman murmured.

The man nodded, a taut movement that emphasised his fear. His eyes darted from side to side as they attempted to pierce the gloom. 'Don't worry,' he said loudly. 'It'll be fine.'

Devereau could smell his terror. Literally. He licked his lips again.

The man reached across and took his girlfriend's arm. 'Come on.'

They started moving, hurried steps that took them away from where Devereau was watching. 'What if he comes after us?' the woman whispered urgently.

Devereau Webb smiled.

'I'll fight him off.' The man's grip on the shoes tightened. The blustering bravado in his voice was almost painful. 'He won't hurt us.'

Devereau stood up and stretched then stepped out from the cover of the trees and padded silently after the scurrying couple. They turned down a path to the left, heading to a block of flats a mere stone's throw from his own high-rise building. As they did so, the woman glanced over her shoulder. When she saw him, less than twenty metres away, she let out a tiny squeak.

The man's head turned. His eyes widened as they travelled the length and breadth of Devereau Webb's massive wolf body.

I know, Devereau thought. Bigger than you imagined, right?

The man yanked his hand from his partner's, dropped the shoes to the ground where they fell with a loud clatter, and spun round. A heartbeat later he started to sprint, pelting away as fast as his matchstick legs could carry him.

The trouble with running, Devereau considered, was that it made you look like prey.

The woman didn't move. Devereau was well aware that it wasn't because she didn't want to, it was because sheer terror had rooted her to the ground. Her body was quivering, shaking visibly from head to toe. Even her teeth were chattering.

Devereau didn't alter his speed. Keeping his movements smooth and steady, he strolled up to her. She couldn't tear her eyes away from him.

He gave her one long look, and then forced the change. Golden-tipped fur gave way to smooth skin, and his scars and tattoos became visible again. His bones snapped and his blood fizzed… And then he scooped up the woman's shoes with a human hand and held them towards her. 'I believe these are yours.'

At first she was unable to speak. She swallowed, still shaking uncontrollably. After a moment, though, she pulled back her shoulders and raised her chin a fraction of an inch. There. That was better. 'Thank you, Mr Webb,' she murmured. Her trembling fingers took the shoes.

He grinned. 'Call me Devereau.' He nodded after her boyfriend who had flung himself into the lobby of his block of flats and was desperately trying to barricade the door with a plant pot. 'You can probably do better than that, you know.'

All she could manage was a tiny nod. Devereau shrugged. On two feet rather than four, he wandered stark bollock naked towards his flat, pausing only to reach down and give himself a damned good scratch.

***

It had been easy to resist the urge to attack the couple; it was less easy to resist the urge to attack the four-inch-thick rib steak that he'd left on the kitchen counter. He'd been planning at least to sear it round the edges first, but his hunger got the better of him and he devoured it raw like a wild animal. He probably ought to work on that, he decided, as he licked his fingers.

He went to the fridge, took out a second steak and devoured that too.

His tastes had changed as well as his body. He no longer wanted curries with their clever layers of spice, and the bottle of hot sauce that he used to apply liberally to most of his food now lay unopened. He didn't even need to sprinkle salt on his meals any more. As long as there was meat, and lots of it, he was happy.

Tossing the plate into the sink, Devereau tilted his head slightly. He grabbed the dressing gown that hung over the back of a chair and shrugged it on before moving to the front door. He opened it to

—

reveal a short, dark-haired man whose fist was raised ready to knock. 'You're late, Gaz,' he murmured.

'Yeah.' Gaz shuffled his feet, dropping both his gaze and his hand. 'Sorry about that.'

Devereau stepped back and gestured him inside. 'What are the overnight numbers looking like?'

Gaz thrust a crumpled newspaper in his direction. 'I picked you up the morning edition,' he said, ignoring the question. 'I thought you might want to read it. You're only mentioned on page six today, so that's progress.'

Devereau took the paper without looking at it. 'Gaz...'

'Mrs Ford up on the eighteenth floor has complained again about her boiler. The plumber's been round and says it's fine, but she reckons he's pulling a fast one and wants you to speak to him.'

'What happened to McGann? Doesn't he usually fix the in-house plumbing problems?'

Gaz coughed. 'He, uh, moved out on Monday. He has a young family so, you know...'

Devereau's gaze hardened. 'No. I don't know.'

'Uh.' Gaz twitched. 'I think they wanted more space. And a garden.'

Devereau folded his arms. 'Did they, indeed?' He glared. Gaz shrank. 'What about the overnight numbers?' he repeated. 'How did we do?'

'The boys picked up a few wallets,' Gaz said reluctantly, his eyes shifting so that he no longer had to meet Devereau's hard gaze. 'But there's not a great haul. People don't carry much cash these days, especially the rich ones.'

'It's also the start of summer. Plenty of people are heading off on holiday. There are vacant flats and houses lying all over the city that are ripe for the picking. It's not rocket science. Jemmy a few locks, slip inside, take the odd valuable or two...' Devereau stretched out his arms. 'Not to mention all the damned Gucci, Armani and Louis Vuitton toting tourists who are too busy taking photos to pay attention to their bags. This is supposed to be peak season.'

Gaz didn't disagree. 'Yeah.'

'So? What's the problem?'

Gaz looked away.

Devereau sighed. 'Just spit it out.'

'Fucking coppers are still all over us, boss.' The words emerged in a nervous rush. 'Nobody can move without being followed. They can't nab *you* because you've gone supernatural, so they're going after the rest of us instead. And there's plenty of journos hanging around. You might be on page six but you're still big news. They're offering cash to anyone with an inside scoop. Things will die down sooner or later.' He sniffed. From his tone of voice, he didn't believe his own words. 'It's hard right now, innit? But things will go back to normal soon.'

Devereau felt a flare of rage. There was far worse than his Flock out and about in London. His people were non-violent. They didn't threaten and they didn't do any physical harm. They didn't even steal any sentimental shit. On the few occasions that a crew member nabbed something irreplaceable, such as a lock of baby hair pressed into an old key ring or a grubby old wedding band, Devereau had always made sure that it was returned anonymously.

The Flock skimmed the top, targeting the rich in order to help the poor. He gave to charity and he helped his community – it wasn't about merely lining his own pockets. Unfortunately, where Robin Hood and his Merry Men were venerated, the Shepherd and his Flock were despised.

Thanks to their efforts in the area, crime was at an all-time low. Muggings, rapes, stabbings … they didn't happen on the Shepherd's turf. The police should be giving him a fucking medal. Three successive mayors and four different governments hadn't been able to achieve what he'd done. His targets might feel like tragic victims but they only had to deal with the minor injustice of violence-free crime, unlike the people here who'd suffered generations of social injustice that affected their education, job prospects, housing and health. *His* people were the real victims.

'For fuck's sake,' he muttered. He strode over to the window and gazed out. It was barely seven in the morning and London was already wide awake. He glowered at the city laid out in front of him before dropping his gaze closer to home. There was a couple he didn't recognise standing near the car park. Even from this distance, they looked far too smart and well-dressed to belong. The woman was brunette with long hair clipped back in a tight bun, while the man wore an immaculate blue suit and held himself too stiffly. They stuck out like a sore thumb.

Devereau narrowed his eyes. No doubt they were more of the journalists Gaz had been talking about. He considered marching down to confront them and make it clear that they weren't welcome. It was tempting, but it wouldn't improve his current situation. He tore his eyes away.

Fourteen storeys below his window, three people barely out of their teens were milling around on the path. He recognised them immediately. Unlike the journos, this lot had grown up here. He'd seen them change from cheeky kids to horny teenagers to young adults who cared about their community. Hell, last year one of them had baked him a bloody cake for his birthday. They were *his* people; he wasn't going to abandon them just because every so often he turned furry. His tastes might have changed, but his motivation hadn't.

He watched the glum trio. It didn't take an expert in body language to recognise how unhappy they were. Devereau unfastened the catch on the window and opened it slightly. Two weeks ago, he couldn't have made out much more than the murmur of their voices from this distance but since he'd been bitten things had changed. No, not things. *Everything* had changed.

'None of this is our fault,' the dungaree-clad young woman complained.

'Yeah,' her friend muttered. 'We're being treated like animals just because *he's* an animal.'

'I saw him the other night, you know. He's not an animal.'

Devereau relaxed slightly.

'He's a monster.'

He slammed the window shut and turned away.

'Boss?' Gaz asked. He twisted fingers together and looked anxious.

'How many people have come forward so far?'

Gaz swallowed. 'Come forward?'

'To be bitten,' he growled. 'To be *turned.*'

Gaz paled slightly. 'I thought the law meant that…'

Devereau felt his anger hardening into something colder. 'Since when did we care about the law?'

'Boss,' Gaz whispered, 'nobody else wants to be a werewolf.'

The door swung open and Alice stomped in, pigtails whirling. She threw herself onto the sofa and reached for the remote control.

'What's wrong with you?' Devereau asked. She didn't answer immediately. He nodded at Gaz, who got the message and withdrew, relief written all over his face at his temporary reprieve from further questioning.

Devereau walked over and sat beside his niece. 'Alice,' he said gently, 'has something happened?'

Her bottom lip trembled. 'I was supposed to be going swimming with Becky and Chloe. I got up early especially.'

Until recently, when her cancer had gone into remission, Alice hadn't been able to go swimming. Being healthy enough to go out for the day with friends and do normal kid things was a big deal for her.

'They've changed their plans?' he prodded.

'Chloe's mum said they were going to visit family instead.' She threw him a baleful glance. 'But I saw their bags. They're not going to see family. They're still going swimming.' Her mouth set into a mutinous line. 'They just don't want me to go with them.'

The cold rage in his veins turned to brittle ice and his right eyebrow started to twitch and spasm. 'Go back to your mum, Alice,' he said. He considered himself Alice's guardian as much as his sister Natasha was her mother. Being a werewolf didn't change that, but he wasn't best placed to look after Alice right now. 'Stay with her today.'

Her hurt was palpable. 'So now you don't want me either?'

He took her hands in his and squeezed them gently. 'I'll always want you. But I'm going to take a shower and head out.'

'Where are you going?'

He set his jaw. 'To see a woman about a wolf.'

Chapter Two

The building that housed Supernatural Squad didn't look anything like a police station. It was a terraced structure with a small supermarket nestled to the right and a boutique hotel on the left. Devereau had been there before – hell, he'd made his first werewolf transformation outside it, although he'd never actually darkened its doors and gone inside.

He looked up at the crumbling stonework. Four storeys high and goodness knew how many secrets inside. He ran a hand through his hair. Coming here was a mistake. Despite her choice of career, he quite liked Detective Constable Emma Bellamy but she would never help him. They were natural enemies.

The bellman outside the hotel, whose burgundy liveried outfit made him look like a clown, was staring at him. Devereau's lip curled as he stared back. He might be undergoing something of an existential crisis but he was still Devereau Webb.

'There's nothing to be afraid of,' the bellman called. 'Supe Squad are strange but they don't bite.' He smiled slightly. 'Unlike you.'

Devereau straightened his shoulders. So his reputation preceded him. 'I'm not afraid.' There was more distaste at the notion in his tone than he'd intended.

'That was probably the wrong choice of words,' the bellman said. His expression remained friendly but Devereau still eyed him suspiciously. Perhaps he was an alright guy. Or perhaps he was in the police's pocket.

'I'm Max,' the bellman offered.

'Devereau.'

'I know. I saw you out here the other week. You know – when you caused all that commotion and showed the world that you'd been transformed into a wolf without anyone knowing about it. Our guests were all aflutter. Bookings have been up by a third thanks to you.'

Devereau grunted, 'You're welcome,' and nodded at the man. He could hardly walk away from Supe Squad now, not without losing considerable face. He sighed, set aside his regret at coming here, then stalked up to the door and rang the bell. Maybe no one would be in. He picked absentmindedly at the peeling varnish on the door frame and waited.

When the door finally opened, it wasn't DC Bellamy who peered out but a redheaded woman in a smart skirt suit whose mouth was puckered in disapproval. She gazed at him for a long moment, her expression inscrutable. She didn't even say hello before she turned her head and shouted over her shoulder. 'Fred! You'd better get out here!'

Devereau frowned. A moment later, the young police constable he'd seen with Bellamy on a few occasions appeared. It might be an old adage that police officers were becoming younger, but here was the truth right in front of him. This Fred fellow didn't look as if he were old enough to vote, let alone wield a Taser and uphold the letter of the law. However, he was wearing a uniform so unless he was playing dress up he really was a police officer. Devereau shrugged. Whatever. It wasn't his business if the coppers wanted to employ children.

'I'm here to see DC Bellamy.'

'Why?' asked the redhead. 'What have you done now?'

Devereau chose to ignore that question.

The young constable blinked at him. 'Er, she's not here.'

He could have worked out that for himself. 'What time will she be in?'

'In a fortnight. Give or take. She's on leave.' He smiled apologetically. 'I can probably help.'

Devereau wasn't sure whether he felt relieved or disappointed at Bellamy's absence. 'That's alright.' He waved a hand. 'It's not important.' Much.

'Who's out there?' called an imperious voice from inside the building. 'Liza, who is it?'

Fred stiffened while the redhead, presumably Liza, rolled her eyes. 'A werewolf,' she shouted back.

There was a loud clatter as something fell to the floor. Devereau glanced round Liza and Fred and into the building. Any normal police station had stringent security systems and self-locking doors to prevent members of the public wandering in where they weren't supposed to be. Such measures didn't appear to have caught on at Supe Squad; anyone could enter easily. Interesting.

He considered this anomaly as a man in his early forties emerged from a room at the end of the corridor. He was rubbing his palms together and blinking owlishly out at the light.

'You dropped your mug of tea, didn't you?' Liza muttered. 'And I'm going to be the one who'll have to clean it up.'

The man didn't appear to hear her, or he chose not to. As he strode forward, Devereau gave him the once over. He was wearing a blue suit and tie, both of which looked far too formal for the decaying Supe Squad building. His hair was thinning and dyed an unfortunate shade that was too dark for his complexion. He had a lanyard hanging round his neck with his ID clearly displayed. Supe Squad was a tiny operation: surely its size would negate the need for such security measures. Devereau peered more closely to try and read it.

The man smiled and held it up. 'I'm Detective Sergeant Owen Grace. I'm here on secondment while DC Bellamy is away.' He grinned broadly, adding to his air of pomposity rather than detracting from it. 'But I'll soon be posted here permanently.'

Devereau's gaze slid to Fred and Liza. Neither of them appeared particularly happy at that prospect. He shrugged again; it made no difference to him because the only police officer he'd speak to was Bellamy. And if she wasn't here, he was wasting his time. 'I'm here to discuss a personal matter with DC Bellamy. As she's not in, I'll be on my way.' He turned away.

'Who is that?' he heard DS Grace ask.

'Devereau Webb,' Liza answered.

There was a sharp intake of breath, then Grace barrelled out and blocked Devereau's path. The smile had gone from his face. 'We've been planning to get in touch with you, Mr Webb.'

Fred coughed. 'Actually, DC Bellamy said she was going to speak to him after she got back from her holiday.'

'There's no time like the present, PC Hackert.' DS Grace gave him a hard look. 'I'm not a soft touch like Detective Constable Bellamy. I don't believe in adjustment periods. The law is,' he paused for dramatic effect, 'the law.'

Devereau rolled his eyes. 'Go on, then.' He stepped towards the policeman, deliberately encroaching on his personal space, not close enough to be deemed aggressive but enough to be annoying. 'Why do you need to speak to me?'

Grace stood his ground, ignoring Devereau's proximity. 'Are you,' he enunciated carefully, 'a werewolf?'

'Why?' Devereau answered. 'Are you looking for a demonstration?'

'A simple yes or no will suffice, Mr Webb.' Grace licked his fingers, took out a notepad and pen and turned to a new page, poised to write.

Devereau leaned forward. 'Yes.' He smiled. 'That's spelled F. U. C. K. Y. O. U.' He pulled back. 'In case you're not sure.'

'I'm perfectly capable of spelling without your help, thank you.'

—

Grace scrawled something on the paper. 'Your transformation was not legally sanctioned, was it? In fact, you ensured you were bitten illegally so that you could become a werewolf and avoid prosecution for your past crimes. Right?'

Devereau didn't blink. 'I'm not obliged to answer that.' Even though that wasn't true. 'And you know what? I'm not obliged to stand here and listen to you either.'

DS Grace's eyes rose to meet his. 'No,' he said. 'You're not. But you are obliged to remove yourself from your current address. All werewolves must reside with a one mile radius of Lisson Grove. It's the law, Mr Webb. And the law…'

'Is the law. Yes. You've already said that.' Devereau folded his arms. 'Tell me, do you honestly believe that ghettoising supernatural creatures, who have more power at their fingertips than humans can ever dream of, is a good idea?'

'It doesn't matter what I believe,' Grace said stiffly. 'I am here to uphold the law. And the law states that you need to live in or near Lisson Grove.'

Devereau reached inside himself. Within a second, fur sprouted from his face. His teeth grew, sharpening to fine, predatory points and his mouth started to change shape to accommodate them. 'Make me,' he rumbled. He unfolded his arms and raised one hand.

Grace flinched.

Devereau snapped his fingers and his features smoothed back to those of a human.

Grace's jaw worked silently. To give him his due, he recovered quickly. 'You have seven days to move your residence, Mr Webb. Seven days from this moment. One-hundred-and-sixty-eight hours.'

'Or what?'

'There are not many legal bindings when it comes to your kind,' DS Grace murmured, 'but some things are immutable. Your address is one of them. If you do not accede, we will act.'

Devereau raised an eyebrow. 'We?'

'The police, Mr Webb. And the government.' Grace snapped his notebook closed. 'Society deserves to be protected from any and all dangers. There are innocent people who could be put at risk by your very existence.'

He was remarkably earnest and Devereau itched to punch him hard in the face.

'You're subject to the vagaries of the moon,' Grace went on. 'You could endanger others. It's for the good of everyone that you move to a secure area where you can be monitored more easily. I know it's not fair, but it's my job to ensure that people are safe. It's why I signed up to the police in the first place. We help. We don't harm.' He nodded meaningfully. 'Have a good day.' Then the detective walked back into the Supe Squad headquarters without another word.

When Devereau Webb was a child, he'd frequently run foul of authority figures. There had been one physical education teacher who'd taken grotesque joy in getting into his face and yelling at him, spittle flying from his mouth. Sometimes it was because Devereau had forgotten his kit or hadn't tackled an opponent effectively during a football game. Often, though, the yelling wasn't for any good reason. Mr Stone had simply known that his aggression would get a reaction. And every time that Stone had achieved his goal and driven him to the brink, Devereau had felt a stiff knot of pain form between his shoulder blades, jabbing at him. Seconds later he inevitably snapped and shouted back – or worse. When he'd finally slammed his fist into Stone's nose and broken it, he was immediately expelled. The school had assumed the expulsion was a punishment, although that couldn't have been further from the truth.

Devereau had learned that the knot between his shoulders was a sign that he was reaching his emotional limit. The last time he'd felt it was when he'd confronted the werewolf clan alphas on Alice's behalf and asked them to turn her so she could beat her leukaemia and they had refused. That had resulted in his extreme – and some might say illogical – efforts to be transformed into a wolf himself. Now he felt the same knot of tension building up again.

He breathed in deeply through his nose. Fuck this guy.

Fresh-faced Fred Hackert sidled up to him. 'Are you sure you've really only been a werewolf for a couple of weeks?' he asked, doubt colouring his words. 'Because I've never seen a wolf, even a naturally born wolf, with the sort of control you just displayed. Transforming your face just like that…' He shook his head. 'Wow.'

'So you're some sort of werewolf expert, are you?' Devereau snarled.

Fred paled and took a step back. 'No, just…' he swallowed. 'Never mind.' He scratched awkwardly at his hand. 'Look, Emma – DC Bellamy – was honestly going to give you more time before she approached you about joining the others in Lisson Grove. She would have done it differently to DS Grace. But there are a couple of occasions when human law really does affect supernaturals. Firstly, if more vamps and wolves are turned than is allowed, and secondly if they are found living outside their designated area. I know it doesn't seem fair, but in return you're exempt from all other human interference. As long as you don't harm any humans, of course,' he added hastily. 'But usually supes deal with that sort of thing amongst themselves.'

Devereau forced himself to breathe normally. The knot was already starting to ease. 'So what *does* happen if I refuse to move?'

Fred glanced at Liza. Her lips pursed before she explained. 'It happens from time to time and usually the supes would sort you out. Unfortunately, Mr Webb, I suspect that your case will be treated differently. There is some precedent. Chances are that you'll be locked up in a specially designated institution that's run by humans. I rather think the government will enjoy making an example out of you.'

'You're talking about sending me to prison?' He paused and glared at her as if it were all her fault. 'Because I refuse to move house?'

Liza ignored his expression and shrugged. 'Essentially. It's worse than you might think, though. It'll be worse than prison.'

'How so?'

She didn't look away. 'You're a werewolf now. Everything is different for you. You've not experienced a full moon yet, and when you do its power over you will be extraordinary. If you're shut away and unable to exert your full lupine abilities during the moon's change, you'll go crazy. It used to be called lunacy for a reason, you know, and there have been plenty of cases like yours. Besides, wolves are pack animals. Most of them are grateful to live with their own kind.'

'I'm not most wolves.'

'No,' she said quietly. 'I can see that.' She hesitated for a moment, as if unsure whether to continue. Then she went on, 'There are supernatural beings who don't live in London. There are vampires and gremlins and pixies – and even werewolves – who choose not to accept the law as it currently stands. But they stay out of sight and they keep their true selves hidden. That wouldn't be so easy for you to manage.'

'Because I'm a career criminal who can't keep his head down?' Devereau asked with only a faint trace of rancour.

'Because your face has been plastered all over the tabloids since you transformed for the first time right on this spot,' Liza said simply. 'You're not exactly inconspicuous, Mr Webb.'

He stared at her for a moment, then glanced at the bellman who was still standing outside the hotel and trying desperately hard not to eavesdrop. 'Max?' he called. 'Where can I get a drink around here?'

'There's a bar in the hotel but it doesn't open till later,' the bellman answered. 'There's a Clan Carr pub not too far away that might be open in the next hour or so. Or there's Heart. It'll be quiet at this hour, but I don't think it ever shuts.'

'Heart is the vamp hangout? The one owned by Lord Horvath?'

Max nodded. 'You don't often see werewolves in there.'

In that case, Devereau decided, it was perfect. It was barely ten o'clock in the morning – and all he wanted to do was to get blindingly drunk.

Chapter Three

Max was right: despite the hour, Heart was open to all comers. The neon sign, shaped into the glowing image of a biologically accurate heart, was lit up and the door was wide open. There was a fanged bouncer outside who was doing a good job of looking alert, although Devereau suspected he was only there for effect rather than a genuine need for security at ten o'clock in the morning. Certainly the American tourists on the other side of the street weren't going to cause any problems; they were happily snapping away with their iPhones before finding the courage to dart across and take selfies with the tuxedoed vamp.

Devereau waited until the tourists had departed before making his approach. At first the bouncer didn't react but, when Devereau drew closer and it became obvious that he was planning to enter the club, he straightened up with a glint of recognition in his eye.

'Good morning, Mr Webb.'

Devereau offered a brief nod in return. He wasn't in the mood for small talk and he wasn't going to pretend to be surprised that the vamp knew his name. The faster he could get to a bottle of whisky, the better. Unfortunately, the bouncer didn't appear keen to allow him to pass through Heart's front door.

'Are you here to see Lord Horvath?'

'No.'

'Because he's at home at the moment. I can call him and make an appointment, if you like.'

'I'm not here for Horvath,' Devereau growled.

'Are you here to make trouble?'

'I'm here for a fucking drink.'

The vamp didn't react to his snarl. 'Wolves don't usually come here.'

'So?'

'It's probably best if you find an alternative venue.' The vamp smiled nastily, opening his mouth just enough to display his fangs. He tilted his head a fraction to the left and Devereau noted his earpiece but, even with his newly enhanced hearing, he couldn't make out what was being said.

The vamp stepped back and, with a grimace, gestured to the door. 'However,' he said, 'if you really do want a drink then you're welcome to come in and have one.'

Finally. It was tempting to rub the vamp's face in the fact that he'd been told by some blood-loving middle manager to let him in, but Devereau knew better than to make an issue of it. After all, you never knew when you'd need a favour from a toothy vamp bouncer.

He swallowed his ego and nodded. 'Thank you.' The look he received in return was nothing but suspicious but Devereau chose to ignore it and ducked inside.

The gloomy interior was at odds with the daylight outside. Although vampires didn't turn to dust in sunshine or burn up at the first hint of dawn, Devereau knew that they preferred the dark. Perhaps Heart was trying to give the illusion that it was permanently night.

He looked around. Despite the low light, the club's opulence was striking. This was only the main lobby and it reeked of money. Devereau had an eye, and a penchant, for such things. He reached out to brush his fingertips against the dark-red flocked wallpaper. It felt expensive and the colour matched the faint tang of blood clinging to the air. Well, this was a vampire club...

He walked through to the main club floor. The smell of blood was now overladen with something else, a herbal concoction that made his nostrils twitch. Whatever it was, it smelled incredibly alluring. His pulse accelerated and a curious sensation of delight zipped through his veins. Glancing round, he spotted the cunningly disguised air vents. Whatever the scent was, it was obviously being pumped through the whole room. He doubted that it was purely to conceal the tang of iron-rich blood; no, the herby smell was designed to enhance the customer's experience. If the vamps packaged it and sold it on the open market, they'd probably make a fortune.

There was music to accompany the enticing aroma, although it was a chilled-out melody rather than the harder dance beats that probably vibrated from the speakers later on. He noted the rather large and showy throne on the empty balcony area and the various booths dotted around the mezzanine floor. There were fewer than twenty people in the club; they all appeared to be either staff members or hardened drinkers who didn't let the time of day stop them from getting their alcoholic fix.

Hoping that they would all be more interested in their drinks than making conversation, Devereau walked up to the bar. 'Double whisky,' he grunted.

The barman put down the glass he'd been polishing meticulously and raised an eyebrow. 'What kind?'

'Whatever's nearest.'

The barman nodded and turned away, reaching up to the Famous Grouse optic to pour Devereau's drink. Before he could, however, there was a delicate cough. 'Not that one. Mr Webb is a special guest. Give him the Balvenie instead.'

'Are you sure?'

The female vampire standing less than a metre away stared hard at the barman. He swallowed and moved to a glass cabinet, almost tripping over his feet in his haste to do so.

Devereau glanced at her. All of a sudden, his day was looking up. Clever dark eyes, smooth brown skin covered with a smattering of tiny freckles, a cute button nose and perfect red bow lips confronted him. He already knew that vampires were physically attractive. All the better to seduce you with. In the same way that scorpions had stingers, vampires had good looks. He had never seen any vampire who looked quite like this, though.

His gaze travelled down. She was dressed head to toe in a tight leather catsuit that accentuated her tiny waist. When he saw the fuzzy purple slippers on her feet, however, Devereau couldn't stop himself from barking out a short laugh.

The vamp grinned and shrugged. 'What can I say? I wasn't expecting a guest of your stature to wander in this morning.'

There was something oddly contagious about her smile, or maybe it was the heady herbal scent in the air. Either way, Devereau felt himself grinning back. His tension was already easing. 'Let me guess,' he said. 'You're the one responsible for allowing me inside. Your bouncer was going to turn me away.'

'Don't take it personally, Mr Webb. We've learned to be wary of lone wolves. Usually when one tries to gain entrance, it's because they're looking for a fight.'

'I'm not looking for a fight. And you can call me Devereau,' he murmured.

Her eyes glinted. 'Very well.' She extended a manicured hand. 'I'm Scarlett.'

He took her hand and shook it, resisting the temptation to kiss it. He had the sudden notion that everything about this woman, from her words to her clothes to the way she smiled at him, was deliberate. Even her ridiculous slippers. There was something slightly odd about her. He couldn't quite put his finger on what it was, but he was sure it would come to him.

The barman placed a heavy crystal glass in front of him. 'The Balvenie,' he said.

Devereau could already smell it. Hints of vanilla, cinnamon, nutmeg combined with earthy peat.

'It's fifty years old,' Scarlett told him. 'And to buy the bottle, you'd have to fork out almost fifty thousand pounds.'

He looked at her. 'Are you trying to impress me?'

Her gaze remained steady. 'Yes.'

Devereau reached for the glass, lifted it to his lips, then threw the contents down his throat. Scarlett winced. He licked his lips and shrugged. 'It's alright, I suppose.'

She laughed, a crystal-clear sound that rang across the near-empty club and made the other punters look up from their drinks. He caught a few knowing glances and he realised what was going on. Vampires were predators – and Scarlett here had just found new prey. Him. Strangely, the knowledge didn't bother him.

'So, Devereau,' she said, drawing out his name with a deliberate purr, 'what brings you here at this hour of the day?'

'I hear that Heart is the place to be. I thought it was about time I checked it out.' He continued watching her. Right now it was Scarlett he was checking out, not the club. She looked back at him, doing exactly the same thing.

'And?' She moved forward slightly until her hips were touching his. 'What's the verdict?'

'I'm withholding judgment for now.'

She placed a hand on his arm, a light touch that still made him shiver. 'Well, let me know if there's anything I can do that will help you make up your mind.' She stepped back and sat on a bar stool nearby.

Devereau let a moment or two pass before glancing at her again. 'You don't have to babysit me. I won't cause any problems. I wasn't looking for conversation or company.'

'I know,' she answered. 'You have the look of someone who's having a very bad day and wants to drink himself senseless. You might not want company, Devereau, but you need it. I'm here to offer a sympathetic ear. And I promise you won't even have a hangover afterwards. Call it your first dose of supernatural therapy. Whatever you say here won't go any further. Here at Heart we offer all sorts of services.'

He considered telling her to get lost. 'And what will you demand in return?'

A smile played around her lips. 'Nothing that will harm you in any way. Besides, I'm a vampire – I've been here for fifty years. There's nothing you can say that I've not heard before. There's nothing to be afraid of.'

He gave her a look of mild irritation. That was the second time in as many hours that someone had accused him of being frightened. These people had a lot to learn. 'I'm not afraid.'

'There you go, then.' She gestured towards him. 'Tell me all your woes.'

Devereau sighed. He supposed he had nothing to lose. He needed advice and, in the absence of Emma Bellamy, it appeared this vampire was all he was going to get. He hesitated for a moment, considering where to start. 'It's taken years to get to where I am. The Shepherd. The man who looks after his flock. I've earned my respect. I've built a community.'

Scarlett raised a dark eyebrow. 'A community? Is that what criminal organisations are called these days?'

He growled. 'We might be based on crime but our success goes far beyond that. I only did what was necessary to help my people.'

She tapped her long fingernails on the bar. 'I'm sensing a but.'

He gave her a long look. 'Nothing I do is by accident. I deliberately allowed myself to be bitten enough times to be transformed into a wolf. I wanted the power that the werewolves have. And I wanted to show the clans that they're not as special as they like to think they are.'

'You wanted revenge because they refused to turn your niece,' Scarlett said mildly.

'You know about that?'

'You'd be surprised at how much I know.' She waved at him. 'Carry on.'

His eyes flashed. 'I don't like it when people say no to me.'

'Your niece is a child. To turn her into a werewolf would have caused far more problems than it would have solved. But, hey,' she raised her shoulders, 'I'm not judging.'

Devereau raised his empty glass at the barman who nodded. 'I think that's exactly what you're doing,' he said softly. 'In any case, I thought it was a clever next step. Create a new clan with my own people. Take what power and strength I already have and turn it into something else.' He grimaced. 'Except it's not turned out that way. I misjudged how far my people were prepared to follow me.'

The barman placed a fresh glass in front of him. Devereau eyed it for a moment and then, like before, downed it in one.

'Oh you poor baby,' Scarlett mocked softly. 'You thought becoming a werewolf would turn you from a prince into a king. You thought your people would love you even more. Instead, they fear you. They might even hate you.'

Devereau couldn't deny it. 'I expected some resistance. I thought they'd come around eventually but there are people moving away to escape the supposed threat that I've become. People I used to trust. People I've helped. There are others who see me and turn in the opposite direction.'

'They're weak. And stupid. People often are.'

'My niece's friends no longer want to spend time with her.' The bitterness gnawed at him. 'She's done nothing wrong but they're afraid to be with her because of me. And now I'm being told that if I don't pack my life up and move to Lisson fucking Grove, I'll be locked up. Locked up! Not because I've done anything wrong but because of my postcode.' His jaw clenched. 'I can't abandon my people.'

'It sounds to me as if they've already abandoned you.'

Devereau's face spasmed into an angry snarl.

Scarlett rolled her eyes. 'What?' she asked. 'Do you want a glass for that whine? Or are you simply looking for sympathy? That's not the sort of therapy I offer. I didn't realise big bad Devereau Webb was such a moany bastard. You said it yourself – you planned this. You *wanted* this. You've got more power at the tips of your furry paws than you could have ever imagined and all you're doing is complaining about it. Some members of the supernatural community haven't had the choice you've had. They're supe whether they want to be or not, but they still have to deal with the rest of the world's derision. Humans will always hate what they fear. And you're hardly alone in the world. There are hundreds of werewolves. Pick a clan to join, and you'll have your new little world all ready for you.'

'Follow *their* rules, you mean. Be *their* leashed dog.'

'Big fucking deal. From what I've heard, you're already strong enough to make a splash. You'll rise through the ranks quickly enough. Get over yourself and adapt. You're not a teenager, so stop sulking and move on. You know you have to.'

Devereau's fingers tightened round the glass until it cracked. He hadn't gotten himself bitten to become someone else's lapdog, he'd done it to prove to the four clans that they didn't hold all the cards. It had been a petty act, but that didn't mean it wasn't justified.

He cursed and released the glass. 'So which clan then? Which one would you join?'

'I'm not a wolf.'

He folded his arms.

Scarlett smiled. 'Fairfax is a possibility, but they're a mess right now. They've been weakened because their previous alpha was an idiot, and they won't establish a new leader until the next moon in just under a week's time. You'll rise quickly through the Fairfax ranks, but you won't learn as much as you could as with the others, and you'll always be viewed as weak for joining them. Sullivan is out – Lady Sullivan will recognise you for the threat you are and probably refuse you. If she does accept you, she'll do everything possible to keep you down. And Lady Carr eats boys like you for breakfast.'

'So McGuigan, then.'

'They're broke, so they don't have the resources to do much. Someone of your capabilities could help them with that.'

'Create wealth for someone else, you mean.'

Scarlett simply looked at him.

'It's not much of a choice.'

'No,' she agreed. 'Unless you go back to your original plan.'

His eyes narrowed. 'Ignore the law and stay with my own people? Force them to accept me whether they want to or not?'

'Not that.' Scarlett leaned forward until she was so close he could feel her breath hot against his skin. 'Start anew. Create a new clan with yourself at the top. You still own the full moon rights to Regent's Park, don't you? For three nights you have sole access to run around it with as much wolfish abandon as you like. The other clans have to make do with St James's Park, which is far smaller. You have five times that space all to yourself. That's already quite a lure for any wolves looking to jump ship. Poach the best wolves from all four existing clans for yourself, for Clan Webb.' Her lips curved. 'You could do a lot worse. The rather pesky human authorities might take umbrage, but you strike me as the kind of person who is adept at getting around the law when it suits him.'

Devereau considered what she'd said as he met her eyes. 'Why do I have the feeling that this is the reason you sat down next to me?' he murmured. 'You want me to cause trouble for the clans. You're a vampire. You want to see the werewolves in chaos and the government up in arms against them.'

'No,' she said, 'I don't want that. I want to see supes succeed. *All* supes.' She bared her teeth. 'Even the furry ones who sulk.'

He gazed at her, finally realising what it was about her appearance that wasn't quite right. 'You only have one fang.'

She displayed it to him. 'I lost the other one. It was very careless of me.'

'One-Fanged Scarlett,' he said. 'It kind of suits you.'

She ran her tongue over her lips. 'Good,' she said. 'I'm pleased to hear it appeals to you.'

The stirrings of hot lust Devereau was feeling were reflected in Scarlett's eyes. He reached across and brushed a dark curl away from her face. 'Why don't we continue this conversation somewhere more intimate?' he suggested.

Something flashed across her face: triumph – or was it regret? 'I can think of nothing I'd like better,' she said. 'But let's take a rain check until you're in full control of yourself.'

He frowned. 'What's that supposed to mean?'

With the tip of one finger, Scarlett drew a line from his cheekbone down to his mouth and briefly caressed his bottom lip. Then she pulled away. 'I'll see you soon, Devereau Webb. I can promise you that.'

Chapter Four

Gaz's hands were crammed into the pockets of his jeans and his shoulders were hunched, guarding him ineffectively against the incessant drizzle that had turned everything grey. England in early summer. What joy.

'Are you sure about this, boss? It looks kinda … skanky.'

Gaz was nothing if not a master of the understatement. The building they were standing in front of had definitely seen better days. Three of the grimy windows had been smashed in and replaced with flimsy plywood. The guttering was filled with overhanging moss, and the front door had several dents in it where it had been kicked in on at least one occasion.

Devereau knew that things weren't any better inside. There was a definite aroma of damp seeping through the walls, and the grubby floorboards were less rustic chic and more rotting death traps. The wallpaper might have once been pristine white but now it was stained yellow with years of nicotine and all manner of other, indefinable stains. Still, he'd stayed in far worse places when he was younger and this place did have two things going for it: firstly, it was as close to the boundary of where he was allowed to reside as he could get, and secondly, the landlord had been willing to rent it to him. Most of the others had taken one look at him and slammed their doors in his face. That was their prerogative, of course, but Devereau Webb had a long memory and he never forgot a slight. They'd live to regret their lack of courtesy.

'It'll do,' he answered. For now.

'Maybe I could round up some of the others,' Gaz said. 'We could get a team together to do the place up a bit.'

Devereau's eyes narrowed a fraction. Gaz was the only person who'd chosen to help him move in today. He was above grovelling, especially to those who'd decided to turn their backs on him after years of loyal service. Alice had wanted to help, but he wouldn't have her here. She was better off back at home with his sister, Natasha, where she'd be safe.

'I don't need any help.' He glanced at Gaz. 'You can get yourself home now, if you want.'

He didn't miss the look of relief on Gaz's face. 'Are you sure? Because…'

'I'm sure,' Devereau said shortly.

Gaz nodded and turned, trotting away as quickly as he could before clambering into his car and switching on the engine. He offered a single guilty wave and drove off.

Scarlett the sexy vampire had been right about one thing, Devereau reminded himself: he'd brought this on himself. He'd connived to be turned into a werewolf and now he had to suck up the consequences. Fortunately, he was more than man enough to meet the challenge.

Ignoring the ugly lace curtains that were twitching in at least three of the other houses along the street, he strode up to his new front door. He'd barely set foot across the threshold when he heard the rumble of several engines approaching. Several expensive engines.

He glanced round and saw three sleek black cars pulling up. Well, well, well. The werewolf clans were bringing out the big guns – and they were working together. This would be interesting.

The driver of the first car stepped out and walked round to open the passenger door. Devereau wasn't surprised to see Lady Sullivan, the alpha wolf of the Sullivan clan, step out. Her steel-grey hair was pulled back into a severe bun and her iron-hard eyes flicked once at him before glancing towards the other cars. Their doors opened to reveal Lady Carr and Lord McGuigan.

None of them were smiling so Devereau plastered on the cheesiest grin he could muster. 'A welcome party! How lovely! I expect the ticker-tape parade in my honour will be happening later. Is no one from Clan Fairfax coming?'

Not one of the werewolf alphas reacted; instead they strode up and formed a semi-circle around him.

'I didn't realise that werewolves were famous for their marching bands,' Devereau drawled. 'There's no other way you could have learned those sorts of synchronised movements.' He pointed at Lord McGuigan. 'Piccolo, right?' He glanced at Lady Sullivan. 'And I'm betting you're a triangle kind of gal.'

Lady Sullivan inspected her fingernails. 'Your pathetic attempts at humour aren't going to impress us, Mr Webb.'

'Please,' he said, 'call me Devereau. We're all friends here.' He paused deliberately. 'Right?'

Lord McGuigan folded his arms. 'We've been waiting to talk to you in person for some time now. Let's just get to the point, shall we? How many times were you bitten before you turned?'

'That's already been covered.'

Lady Sullivan sniffed. 'Just answer the question.'

Fine. 'Four times.'

'We only have a record of one bite, which occurred when you deliberately antagonised a Sullivan wolf.'

Devereau shrugged. 'Well, I can guarantee I received four bites, one from each Clan. I'm an equal opportunities kind of guy, you see.'

'That's not possible.' Lord McGuigan glared at him, clearly convinced he was lying. 'Our records are very detailed. They have to be. We always know exactly who has been bitten and when. You were bitten once, by one werewolf.'

'Let's just say,' Devereau replied, 'that I made use of a certain potion that encourages … absentmindedness in others.'

'What potion?' Lady Sullivan snapped. 'What are you talking about?'

A potion that was far too dangerous to speak of; a potion that enabled the drinker to re-live the same twelve-hour period up to four times. 'I couldn't possibly say.'

McGuigan let out a loud snort. 'He's probably too embarrassed to admit that he's so weak it took only one bite to start his initial transformation.'

'Except,' Lady Carr purred, 'nobody, no matter who they are, is turned after only one bite.' She broke away from the semi-circle, moved towards Devereau and reached out to stroke his arm. He didn't react. 'Devereau Webb, get onto your knees.' Suddenly there was an odd note in her voice.

He raised his eyebrows. 'Why would I do that?'

Lord McGuigan frowned. 'Your compulsion doesn't work, Lady Carr. That means he is strong after all.'

Devereau grinned.

'Let's set aside the question of Mr Webb's bites for now and move on to Regent's Park,' Lady Sullivan said. She looked at him coolly. 'You possess the rights to its use during the full moon.'

'I do.'

'Once upon a time, you offered us those rights.'

'I did.'

Her gaze hardened further. 'What do you want for them now?'

'Nothing.'

McGuigan jerked. 'You'll give them to us for free?'

'I didn't say that,' Devereau said. He smiled broadly. He was enjoying this.

'Join me,' Lady Carr told him. 'Join Clan Carr and you'll receive considerable bonuses in return. We'll rank you immediately. No

---

other wolf has ever received such a boon, most have to fight for their right to become a ranking wolf.'

'You only want the park rights,' McGuigan sneered. 'You'll leapfrog our traditions and rules just to feather your own cap.'

'You mean you won't?' Lady Carr shot back.

'I have a better idea,' Lady Sullivan interrupted. 'Hand over Regent's Park to me, and I'll see to it that you don't meet an untimely end.'

Devereau gazed at her. 'Why, Lady Sullivan, I do believe you just threatened me.'

For the first time she smiled. 'Why, Mr Webb,' she trilled, 'that was no threat. That was a promise.'

Devereau looked from one clan alpha to the next. 'You know, until now I had no idea what I was going to do. I was open to all options. But your visit has helped me to make up my mind.'

'And?' Lord McGuigan demanded.

'None of you has impressed me enough to want to join your clans. And none of you has frightened me enough, either.'

Lady Sullivan snorted. 'If you think that you can waltz into Clan Fairfax and take the top spot as alpha because it happens to be free, you're sorely mistaken. We wolves don't work that way.'

Devereau laughed. 'I'm not interested in Clan Fairfax. In fact, I think I'm going to keep Regent's Park for myself.'

'And what?' she scoffed. 'You certainly can't start your own clan, if that's what you're thinking. The humans will never allow it. You'll end up a lone wolf, and what you fail to realise is that we're pack animals by nature. Before the new moon appears, you'll be begging to join us.'

'Well,' Devereau said, 'I'll guess we'll just have to see about that.'

The three alphas were clearly rivals rather than allies, yet they exchanged glances that suggested they were considering banding together to bring him down right then and there. In the middle of the street. In broad daylight.

Out of the corner of his eye, Devereau saw one of his new neighbour's curtains twitch again. He hadn't got this far in life without knowing when to raise his fists and when to back down from a fight. He smiled and waved at the window. 'People around here are very nosy,' he said to no one in particular.

Lady Carr met his eyes. 'I have the feeling that you planned this. You were never going to agree to join one of our clans.'

'Do you know, I think you might be right,' Devereau said softly.

There was a sudden loud beep. Lady Sullivan's brow creased and she withdrew a slim, silver-coloured phone. At the same time, the driver from McGuigan's car walked over and murmured in his Lord's ear. Then Lady Carr's phone started ringing.

Devereau took a step back and watched them. In a few swift seconds, each alpha's attention had been diverted away from him to something entirely different. The question was what. And how could it help him?

None of the werewolves bothered with farewells. They departed as smoothly as they had arrived. One by one, they pulled away from the curb.

Devereau tapped his mouth thoughtfully then strode to his car. He didn't bother locking the front door of his new home. Frankly, there was no point.

***

He followed the trio of cars for a few streets. At first he'd assumed something had occurred at Lisson Grove, where all four clans were based. Rather than turn right to the werewolf stronghold, however, the cars turned left. Interesting.

Devereau reached for the illegal radio in his glovebox. It had come in handy on more than one occasion in the past, and he didn't think it would let him down now. He fiddled with it for a moment until the crackles told him he'd tuned in to the right frequency.

'The scene has not been secured. Paramedics are not safe to approach. I repeat, paramedics are not yet safe to approach. Stand by for now.'

'Acknowledged, Dispatch. We're waiting round the corner for now.'

There was another crackle and a different voice filled the air. 'We're going to need more officers on site. This place is a mess. We believe there are two victims so far, status unknown.'

'Any sign of the werewolf?'

Devereau hissed through his teeth.

'Not yet.'

'Armed police are on their way. They have authority to take down the wolf.'

He heard a satisfied grunt. 'Good. Those damned animals can't attack people like this and get away with it.'

Devereau's hands curled round the steering wheel and his grip tightened. No wonder the alphas had departed in such a hurry.

Despite what the general public – and his own community – might think, werewolves rarely attacked humans without provocation. But it sounded like that was exactly what had happened.

'This is Dispatch. Supe Squad have been informed. DS Grace is heading to Goodman's Alley. ETA twenty-five minutes.'

Devereau straightened. He knew Goodman's Alley: it was a tiny street in Whitechapel in the East End of London. He also knew exactly how to get there. While the three black cars in front of him turned right to take the most obvious route, Devereau turned left. His route was faster. Whatever was going on was something to do with werewolves and that meant he was involved, whether anyone else liked it or not.

Chapter Five

As he'd expected, the police had blocked off all the roads around Goodman's Alley. Prepared for such an eventuality, Devereau parked at the small Tesco Metro and continued the rest of the journey on foot. He moved swiftly and purposefully, noting the gathering crowd as people craned their necks to try and get a peek at whatever macabre drama was unfolding beyond the cordon.

Devereau gazed over the onlookers' heads and watched the tense-looking police officers outside the shabby terraced house. DS Grace, his expression harried and anxious, had already arrived but there was no sign of the three clan alphas. Satisfied that his knowledge of London hadn't let him down, Devereau nodded. Then he looked around for a way through.

Directly behind the house there was a small pub, the sort where old men gathered around a tiny bar to share stories of the good old days. Its front entrance was on the street parallel to Goodman's Alley, but fire regulations meant that there would be a rear exit which no doubt backed onto the house itself. All he had to do was to get to the pub without being seen and he could nip through and gain access to the crime scene before anyone else.

The street on which the pub was situated had also been evacuated; clearly the police were taking no risks. There was a policeman at the far end directing people away and Devereau watched him for a moment or two. He might be a uniformed officer rather than a plain-clothes detective but it was obvious he knew what he was doing. From the way his eyes flicked around, never settling on one person for too long, the officer had the age and experience to do his job properly and ensure no member of the public got too close. Getting into the pub unnoticed wouldn't be easy – but it was far from impossible.

Stepping back, Devereau's gaze fell on a group of teenage lads. They were jostling each other and laughing. 'Drugs,' one of them said knowledgeably. 'Betcha.'

'Nah. It's a bomb. If it was drugs, they'd have raided the place already.'

'We should go round the other side and get a better look.'

No, don't do that, Devereau thought as he sidled up to them. 'Hey,' he said.

The nearest lad turned to him, obviously prepared to tell him to get lost. He looked Devereau up and down and thought better of it. 'What?' he asked suspiciously.

'I'll give you fifty quid if you go and tell that copper that you just saw someone running down the street to the left carrying a knife.'

'No chance,' the lad scoffed.

His dark-haired friend glanced round with interest. 'Hundred.'

Devereau didn't need to think about it. 'Done.' He reached into his pocket and drew out the cash.

A flicker of indecision crossed the boy's face as he weighed up whether he could keep the cash without completing the task. Then he looked again at Devereau, glancing at his hard features and visible tattoos, nodded and trotted off.

Devereau waited just long enough for the copper to turn to the boy and frown, then he slipped past the rest of the boys and darted to the pub's front door. The landlord hadn't locked it. He exhaled and went inside.

Ignoring the half-empty pints of beer and yeasty smell of alcohol, Devereau hopped over the top of the narrow bar and headed for the door marked Staff Only. He emerged into a narrow corridor. A kitchen to one side smelled strongly of grease, and a store room on the other side was stacked high with beer kegs and boxes of crisps. Devereau reached in and grabbed a pack of pork scratchings. He tore it open with his teeth then pressed on, exiting through the fire door into the scrap of garden beyond.

Popping a few of the scratchings into his mouth, he examined the rear of the house. At first glance it was smart and well maintained but, when he looked more closely, it was clear that the building had problems. It wasn't quite as bad as his new home, but the drainpipe was rusting and barely attached to the exterior wall. A pigeon seemed to have made a nest on top of one of the chimneys. There was no back door, but an old-fashioned sash window on the second floor had been propped open with a wooden stick.

Devereau eyed it. Even before he'd turned wolf, he would have managed that climb – there were more than enough footholds in the uneven wall – but he knew that he probably only had minutes before the armed police on the other side of the building made their entrance. He had no desire to get caught in any crossfire. His decision was made, however, when he heard a low, keening moan from inside the house. He was new to this game but it definitely sounded like it came from a werewolf.

He wasted no more time. Swallowing the last of the piggy

snacks, he tossed away the empty bag and vaulted over the rickety fence between the pub's poor excuse for a garden and the house. He scrabbled up the wall, his fingertips and toes using the uneven surface to gain purchase. Within seconds he was at the open window and shimmying inside.

The first thing he noticed was the smell of blood that permeated the air. It distracted him from all other considerations, even though the room he found himself in was beautifully decorated in the Scandinavian style that seemed so popular these days. There were numerous objects that he could easily make money on if he chose to nick them, but he wasn't here for that.

Devereau knew instinctively that the blood was fresh and had been spilled only recently. It overtook almost completely the lingering scent of floral perfume from whoever lived here. He pushed down his involuntary nausea and, more carefully now, edged towards the door and peered out. The moaning hadn't ceased – and it sounded like it was coming from only metres away.

Stepping into the hallway, he glanced up and down. There were three rooms to his left, each one smartly decorated in the same hygge style. Nothing about the house suggested supernatural, so why would a werewolf come here?

Devereau's eyes narrowed and his skin itched. It felt as if his own wolf was scratching at him, desperate to be set loose. He squashed it down as best as he could and turned right. The smell of blood was strongest from that direction – and it was also the source of the moans.

The floorboards next to the narrow staircase creaked, advertising his presence. He couldn't worry about that now. Throwing his remaining caution to the wind, he leapt to the last door and threw it open to reveal the horrifying scene beyond.

Devereau had witnessed a lot of things in his time but he'd never seen anything like this. The whole room was drenched in blood. It was everywhere: coating the floor, sprayed across the walls, splattered on the window and soaked into the clothes of two corpses lying, glassy-eyed, in the corner. Two men, both in their fifties.

Devereau swallowed and ignored them, focusing instead on the huddled shape by the window. It was a girl, thin boned, shivering and completely naked. Her face was buried in her arms, which were wrapped round her knees. He spotted a strange mark on her shoulder, a birthmark perhaps. It was difficult to be sure because her hair covered most of it.

Devereau sniffed, searching through the overpowering scent of blood to what lay beneath. The corpses were human but the girl was wolf. It didn't take a genius to work out what had happened. The question was why.

No doubt the smart thing to do was to turn and leave as quickly as he'd arrived. The police were preparing to enter and it was highly likely that they'd take no prisoners. Nobody knew Devereau was here; he could walk away and forget he'd ever entered this hell-hole. He hadn't become The Shepherd by chance; he'd survived on his instincts and grown his crime syndicate by avoiding unnecessary risks. He took a step back. It was definitely time to go.

And then the girl looked up.

She was young, far younger than he'd expected. Even with blood streaking her face, it was clear she couldn't be more than twelve years old, barely older than Alice, in fact.

He'd been told many times in the recent past that human children were never turned because their hormonal changes during puberty and adolescence made the process too dangerous. It was the reason the clans had refused to turn Alice, despite the very tempting carrot of the use of Regent's Park at full moon, which he'd dangled in front of them.

There were naturally born werewolf kids but their bodies were built to cope with the physical demands of lupine transformation. This girl didn't look like those children. She didn't possess their squat, heavy bones or their unruly hair. This girl had started life as a human.

She gazed at him dully, barely registering his presence, then she squeezed her arms tighter around herself and moaned again. He could still leave. In the unlikely event that the police didn't shoot her dead on sight, she was nowhere near clear-headed enough to identify him. Nobody knew he'd been there.

Devereau took another step back and cursed. Fucking hell. He peeled off his T-shirt and tossed it to her. 'Put that on. Now.'

The girl simply stared at him.

Devereau clenched his jaw. Lord McGuigan had tried to compel him through his voice and he knew that it was possible for supes to do that. He was also aware that it was far easier when you had the other person's real name. He had no clue what this girl was called or if he could compel someone to act, especially when they were in a state of deep shock like she was. But if he could use his authority to scare away drug dealers and force violent hoodlums to give up trying to kill people and join his Flock, he could deal with one small girl.

He drew in a breath and tried again. 'Put on the T-shirt.' Then he blinked. Man! He could feel it. He could feel the power beating through every word. He tried it again, even as the girl was already mechanically doing as she'd been told. He averted his eyes. 'Put on the T-shirt and stand up.'

She got up on shaky legs. His T-shirt swamped her but at least it covered her thin body. Devereau held out his hand and beckoned her towards him. He couldn't risk stepping in the pools of blood. He couldn't leave any trace of himself or he was likely to be indicted for the murders. But what he would do was to help the real murderer make her escape.

The girl stumbled forward and placed her hand in his. She was emaciated and hollow cheeked, her bones fragile and bird-like. He gave her hand a brief, reassuring squeeze. 'We're going to get out of here,' he promised. 'You just have to do what I tell you. Alright?'

The girl managed a tiny nod.

'I'm Devereau,' he told her. 'What's your name?'

She didn't answer. He saw her cracked lips and the bruises on her neck and a ripple of rage ran through him. Someone had done this to her; she hadn't done it to herself. 'Never mind,' he said. 'You can tell me later. Let's go.'

She let him lead her out of the room and down the hallway. As Devereau pulled her gently towards the window he'd come through, he realised the girl would struggle to get down to the ground. 'I'm going to give you a piggyback,' he said. 'Put your arms round my neck and hold on as tightly as you can.'

She did as he said. He hoisted her up until her bare legs were hooked round his waist.

'Hang on.' He stepped towards the window and then he paused. Everything had gone silent. The muted buzz from the outside world had all but disappeared. That meant only one thing: the armed police were about to enter.

Devereau moved fast. He swung out of the window arse first with the girl still clinging to him, and lowered his body until only his fingertips were curled round the windowsill. He let go as he heard the sound of the front door thudding open, booted feet running up the stairs and bellowed shouts of 'Armed police! Nobody move!'

He landed on his feet. The girl's body jolted against his back but she held on. 'Well done,' he muttered. 'We've got this.'

He hauled both of them over the fence and into the pub. Leaving from here was incredibly risky – he had no way of knowing what was waiting for him outside or whether the police presence had been beefed up – but he had no choice. There was no other way out.

He jogged back through to the bar and leapt to the door while the girl buried her face in his neck. He opened it an inch and peered out. There was no sign of the group of lads; no doubt they'd been forced to skedaddle after giving a false report to the police. The street was empty and the cordon had been pushed back in both directions. Devereau counted several uniformed officers at either end, some watching the crowd and some watching the street. Fuck. Getting out of here without being noticed was going to be next to impossible.

Should he find a hidey-hole inside the pub and wait until the hubbub died down? Given the bloody scene inside the house, he suspected that would take days rather than hours. Besides, when they discovered that their murderer had managed to escape, the police would probably initiate house-to-house searches. If he was going to get the girl away safely, he had to think of something else.

Closing the pub door again, Devereau moved to the grubby window and searched for another escape route. His brow furrowed. There was a narrow snicket on the other side of the street about thirty metres away from the pub door. He didn't know where it led and it could be a dead end, but it was unguarded. As soon as he made a move towards it, though, the police would swarm all over him. The only way he could get there unnoticed was if there was an appropriate diversion – and with police and onlookers to his left and right that wouldn't be easy.

'I'm going to let you go for a moment,' he murmured to the girl. 'I need you to stay here. Understand?'

He received a tiny grunt in response. He slowly eased her to the floor and waited to check that she was going to do as he'd asked. When she simply stood there, her bare feet planted on the grimy boards and her expression vacant, he nodded and got to work. This was a pub. It shouldn't be hard to find what he needed.

Devereau grabbed a large plastic bottle full of cheap lime cordial and emptied it in the sink behind the bar. There was a pot of pencils near the till; using three of them and a roll of yellowing Sellotape, he taped them to the bottle to make a shaky stand. Then he headed back to the staff area and into the kitchen.

He doubted the pub menu was extensive but they would definitely serve chips, and where there were chips there would be vinegar. Within seconds, he'd found a large bottle of the stuff and decanted a generous amount into the empty cordial bottle. Now for the store room. He resisted the urge to take more pork scratchings and looked around for the last of his ingredients. At the back of the room, next to an array of cleaning products, was a huge box of baking soda. His nan had worked in an old London pub just like this one and she always swore that nothing was better for scrubbing down the sticky mess left by drunken punters than good, old-fashioned baking soda.

Locating a cork from a long-since discarded champagne bottle, Devereau took all his equipment into the yard. He could hear the police searching inside the house so he moved quickly in case any of them paused and glanced out of the upper windows. He poured baking soda into the cordial bottle, rammed the cork into its neck and turned it upside down on its makeshift stand. He darted back inside the pub, threw the girl over his shoulders, went to the front door and reached for the handle. Any second now. Any second … NOW.

There was a spurting sound from the pub's garden followed by several screams from outside as shocked onlookers mistook the miniature home-made rocket for something far more sinister. They were still screaming when Devereau wrenched open the pub door and sprinted across the street towards the narrow alley. The girl's arms tightened round his neck and she hung on for dear life.

He didn't stop when he reached the alley. He couldn't be sure that his makeshift science project had drawn everyone's attention away from the street and up to the sky, so he kept moving, praying that there'd be a way out.

He swung to the right. The alleyway ended in a row of flat-topped garages. He climbed onto the nearest one and ran along the roofs before dropping down to the left and into another back street. As he sprinted down it, he wondered if he should turn wolf. He'd move faster, but he'd also risk drawing attention. And could he still carry the girl while in wolf form? He had no idea.

He didn't think anyone was on his heels but he was still far too close to the danger zone. Then he heard a screech of wheels.

Devereau glanced towards the end of the narrow lane as a car pulled up and blocked the exit. He hissed. Shit. Someone had seen him after all. They weren't going to escape – and there was nowhere else to go.

He slowed to a halt. He was a werewolf; he could still fight his way out and worry about explanations later. 'Listen kid,' he started, 'this is going to get messy. You need to…'

The car door opened and a hand beckoned him. Devereau stopped mid-sentence. Was that really who he thought it was?

The hand beckoned again and Devereau blinked. A moment later, he jogged forward.

'I suppose,' Scarlett drawled, 'you'd better get in.'

Chapter Six

Devereau bundled the kid into the back seat of Scarlett's car, clipping in her seatbelt when she seemed unable to do it for herself. Then he walked round to the passenger side and got in. 'Were you following me?' he asked conversationally.

Scarlett offered an arch grin. 'No.' She raised her eyebrows. 'Why? Would you prefer it if I had been?'

'I was merely commenting that it's something of a coincidence that you happened by when you did.'

'There's no coincidence, Devereau.' She put the car in gear and moved into the road. 'All three clan alphas are here because of a violent incident involving a werewolf. I'm surprised that Clan Fairfax didn't send their own representative in lieu of an alpha. Whatever, in the current climate any incident involving any supe is also the business of us vampires since we all tend to be tarred with the same brush. I was asked to offer my assistance to the alphas in tracking down the killer.' She glanced in the rear-view mirror. 'Lord Horvath will be pleased to see that she's already in supe custody.'

Devereau stiffened. 'She's not in custody. I'm not the fucking police. And there's nothing to prove that she was involved in whatever was going on back there.'

'Nothing apart from the fact that she reeks of at least three different people's blood. And when I say reeks, I mean she smells like she's been bathing in it in a way that most vamps only dream of.'

He looked sharply at the girl. His newly enhanced werewolf skills included a very keen sense of smell but he couldn't discern blood types. Scarlett obviously could. Three people? Not two? So who was the third?

'That means nothing,' he said. He pointed to the crossroads ahead. 'You can drop us here. I'm parked around the corner.'

'The Metropolitan Police aren't stupid, even if they occasionally appear that way,' she told him. 'They've already identified your car. If you go anywhere near it, they'll slap you into custody regardless of the girl back there. You know they're only looking for an excuse to put you away for good whether you're a werewolf or not.'

Devereau curled his fingers into tight fists. 'I didn't have anything to do with what happened in that house. Besides, I'm supposed to be answerable to supe law not human law.'

'Exceptions can be made to every rule, as I'm sure you're aware. And I don't think any of the clans will be jumping to your defence at any point in the near future.' She took her eyes off the road for a moment to look at him. 'Am I right?'

He exhaled sharply. That damned knot of tension in his back was tightening up again and his eyebrow was starting to twitch.

'That girl is dangerous whether she's killed anyone or not,' Scarlett told him. 'You can't deny that she's a werewolf, but she's obviously not naturally born. Her very existence threatens all of us.'

'So you're suggesting that we should put her down like a dog? She's a *child*.'

Scarlett didn't respond immediately. When she did, her voice was sad. 'When people think of supes, they think of power and wealth and strength beyond measure. They imagine that our lives are filled with nothing but parties and dancing and drugs and sex.'

Devereau put up his hands in mock horror. 'Wait. You mean they're not? But that's the only reason I became a werewolf. If I can't have sex and dancing and drugs on tap twenty-four hours a day, I want a refund.'

Scarlett clicked her tongue but he didn't miss the glint of humour in her eyes. 'We deliberately make ourselves appear that way because then the rest of the world views us as less of a threat. Yes, we've got money. Yes, we've got power. And yes, we've even got super strength. But, as you've already discovered, we are also despised. All supes are. Even those humans who come to play with us hate us deep down for having what they don't have, for being different. They're jealous of what we have and scared of what we can do. Our numbers are deliberately curtailed by the government, and we're told where to live so that we can be kept in check. We are fighting to make things better for all supes and we're making inroads but that girl threatens to put all our efforts back by several decades.'

Devereau gritted his teeth. 'Whatever she's done, it's not her fault.'

'No. It's not.' She looked in the mirror again and sighed. 'But nobody ever said life was fair.'

He turned his head to see how the kid was taking Scarlett's words but it was hard to tell. Her head was bowed and she was staring down at her bloodied hands. 'What's the point in fighting for supe rights if you're going to abandon your own kind along the way?' he asked softly. 'The girl stays with me. I'm taking full responsibility for her.'

'You're already a pariah because of how you got yourself turned.

———

If you don't hand her over to the clans, you'll only make matters worse for yourself.'

Devereau shrugged. 'So be it.' He looked at Scarlett, challenging her to argue further.

She smiled. 'I knew there was a reason I liked you.'

His eyes narrowed. 'Was this a test? Were you trying to goad me into giving up the girl to see what kind of person I really am?'

'It was no test.' She hesitated. 'I was curious how far you're prepared to go to help her. And I wasn't sure if you fully understood all the ramifications.' She stopped the car as the traffic lights ahead turned red. 'You have to understand that I am wholly loyal to my Lord. If Lord Horvath asks me what I know about the girl or where she is, I am bound to tell him. However, he's somewhat distracted these days so if he doesn't ask I won't tell. But you won't be able to keep her hidden for long. You'll have to come up with a better plan than hide-and-seek if you want to keep her safe. And if she kills anyone else, all bets are off.' Scarlett gave him a hard look. 'I mean it.'

'Noted,' he growled.

A car pulled up alongside them, music blaring from its rolled-down windows. A man in his early twenties in the passenger seat looked at Scarlett. It was obvious he immediately recognised her as a vampire. His blue eyes widened with morbid delight and he started to wave vigorously. 'It's daytime, bloodsucker! Why aren't you burning up, like the monster you really are? You know what God thinks of your kind, don't you? You're going to hell, bitch!'

Devereau put his hand on the door and prepared to get out. Scarlett touched his arm. 'No,' she said. 'I've got this.'

The man pointed to his neck. 'You gonna bite me? I'd like to see you try!'

Scarlett left the engine running as she unclipped her seatbelt and calmly got out. The man blanched slightly but he was too much of an idiot to back down. 'Whatcha gonna do? Eh? You don't know who I am. If you so much as breathe your foul bloody breath on me, I'll...'

Scarlett didn't give him chance to finish his sentence. She leaned down, grabbed him by the arms and yanked him out of the window. He screamed. She hauled him up against the car, pressing his spine against it, then she moved her face into his and deliberately exhaled.

'Let me go! Let me go!' He struggled against her, unable to free himself.

Scarlett rubbed her body against his and opened her mouth to display her single fang. 'In a moment,' she murmured. 'I just want a little taste first.' She grinned and looked down at his crotch. 'Well, well, well. That's quite some reaction you're having there. All that blood pumping to one place.' Her hand reached down until it was hovering just above his tented trousers.

The man screamed again. 'No! Don't touch me! I'm sorry!'

Scarlett tapped her mouth thoughtfully. 'Make it up to me. Get on your knees.' He threw himself down, desperate to do as she asked. She lifted one stilettoed boot. No furry slippers now. 'Lick it.'

Devereau could see that the man was shaking and he frowned. This was going a bit too far. He was all for standing your ground but he drew the line at humiliation. But this was Scarlett's gig so he held himself back and continued to watch.

The man's tongue darted out and he gave Scarlett's foot a single, delicate lick. She smiled again and kneeled down. 'Say thank you.'

'Th – thank you.'

She patted him on the head. 'You're welcome.' She winked. 'Watch that mouth of yours in the future.' She turned and sauntered back to the driver's seat while the hapless man scrambled up and threw himself back into his vehicle. His friend who was driving stared at him with wide, frightened eyes.

'And you're surprised that humans despise supes?' Devereau commented.

She turned on the engine. 'You're right,' she said. 'I probably shouldn't have done that. But sometimes the only thing you can do is fight back.' She glanced at him. 'You're turned on right now, aren't you?'

He didn't get the chance to answer. From the back seat, a small thready voice piped up, 'That was so cool.'

***

Try as Devereau might, he couldn't get the kid to speak again. He coaxed and cajoled but she returned to staring at her lap, her lank brown hair covering her face. At least he'd learned that she spoke English – and with a London accent. Unfortunately he'd also learned that she took a macabre pleasure in violence, or at least in the potential for violence.

He was glad that Scarlett chose not to comment on it; in fact, she even joined in his attempts to get the kid to speak. Her efforts were to no avail, but he was starting to sense that he could trust the vampire, as well as fancying the skin-tight pants off of her. He couldn't blame the idiot bloke who'd licked her shoe for his physical response to her; he'd probably have reacted in the same way if she'd pushed him up against a car. He was almost disappointed when their journey ended and she pulled up outside his house.

'So,' Scarlett said. She drummed her fingers on the steering wheel and wrinkled her nose thoughtfully. 'So.'

'So what?'

'You strike me as a man of deed and action rather than thought. That's not a criticism, by the way, but an observation. If I'm right, it will stand you in good stead. You can't simply hide yourselves away. For one thing, the police are going to come asking questions about your car. For another, if you can find out what really happened at that house you'll be in a better position to help the girl. You were right that she's a victim. She didn't turn herself into a werewolf – someone did that to her. The more you can find out what happened to her, the more sympathy you'll drum up for her. I'm not saying it will save either of you in the long run but it's a good start.'

Devereau considered her words. 'I'm not averse to a little investigation,' he said. 'It's not as if I've much else to do at the moment.' He met her eyes. 'Will you help?'

Scarlett's mouth twitched. 'A vampire help two werewolves?'

'I'm sure stranger things have happened.'

'Mmm. What's in it for me?'

'What would you like?' he countered. 'I'd offer to lick your boots but someone's already done that.'

She ran her tongue across her teeth. 'You can owe me. A favour of my choosing to be performed at a time of my choosing.'

'Very well.'

Scarlett raised an eyebrow. 'No caveats? You shouldn't agree so quickly without negotiating first.'

Devereau smiled slowly. 'Perhaps I don't want to negotiate. Perhaps I want to be in your debt.'

'Careful, Mr Webb. Sometimes I bite.'

He gazed at her. 'Sometimes I bite too.' He felt the girl's eyes on him from the back seat and pulled back; there was a time and a place, and this definitely wasn't it. 'Let me get her settled. Can you meet me back here later? This evening?'

She nodded. 'I can do that.'

He smiled and started to get out of the car. Scarlett called him back. 'Devereau.'

He half turned. 'Yes?'

'The full moon is almost here. You've never experienced one and I'm guessing that she hasn't either. It's not going to be easy for you, and the closer it gets the harder things will be. Your control will slip with each day and you'll have more power and strength within you than any other werewolf I've met. You should avoid close contact with others. You don't know what might happen otherwise.'

He flashed her a grin. 'You just want me all to yourself, don't you?'

She didn't smile back. 'I wish that were true.'

Chapter Seven

Wary of the curtain twitchers, Devereau hustled the kid inside as quickly as he could. She made no move to resist. Once the door was safely bolted, he felt the need to apologise. It was most unlike him.

'I know it's not much and it smells like someone's died. And the furniture is probably riddled with fleas. And the electric wiring is probably…' He didn't get chance to finish his sentence. The girl walked away from him up the creaking staircase. He followed on her heels. 'There's a bathroom to the right. I've checked the plumbing and there is hot water.'

Her expression didn't flicker and he had no idea if she'd even registered his words. She didn't glance towards the bathroom but turned in the opposite direction, into the nearest bedroom. There was a single bed with a bare mattress against the far wall and she made a beeline right for it. While he watched, she clambered on top of it, curled into a ball and closed her eyes.

Devereau blinked and took a step forward. Her chest was already rising and falling with the regular rhythm of sleep. She must have been exhausted.

He watched her for a moment or two then went back downstairs. He searched through the few boxes he'd brought with him until he found what he needed, returned and carefully tucked the duvet round her. She didn't move.

As soon as he was downstairs again, he got to work. He made a couple of phone calls before unpacking his things in a bid to make the drab house look a bit more homely and less threatening. Once that was done, he brewed some coffee and sat down with his laptop. Somebody somewhere had to be missing their daughter.

There was nothing on the recent local news or the Metropolitan Police's website, and nothing on any missing persons' websites. He tapped the keyboard and frowned. The police might take up to seventy-two hours before searching for missing adults but children were a different matter. If somebody had reported the girl missing they would have sprung into action, but he couldn't find a damned thing. He considered his options and then he made another call.

'Good day,' burbled an efficient robotic voice. 'You have reached St Agnes School. To report an absence, press one. To make enquiries about admissions, press two. To…'

Devereau rolled his eyes in exasperation. Fortunately, he already had the extension code he needed and he jabbed it in before he had to listen to any more of the monotonous droning. With any luck, Mrs Foster would be in her office.

'Rachel Foster.'

'Good afternoon, Mrs Foster. This is…'

'Mr Webb.' She sounded considerably more cautious than the last time they'd spoken. 'I would recognise your voice anywhere. I was planning to contact you this week. We need to speak about the library.'

Devereau's eyes narrowed. 'I was given to understand that it was on schedule to open before the half-term holiday in October.'

'Yes, yes, it will be ready. We're very proud of it and we'd be happy to give you a tour on a Saturday or Sunday so you can see where all your money has gone.'

'I'd rather get a tour during the week when there are children using it.'

'Mmm.' She hesitated. 'I'm not sure that's a good idea. Some of our parents are a little concerned, and there are health and safety measures we have to consider. As you know from Alice's time here, we take child protection very seriously.'

'You mean,' he said flatly, 'you're worried that if I come by when children are present, I won't be able to stop myself from transforming into a wolf and eating them.'

'*Obviously*, I know you won't do that but there are others who—'

He clenched his jaw. 'Fine.'

She rushed on. 'Mr Webb, you know how grateful we are for the money you gave us to build the library. We won't ever forget it. But our Board thinks it's better if we no longer call it the Webb Wing. Something more generic will probably be more appropriate.' The headteacher sounded nervous, and with good reason.

He hadn't given the money to the school because he wanted his damned name on a plaque; it had been Mrs Foster who'd suggested they call the new wing after him. That didn't mean he wasn't pissed off that she was backtracking now.

'So you were happy to use my name when I was nothing more than an alleged criminal in charge of my own crime network,' he said. 'But now that I'm a werewolf, my name is no longer good enough?'

'Uh, you see, the thing is—'

'Forget it,' he interrupted.

———

'Pardon?'

'I don't care what the library is called. You happily took a great deal of my money to build it. Call it whatever the hell you like.' His voice hardened. 'But in return for *my* silence on *your* prejudice, there's something I want.'

'I'm not prejudiced against you, Mr Webb. Nobody at St Agnes is. Our first duty is to preserve the safety of our children. Our parents put a great deal of faith in us to look after them. It would be remiss of us not to do everything we could to meet their expectations.'

Devereau didn't say anything.

Mrs Foster sighed. 'Fine. What do you want?'

'You mentioned child protection,' he said. 'That's what I'm interested in. I want to know if there are any schools in London that are dealing with the unexpected absence of a young girl about twelve years old. Caucasian, long brown hair, brown eyes.'

'You want to know *what*?'

'I'm sure you heard me the first time.'

'Mr Webb, even if I were prepared to give you that kind of information, there are three thousand schools in London. We deal with unexpected absences all the time. There's no way that—'

'Try.' He thought about the girl and the fact that nobody had reported her missing. 'She's probably already classed as vulnerable. I'm sure you have contacts and a network you can use.'

'Three *thousand* schools, Mr Webb!'

He gritted his teeth. 'Focus on the Whitechapel ones.' That was where he'd found her. It made sense that she'd be from that area.

'That's still a huge number of children—'

Devereau was done talking. 'I'll expect to hear from you by the end of the day.' He hung up. It was a long shot but worth the punt. Besides, Rachel Foster bloody well owed him.

He heard a car pull up outside and went to the window. A moment later, Alice burst through the front door. 'Oh my God!' she exclaimed. 'This is where you live now? It's a dump! What's that smell?'

A low-pitched growl rumbled from deep in the centre of Devereau's chest. 'You shouldn't be here. And why aren't you in school?'

'She had a check-up at the hospital,' Natasha said, walking in behind Alice with a bag in her hand. 'They called this morning and moved it forward from next week.'

Devereau stiffened. 'Is there a problem?'

She shook her head. 'It was just routine. She's still clear of cancer. The doctor is baffled but happy.'

They exchanged looks. Natasha knew exactly why Alice's leukaemia had vanished but nobody else did; even Alice herself didn't really understand what had happened. Detective Constable Emma Bellamy had given Devereau a gruesome potion that had cured the child. It had been a one-off and there would never be anything like it again. Given what he'd later learned the potion contained, that was a good thing.

'Why do you want some of my clothes?' Alice asked.

'It's a long story.'

She tilted her head, her pigtails falling to one side. 'Try me.' She put her hands on her hips and gave him a demanding glare. Any other time he'd have found it comical.

'Curiosity killed the cat, Alice.'

'And satisfaction brought it back,' she shot in return.

He gave her a long look and glanced at Natasha. 'Thank you,' he said. 'I appreciate the help. But you shouldn't come here again – and you definitely shouldn't bring Alice. At least not for a while.'

'You told me that werewolves aren't dangerous, Dev. You said that I could trust you and any other wolf who happens along.'

'And normally that would be true,' he said. 'But right now…' He didn't get the chance to finish his sentence. The creaking stairs were already advertising Alice's ascent upstairs to where the girl was sleeping. 'Alice!' he roared, running after her. 'Get back here!'

From somewhere above his head there was a loud snarl. Alice stopped dead in her tracks on the first landing. Devereau barrelled towards her and shoved her out of the way in the nick of time. A second later, a small grey-coloured wolf collided with him, jaws snapping.

There was a crazed look in her eyes and he had no doubt that she was out for blood. As he held up his arms to hold her off, her sharp teeth scraped against skin. She didn't stop. Her guttural growls and frenzied actions bore testament to her complete inability to control herself. Devereau shoved out a hand, unwilling to hurt her or to allow her to hurt him, but she was a ball of unstoppable fury. When her teeth couldn't reach his exposed face, her head dipped and she went for his leg instead, her canines ripping through the denim of his jeans and sinking into his flesh. Devereau howled in surprise and pain.

And then his wolf took over.

His clothes burst off, scraps of material flying in all directions. His muscles bunched and twisted and his bones snapped. Suddenly he was on all fours, his hackles raised as he bared his teeth and snarled at the girl. She snarled back. He was four times her size, and in a real fight she wouldn't have lasted a second, but she still wasn't backing down. Her pupils were tiny black pinpricks of madness.

He lifted one paw and swiped her muzzle in warning. He was master here, he was alpha wolf. Unfortunately, the girl wolf didn't care. Her jaws snapped and he registered her body tensing as she prepared to throw herself at him again. Goddamnit, she didn't know when to quit.

Devereau pushed forward, trying to back her into a corner where he might have some chance of controlling her. He only managed a few steps before she launched herself at him again, her white teeth flashing.

Thwack.

There was a soft thud. For a moment she paused in mid-air, her eyes clouding with confusion, then she collapsed in a heap at his feet. He saw the dart sticking out of her hindquarters and turned. When he saw who was there, tranquiliser gun in hand, his shoulders sagged in relief.

Chapter Eight

'You don't have to stay if you don't want to,' Devereau said to Dr Yara. 'I understand.' He wasn't going to force her do anything that made her uncomfortable. After all, nobody else from his former Flock had wanted to hang around.

The doctor fixed him with an irritated glare. 'I stay. I see worse things than furry children with big teeth in Syria. I am not frightened. You help me when I come to this country, Mr Webb. Now I help you.'

He knew better than to look a gift horse in the mouth. 'Thank you,' he said quietly. 'And I've told you before, call me Devereau.'

'Pffft.' She clicked her tongue loudly as if such an idea were completely preposterous.

'Well, I'm certainly not staying,' Natasha said loudly from beside the door. Alice had already been bundled into the car. His niece had protested all the way, but he was aware how close she'd come to being ripped apart. And from the way she'd been shaking despite her best efforts to hide it, so was she.

'I'm sorry about what happened.'

His sister looked at him. 'Me too.' She shook her head. 'First getting yourself turned into a wolf and now this. I hope you know what you're doing, Dev.'

He used to; he wasn't quite so sure now. 'I would never hurt Alice, Tash.'

She managed a smile. 'I know. You've been more of a father to her than her own dad. She's alive today because of you. But I have to put her first. We can't come here again.'

He nodded. 'Good. I'll stay in touch and when things are normal again…'

Natasha held up her hands. 'No, don't make promises you can't keep.' She leaned across and pecked him on the cheek. 'And don't get yourself killed, either.'

'Don't worry about me.'

'I always worry about you.' She smiled again, this time with a trace of self-mockery, and left.

Devereau glanced at Dr Yara. 'Make yourself at home.'

'Mmm.' Despite her willingness to help, she was clearly unimpressed at her surroundings. He didn't blame her.

'Will she be out for long?' he asked, jerking his chin towards the

---

girl.

'A few hours maybe.' She offered him a shrug. 'No more than four. It was not strong sedative.'

He nodded. 'Okay. Would you mind if I left you here and went out for a while? There are a couple of things I need to check out. I'll make sure I'm back before she wakes.'

'Is no problem, Mr Webb.'

'Devereau.'

Dr Yara's gaze didn't flicker. 'Is no problem, Mr Webb.'

He gave in. 'Thank you.'

Dr Yara inclined her head. 'See you later.'

***

With his car trapped in Whitechapel – assuming the police hadn't already towed it away to examine it for evidence that didn't exist – Devereau walked to Supe Squad. Located between the werewolf Clans in Lisson Grove and the vampires in Soho, it wasn't far and it gave him time to work through his thoughts. This certainly wasn't the day he'd been anticipating when he'd woken up this morning, but he was nothing if not adaptable.

He was briefly tempted to go the long way round and avoid bumping into other supes; it would cause fewer problems if he kept his head down. But if the clan alphas knew that he'd moved in nearby, so did every other supe with half a brain cell. And he was curious to see how those who weren't in power reacted to his presence. He knew what the three alphas thought of him but what about the rest?

Whistling tunelessly, he headed north until the elaborate wooden archway that signalled the entrance to Lisson Grove appeared. A group of women of various ages was standing on the corner in front of it. They appeared to be absorbed in their conversation but, as Devereau approached, they fell silent and stared at him goggle-eyed. He tipped an imaginary hat in their direction and grinned. His efforts were rewarded when he heard a muffled whisper as he passed them, 'Well, he's a lot sexier than I thought he'd be.'

Rather than pretend he hadn't heard them, he tossed his head ostentatiously and glanced back coyly over his shoulder. They all burst out laughing, although the one who'd made the comment turned bright red. Devereau smiled. He wasn't above making a fool of himself if it helped him win a few hearts and minds.

He continued on his way and passed beneath the archway. It was

———

probably his imagination but it felt as if the air shifted once he emerged into the official werewolf quarter. It wasn't an unpleasant sensation – quite the opposite, in fact. Some of the knotted tension that had been stoutly refusing to leave his body melted away. He inhaled deeply. Man, that was good.

Then he spotted the couple on the other side of the street. Hang on a minute – he'd seen them before. He growled. It was the same couple who'd been hanging around outside the tower block that he'd assumed were journalists. Devereau shook his head. He wasn't going to let them glide by this time. He turned in their direction.

A shadow fell across his path. A burly, heavyset male with bushy eyebrows and a dark expression moved in front of him. 'You're Devereau Webb.'

Devereau kept his expression neutral. 'I am.'

'They say your wolf is bigger than any that's been seen before.'

'I wouldn't know about that.'

'They say that you're telling everyone you were bitten four times.'

Devereau was starting to sense a theme and he also recognised the belligerent edge to the man's tone. He might not know a great deal about his new werewolf cousins but he knew people; this guy was building up to a confrontation. He wanted to goad Devereau into a fight, either to prove to the world that he wasn't scared of anyone or to prove that Devereau was nothing more than a liar and a weakling.

It would be easy to allow the confrontation to go ahead – and it would certainly discourage further attempts – but it wouldn't make anyone like him. Devereau could work on developing power and respect later; right now, being liked would get him further. 'You're a naturally born wolf, right?' he asked.

'Yeah.' The man bared his teeth and pointed to the tag on his arm. 'And I'm ranked epsilon in Clan Carr.' There was a definite glint of challenge in his yellow eyes.

Devereau didn't blink. 'Oh, I met your alpha this morning. Strong lady.' He leaned forward. 'Listen, maybe you can help me. When I change into my wolf, I get really itchy. You know, down there.' He gestured at his groin. 'Is there some kind of cream or salve I can use to stop it? It's embarrassing to ask, but you've always been a wolf so I figure you'll know better than anyone.'

The Carr werewolf stared at him and Devereau tried not to grin. He'd shocked the man out of his antagonism by referring to something so intimate, and implied a compliment by suggesting that his adversary might have the answer. Everyone, both humans and werewolves, usually responded positively to honesty. Devereau was being truthful: the itchiness *was* a problem.

Nonplussed, the werewolf took a step back. 'There's a Clan Carr shop on Booth Street,' he said grudgingly. 'Herbalist place. The owner's not ranked, but he's an alright kind of guy when you get to know him. He can give you something that will help.' He paused 'Just tell him that Cannon sent you.'

'Cannon Carr?' Devereau raised his eyebrows. 'Cool name. Thank you.'

'No problem.' Cannon nodded and stepped aside to allow him to pass. He didn't seem to realise that his actions indicated that Devereau was the superior wolf. Mission accomplished. Except, while he'd been chatting to Cannon, the two supposed journos had vanished.

Devereau hissed. If they knew what was good for them, they'd stay out of his way in future.

By the time he finally reached the familiar Supe Squad door, he'd had several similar supe encounters, not all of them with werewolves. One was with a pixie, and a couple of gremlins had yelled at him from across the street. Now all he had to do was charm the coppers as well as the supe populace and he'd be well on his way.

He knocked loudly on the door. He wasn't sure if DS Grace would be back from Whitechapel but it would be easier if he were. He mentally crossed his fingers and stood back.

Liza opened the door and scowled at him. 'Devereau Webb,' she sighed. 'Back again. Why are you here?'

'It's lovely to see you again, too,' he said with an easy smile. He pointed at her face. 'You have some crumbs on your cheek. Looks like chocolate cake to me.'

She grimaced and wiped them away. 'Yes.' She glared at him. 'And you're not getting any.'

'I wouldn't dream of asking. But now I know what to get you to thank you for your help. I appreciate the time you took to explain everything to me. I wanted to drop by to tell DS Grace that I've done what he asked and moved to an officially sanctioned address. I thought there might be some paperwork to fill in and this seemed like a good opportunity.'

'Mmm.' Liza looked at him coolly. 'For some reason, I didn't think you were the sort to voluntarily present yourself at a police station. And yet here you are, twice in one week.'

'It's a conundrum,' he said cheerfully. He dropped his voice to a whisper. 'I'm just trying to get off on the right foot and avoid making enemies. This is a good chance for me to turn over a new leaf and be on the right side of the law for a change.'

It was clear from the way she sucked in her cheeks that she didn't believe him for a second, and he liked that about her. He could charm the pants off the gnarliest of werewolves, but Liza would probably always be suspicious of him regardless of what he did. Of course it was her loss in the long run, but he had to admire her stubborn resolution.

'Who is it?' DS Grace called from inside the building.

There was something else that could be said about Liza: whether she worked with the police or not, she wasn't worried about masking her true feelings. A spasm of irritation crossed her face. 'Devereau Webb,' she called back. 'Again.'

Devereau made full use of the opportunity and stepped smoothly past her into Supe Squad. A strange smell lingered in the air but he ignored it and strode down the corridor towards Grace. He didn't want the detective to put him in an anonymous interview room; that wouldn't help at all.

He made it to the end of the corridor before DS Grace appeared from a room to the left and stopped him. 'Mr Webb,' he said. 'What excellent timing. I have a few questions for you.'

'I thought you might,' Devereau said smoothly. He glanced into the room. There were several desks laden with blinking computers, stacks of books and papers. Fresh-faced PC Fred Hackert was sitting on a small sofa with a mug of coffee in his hands. Devereau beamed at him as if they were old friends. 'Hey! How's it going, Fred?'

Surprised at being asked, Hackert jerked and glanced up. 'Oh, it's you. Yeah, things are alright.' He paused. 'Did you go to Heart the other day?'

'I did.'

'Did you meet any vampires while you were there?' There was something deliberately casual about his tone.

'I hardly think this is the time—' DS Grace started.

Devereau ignored the detective. 'I did. There was one lady in particular who was very helpful.'

Fred put down his mug and jumped to his feet. 'Oh yes? What was her name?'

'Scarlett.'

Fred's eyes widened. Behind him, Devereau heard Liza click her tongue in exasperation.

'Scarlett? You met Scarlett?' Fred gasped. 'How was she? What did she say?'

This was perfect. Devereau took full advantage and walked into the room. 'She was really helpful,' he said. 'She listened to all my woes and set me on the right track.'

Liza snorted. 'I'll bet she did.'

Fred frowned at her. There were two vivid points of colour high on his cheek. 'She's a good person, Liza.'

Liza rolled her eyes.

'You're not allowed to be in this room, Mr Webb,' Grace interjected. 'If you follow me to one of the interview rooms, we can get some privacy.'

'Sure.' Devereau shrugged as if it were no problem and stepped back towards the door. Then he stopped. 'Say, what is that smell? It's really strong.'

'It's a mixture of verbena and wolfsbane,' Fred replied eagerly. 'Only supes can smell it. The fact that you can smell it so strongly proves that you're a supe.'

'I kind of thought that turning into a four-legged animal did that,' Devereau smiled. 'But sure, let's go with smell.'

'I expect,' Liza said, 'that you're used to dealing with strange herbal scents after your visit to Heart.'

He glanced at her. 'Actually, I did smell something odd in there.'

'Uh huh.' She smirked. 'The vampires have their own concoction that they pump into the air. Whatever is in it is a closely-guarded secret, but it makes humans euphoric. It's like some kind of legal high.'

Devereau's eyes narrowed. 'And what does it do for werewolves?'

Her smirk broadened. 'It relaxes them. Stops them from feeling angry and aggressive.'

Fair enough.

'And,' she added, 'I'm told it also makes them highly suggestible.'

Something inside Devereau's chest hardened. No wonder Scarlett had made that remark about waiting until he was in full control of himself – and no wonder he'd opened up to her like he had. It had definitely been out of character. His eyebrow spasmed in annoyance.

'All this chat is completely unnecessary,' DS Grace blustered.

'You're right,' Devereau said. 'I only came to tell you that I've done as you requested and moved house. I'll write down my address for you.' He turned, searching for a pen and a piece of paper.

——

Spotting a biro on the desk to his right, he took it and grabbed a Post-it note at the same time. There was a wad of paper and several handwritten notes in front of the computer; he couldn't see the screen because it was angled away from him.

Devereau bent down to write and squinted at the notes at the same time. *12 Goodman's Alley. Registered owner Marsha Kennard.* He scribbled his new address and straightened up. 'Here you go.'

DS Grace snatched the paper from him. 'Why was your car in Whitechapel this morning?'

'I heard there was a ruckus over there and that a werewolf was involved,' Devereau said. He started his explanation honestly, though he wasn't planning to end it that way. 'I wanted to check it out for myself but I couldn't get close. By the time I realised I was wasting my time, the traffic was terrible. I left the car where it was and came back by public transport. I'll pick it up later.'

'You don't seriously expect me to believe that, do you?' Grace demanded.

'Well, I certainly wasn't involved in what happened at Whitechapel,' Devereau said. 'I was moving house when it all kicked off – whatever *it* was. I'm sure my new neighbours will confirm that, as will the three clan alphas who came to welcome me to the neighbourhood. You're free to check with them, if you like.'

'I don't need your permission to check anything,' Grace said. 'And I've already told you,' he added as if he'd just remembered, 'you're not allowed to be in this room.'

Devereau placed his hand on his chest. 'Oh, I'm so sorry.' He moved towards the door but before he reached it, he turned to Fred. 'I'm seeing Scarlett later tonight,' he said. 'Would you like me to pass on a message?'

Fred started to stutter. Devereau smiled politely as his eyes slipped to the computer screen. There was a photo displayed on it; it looked like an official mug shot. He immediately recognised the face grinning unapologetically out at him – it was of one of the corpses from Goodman's Alley. He scanned the text underneath it: *David Bernard. 48 years old.* Then he swung his gaze away.

'Tell her,' Fred said, 'tell her that … that … that … I'm thinking of her.'

Devereau nodded gravely. 'I certainly will.'

'Mr Webb!' DS Grace hissed.

Devereau smiled. 'I'm on my way, detective. Thank you for having me.'

Chapter Nine

When he got back home, the kid was up. She was sitting groggily at the table in the kitchen with a bowl of cornflakes in front of her. That wasn't the only thing that was different: instead of the permeating aroma of damp, there was a lemon freshness clinging to the air.

Devereau frowned at Dr Yara, who was humming away to herself and washing a cup at the kitchen sink. 'Have you cleaned up in here?'

'I do a bit,' she answered breezily.

'You didn't have to do that.'

'I know.' She turned her head and gave him a crooked grin.

'Thank you.' He paused and added, even though he knew it probably wouldn't do any good, 'Don't do it again.' He pulled out the wooden chair opposite the girl and sat down. She didn't look up. 'Hi,' he said gently. 'How are you feeling?'

Nothing. Not even a blink.

'Can you tell me your name?'

The girl raised her spoon and stared at it as milk dripped from its curved underside back into the bowl.

'How about where you're from? Or where your parents are?'

She slowly moved the spoon towards her mouth then chewed several times.

'Can you tell me anything about yourself at all?'

The girl swallowed her mouthful. 'I'm a monster,' she said so matter-of-factly that he jerked.

'No.' He gave her a ferocious glare but immediately regretted it when she flinched. He softened his features. 'You're not a monster.'

'I killed those people. Those two men.' She dropped her spoon with a clatter and stared at her hands. 'They're dead because of me.'

'What happened?'

She went back to resolutely ignoring him.

'Look,' Devereau said, persisting, 'I can help you. But I need you to tell me—'

Dr Yara walked up to him and placed a hand on his arm. She shook her head. 'No. Now is not good time. Martina must eat, bathe, then rest. She can talk later.'

'Martina? That's her name?'

Dr Yara shrugged. 'Is what I call her. It means—' she hesitated, searching for the words '—little warrior.'

Huh. He glanced at the girl. It suited her. Despite her quiet meek appearance, he knew deep down that she was a fighter. 'I want to help her, Dr Yara. But to do that, I need to know what happened to her.'

'When she is ready she will talk,' Dr Yara said serenely. She tipped her head towards the kitchen. Understanding, Devereau headed out. A moment later, Dr Yara joined him. 'Martina, she has great trauma. Lots of pain. She need time.'

'Pain? Physical pain?'

'No. It is in here,' she tapped her skull. 'But in here is worse sometimes.'

He nodded. He could understand that.

Dr Yara wasn't finished. 'But she also has scars. Bruises. I do not think these are from her wolf. Someone do this to her. Someone hurt her before.'

Devereau stiffened.

'And she has mark.' Dr Yara motioned towards her shoulder. 'Here. Is—' she struggled with the word '—like burn.'

'Burn?'

'You take iron and heat it and…' She grimaced.

'A brand?' Horror filled him. Someone had branded the child?

'Yes.' Dr Yara nodded. 'Brand.' She reached into her pocket and handed him a piece of paper. She'd sketched out a facsimile of it: a squiggly line intersected with what looked like the letter M. As he stared at it, Devereau sucked in a breath of pure rage.

Dr Yara looked at him pointedly. 'Your hands,' she said.

He looked down. Wiry hairs had sprouted all over the back of them and his fingers looked misshapen and claw-like. He clenched his jaw and forced his hands back into human form. 'Sorry.'

Dr Yara didn't appear concerned. 'Is no problem.'

'Do you think she'll change again? Is she still … dangerous?'

She shook her head. 'No. Now she is too tired.' She pursed her lips. 'Maybe later. Tomorrow perhaps. She cannot control what is inside her.'

Devereau rocked back on his heels. That was going to be a problem.

'Stress will make it worse. We must be careful. But is okay, Mr Webb,' Dr Yara said calmly. 'I will help her. And you will help her. It will be good.'

He sincerely hoped so.

***

His attempts to persuade Martina to speak postponed for now, Devereau elected to work on the few scraps of information he already possessed. He'd exhausted all of his leverage with the various bigwigs and power brokers in London in his efforts to gain full-moon access to Regent's Park. That was okay – it had been worth it – but it meant that now, in terms of research, Google was his only friend.

He started with the supposed owner of 12 Goodman's Alley where he'd found Martina and the bloodbath, and typed the name Marsha Kennard into the search bar. Scrolling through the results, he found only one listing for a Marsha Kennard in London. Given that it was for a funeral home notice from eight years earlier, he doubted it was going to be any use. Fortunately, when he searched for David Bernard, one of the men who'd apparently been killed by Martina when she was in wolf form, he had more luck.

'Thank you, LinkedIn,' he muttered under his breath. Apparently David Bernard was a high-profile solicitor who worked exclusively in financial law. He had a small office with a swanky address in Canary Wharf that Devereau made a note of. He wanted to know why a man like that had been in the small house in Goodman's Alley because there was no good reason that he could think of. There were plenty of bad ones, however.

With his research attempts completed for the time being, he picked up his phone. Rachel Foster hadn't called him back; she was probably hoping he'd forgotten all about their earlier conversation. She should know better. The school day had finished over two hours ago and she'd had plenty of time to fulfil his request.

'Mr Webb.' There was heavy resignation in the headteacher's voice when they finally connected.

'Mrs Foster.' Devereau smiled. 'Have you done as I asked?'

'Before I answer that, I want to know why you need this information. These are children we're talking about. If there's a chance that they could be in danger from the likes of you…'

He interrupted her. 'I don't hurt children. In fact, I don't hurt anyone.'

She snorted. 'That's up for debate.'

He couldn't blame her for being wary. 'I have a girl with me,' he said. 'I … found her. As far as I can tell, she's a runaway and she's in a great deal of trouble. She won't talk. I'm trying to find out who she is so that I can help her.'

'You should contact social services.'

He couldn't begin to imagine how an overworked social worker would deal with a near-adolescent werewolf who'd killed two people. 'Under normal circumstances that's exactly what I'd do, but I have good reason to believe that her life is in danger. I don't think that social services can protect her.'

'And you can?'

His response was quiet. 'You know I can. And deep down you know that I will.'

For a long moment, Mrs Foster didn't answer. 'I'm not prepared to give you a list of children from local schools. Not for any reason. You can threaten me all you like, Mr Webb, but I won't do it.'

'At no point have I threatened you,' he said, mildly irritated.

Mrs Foster drew in a breath. 'Send me a photo of the girl. If she matches any of the children who have been reported absent recently, I'll tell you who she is.'

'How do I know that you won't share her photo?' he asked. 'Someone is out there looking for her, and that someone probably wants to do her serious harm.'

'Well, I guess we'll just have to trust each other.'

Devereau ran a hand through his hair. 'Very well. Wait a minute.' He stalked back through to the kitchen. The girl had finished her cornflakes but was still seated at the table, staring into space.

'I'm going to take a photo of you,' he said gently. 'Would that be alright?'

She lifted her eyes to his. 'I can't do it,' she whispered. 'I'm too tired to change again.' Her shoulders hunched. 'I'm sorry.'

Devereau went very still. 'It's not a photo of your wolf that I want,' he said. He watched her carefully. 'Has someone taken photos of you like that before? When you've … transformed?'

She nodded mutely, her face pale.

'Who?' He growled the question. He couldn't help himself.

'I can't tell you.'

'Yes, you can. It will be fine.'

'If I tell you, they'll kill you.'

Devereau clenched his fists. He could feel his claws appearing again and the familiar jabbing pain between his shoulder blades. 'What about your name? Will you tell me your real name now?'

She shook her head furiously. 'No. I'm not allowed.'

'But—'

Dr Yara appeared in the doorway and threw him a warning look. He exhaled and nodded to indicate he understood.

——

'Okay,' he said. 'Okay. That's alright. Can I take a photo of your face?' he asked Martina, trying to remain calm. 'I'm going to share it with only one person. She's a teacher. She might be able to help us.'

The girl considered this. 'Okay,' she whispered.

'Thank you,' Devereau said. He meant it. He raised his phone, quickly took a photo then returned the phone to his ear. 'Mrs Foster,' he said, 'give me your mobile number and I'll send you the photo straight away.'

The headteacher didn't respond immediately. For a second, he thought she'd hung up. Then she cleared her throat. 'I heard that,' she said. 'I heard what she said.' She paused. 'Mr Webb, is this girl a werewolf?' Horror traced through her every word. 'Is that why her life is in danger? Because she's … she's … like you?'

Devereau didn't answer. He couldn't.

Mrs Foster spoke again. '0768 412 2085. It's my personal number. Hardly anyone knows it outside of my family and a small circle of friends.'

Devereau typed in the number and pressed the send button. He heard a faint ding as Mrs Foster's phone received it, followed by a rustle of papers. After that there was nothing, just silence.

'Mrs Foster?' he asked.

'She's not here. I don't know who she is.'

Fuck.

'She's not on any of the records I requested. Not from Whitechapel or anywhere else nearby.'

It had been too much to hope that she would be. 'Alright,' he said. 'Thank you for trying. I won't bother you again. I would sincerely appreciate you not telling anyone about this conversation.'

'I can assure you, Mr Webb, that I will speak of this to no one.' Her voice was stiff. 'I will look into other areas of the city and see what I can find out. No child should be turned into…' She didn't finish her sentence; she didn't seem capable of it.

'No,' he agreed. 'They shouldn't.' And then, because there was nothing left to say, he hung up.

Chapter Ten

Scarlett's expression was troubled. 'Those were Martina's exact words? "*I'm not allowed*"?'

Devereau folded his arms across his chest and nodded. 'And yet she let me take her photo and send it to someone else. She knows I'm actively seeking her identity and she didn't stop me.'

The vampire tapped her single fang with the tip of her fingernail as she thought. 'It's perfect kid logic. She's been told not to reveal her name under threat of terrible pain, but if you discover who she is under your own steam she can truthfully claim innocence. She *wants* you to find out who she is.'

'But she's too afraid to tell me herself.' Devereau nodded. 'That makes a sort of sense.'

'There is another explanation, of course,' Scarlett murmured.

He glanced at her.

'She's been compelled by another werewolf to keep her mouth shut.' She raised her eyebrows. '*Someone* turned her, after all. Someone burned that mark into her skin. It stands to reason that whoever did that would be trying to keep her in check. Unfortunately, if that's the case, it won't last. No living werewolf can maintain control of a turned adolescent. Maybe that's why she murdered two people – whoever turned her lost control of her and she flipped. Either way, right now that little girl is probably the most dangerous creature in the whole of London. The werewolves can't afford another PR disaster. Not right now. If they find out she exists…'

Devereau growled. 'They won't.'

It was obvious from Scarlett's face that she didn't believe him. Unwilling to debate the matter, he changed the subject. 'There's something else we need to discuss,' he said silkily. 'Actually, two things.'

'Mmm?'

'Heart.'

The tiniest smile flickered around the corner of her mouth. She reached out her hand and placed it flat against his chest. '*Your* heart, you mean? Is it lost?'

'No,' Devereau said, making no move to remove her hand. 'And no.' A beat passed. 'But there is a certain young police officer who may have lost his.'

Scarlett dropped her hand. 'You mean Police Constable Fred Hackert?'

Devereau held her gaze. 'What happened?'

There wasn't a trace of embarrassment in Scarlett's answer. 'I seduced him, like the evil femme fatale bloodsucker I truly am. Then, when I'd had enough of him, I dropped him.'

'He's in love with you.'

'What Fred feels isn't love. It's nothing more than boyish lust and the desire to possess what he can't have. He'll get over it.'

He folded his arms. 'That's rather cold, isn't it?'

'I made him no promises. It's not my fault if he read more into our brief fling than he should have.' She gave him a cool look. 'Is that it? Or are you going to tell me I'm a naughty vampire for playing with the little policeman?'

Devereau raised a shoulder in answer. 'I don't give a fuck about him. But what does bother me is that you used the shite you pump through the Heart ventilation system to get me to bare my soul to you.'

Scarlett laughed. 'That's what bothers you? You walked into the club like you were already defeated and you walked out like a new man. Nobody forced you into anything, least of all me. I could have had you chained to my bed within twenty minutes, Devereau. Instead I let you go. If you really have a problem with that, you're less of a man than I thought you were.'

'Chained to *your* bed?' He leaned forward and took hold of her wrists, one in each hand. He looked into her eyes, registering the challenge reflected there.

'Go on then,' she murmured.

He allowed himself a small smile then he gently pushed her back against the wall, pinning her in place.

'Do you even have a bed in this godforsaken hellhole of a house?' Scarlett asked.

'I have several.' Devereau's head dipped until his mouth was hovering over hers. He felt her breasts press against him as she held her breath. A faint flush stained her cheeks. Still holding her wrists, his thumbs stroked her forearms and he licked his lips. And then he released her and stepped back.

A tiny frown flickered across Scarlett's face. 'So much for the big bad Shepherd.'

He grinned at her as he tried to control his breathing. 'Maybe later you can become my Little Bo-Peep,' he said. 'But right now we have other concerns.'

Scarlett's gaze dropped to his crotch. 'Is that so?'

He didn't get the chance to formulate a reasonable answer. From the next room, there was the sudden unwelcome sound of breaking glass. A split second later it was followed by a staccato burst of gunfire.

In a split second, Devereau transformed. His clothes burst off, buttons and scraps of fabric flying in all directions. He bounded next door with Scarlett on his heels. Dr Yara and Martina were flat on the floor, glass all around them. The older woman's body was covering the girl's and, for the briefest moment, he thought the worst. Then he registered that they were breathing and uninjured.

Scarlett was at the side of the shattered window, flat against the wall. She craned her neck to peer out before whipping her head back in the nick of time. Yet another shower of bullets zipped through, flying over Devereau's body and thudding into the back wall. Pure incandescent rage flooded his veins.

'Three of them,' Scarlett muttered, her face rigid. 'One on the roof opposite and two on the street behind the blue car.'

From the floor there was a tiny whine. Devereau swung his shaggy head downwards. Dr Yara's arm still held down Martina's body but she wouldn't be able to hold her for much longer. Despite the trace of sedatives still in the child's system and her undeniable fatigue, the brush with death was forcing out her wolf. She writhed, patches of fur appeared on her arms, and he heard the familiar creak as her the structure of her bones snapped.

'Devereau.' Scarlett's voice was low but her warning was unmistakable.

He nodded. He knew.

Another three bullets smashed into the room. Devereau ignored them. Right now, he could either worry about the definite beasts outside or the potential beast inside. He chose the latter; she was closer.

In three steps he was there. Ignoring the distant scream from the street and the sound of running feet, he dipped his head and used his jaws to grab Dr Yara's arm. She squeaked in alarm, her frightened gaze meeting his, then she swallowed and allowed him to nudge her out of the way. She scuttled to the far corner of the room on her hands and knees, hissing in pain when shards of broken glass cut into her skin. Her movement attracted the attention of the gunmen outside and there was another shot but yet again it missed.

Devereau knew their luck wouldn't last and so did Scarlett. With an inarticulate yell, she threw herself to the side, leapt through the gaping hole where the window had been and down into the street. Don't worry about the vampire, he told himself. Worry about the girl.

The sound coming out of Martina's mouth was like nothing he'd ever heard before. It was half animal, half human – and all fear. Her small body was jerking, and he didn't need to speak to her to know that she was desperately fighting the change. It was a battle she was likely to lose. Her spine bulged in a grotesque fashion and her hands and feet were already more wolf than girl.

Last time he'd tried, she hadn't even registered his attempts to subdue her; this time he'd have to do a far better job. Scarlett was out on the street facing down three armed fuckers on her own. There wasn't time for niceties, and he knew that Dr Yara's tranquiliser gun was on the kitchen table in the other room. It wouldn't save them this time.

He didn't want to hurt the child but he had to get her attention. Fast. While her keening moan rose, he opened his jaws again and latched onto her already furry arm. He sank his teeth in hard enough to cause pain without quite breaking her skin. In an instant, her moan changed to a growl and she whipped round, her brown eyes now a pale yellow.

There were more shouts from outside, followed by another gunshot. Devereau did his best to block out the sound and pulled his lips over his teeth in a guttural snarl. He towered over Martina, but she wasn't in a quitting mood. She snapped the air in front of his muzzle. Devereau raised a single heavy paw and cuffed her lightly on the side of the head. Talking wasn't going to help and neither was kindness. They were both wolves, so he had to use that.

He stared into her eyes and she stared back as her body quivered. Although he remained still, he knew that every hackle along his spine was raised. If she didn't back down in the next three seconds, he'd have to knock her out. He lowered his head until the tip of his nose was an inch from hers.

And then she blinked.

Devereau breathed out. He nudged her sharply and Martina whimpered. He nudged her again. Her eyes dropped and, a heartbeat later, she was gasping, her fur melting back into smooth skin, and her eyes changing colour and filling with tears. He offered her a single congratulatory lick, which only made her tears flow faster.

Then Dr Yara was there, tugging Martina over to the dubious safety of the corner of the room, and Devereau was free. In a single bound, he leapt out of the window. Someone was about to pay for

———

what had just happened. And they would pay in blood.

The colours of the outside world were muted as his lupine vision muddied the brighter hues. Despite that, his other senses were now far keener than they were in his human form. He could smell blood seeping into the ground from beyond the blue car and sprang over. One figure lay face down on the pavement, a man, judging from his build and a human, judging from his scent. He was flat out , although his chest was rising and falling with shallow, ragged movements. His balaclava had been pulled up to reveal a patch of pale skin on his neck smeared with blood. Scarlett had acted without hesitation.

Devereau caught of a flicker of movement to his left and swung round to see the vampire, though she was little more than a blur of movement at the far end of the road. She was in hot pursuit of gunman number two and, stiletto heels or not, she was moving incredibly quickly.

Devereau instantly discarded the idea of running after her and looked up instead. Two on the street, one on the roof. He'd lay bets that the bastard on the roof was still there; he had the perfect vantage point and he'd undoubtedly seen Devereau leaving the house. One question remained: was Devereau the target or was it Martina? Both were distinct possibilities and it was imperative that he discovered the answer. Ideally without getting shot in the head.

Adrenalin fizzed through his body. One of his nosy neighbours must have alerted the authorities because he could already hear the wail of sirens in the distance. Time was running out.

His instinct was telling him to find a way to clamber onto the roof and seek out the bastard who'd shot up his house, but instinct wasn't always the best way to go. Besides, if the third gunman was indeed up there he had the higher ground and the stronger advantage. Devereau was liable to end up with a bullet between his ears if he tried to climb up.

The good thing was that the approaching police and paramedics would be putting the gunman under pressure. Make your escape or finish your job, he ordered silently. He glanced at the bleeding bloke by the car. Or rescue your buddy. For some reason, Devereau didn't think that would be a viable option.

He eyed the bloodied man. Sucking air into his lungs, Devereau tightened his shoulders and transformed back into human form in an instant. He reached down, grabbed the unconscious gunman under his arms and hauled him to the narrow side gate just to his right. He opened the latch and shoved the man's body onto the weed-covered pathway beyond. It was an action that wasted precious seconds but it might prove worth it.

Closing the gate, Devereau side-stepped into the doorway of the house opposite his own. He knew he was shielded from view and anyone on the roof above him couldn't tell where he'd gone. They certainly wouldn't know that he'd returned to the danger of the open street.

The sirens were getting louder. The gunman had ninety seconds at best to decide what to do. Devereau smiled grimly. He could wait. The fucker above him didn't have that choice.

One one thousand.

Two one thousand.

Three one thousand.

Four one thousand.

Devereau tilted his head. There. He spotted a jerky movement reflected in the tinted rear window of the blue car. An indistinct face shrouded in black appeared to be holding what looked like a lethal weapon. It wasn't being pointed down at the street but up at the shattered windows of his living room. So Martina was definitely the target.

Devereau's jaw tightened as he spun round. Now the gunman's focus was elsewhere, he had his chance. Plus the fucker was looking for a wolf, not a man.

Throwing himself upwards, Devereau's bare toes found a useful foothold at the first windowsill. If anyone was inside and looking out, they'd certainly be getting a good eyeful of his naked body. He smiled slightly and leapt upwards again, his fingertips curving first round the edge of the second-floor windowsill and then round the sharp corners of the roof slates. A moment later he was there, face to face with balaclava bastard number three.

He briefly registered a pair of shocked blue eyes staring at him – then the muzzle of the gun swung in his direction.

Devereau was already there. With one hard kick, he knocked the gun out of the man's hand. It clattered down to the street just as the first cop cars arrived. The bellows of the police officers could be heard from below as they realised the action was taking place directly above their heads.

The gunman, now unarmed, roared underneath his woollen mask and lunged at Devereau, who raised his arms to block the attack. In theory, his nakedness meant that he was vulnerable but his bare feet granted him greater purchase on the rain-slick roof tiles. The man's right foot slipped as he connected with Devereau's forearms. Limbs flailing, he started to fall.

———

Shit. A dead gunman was no use to anyone. Devereau gritted his teeth and his hand shot out. He was determined to catch the man before he fell over the roof and down onto the pavement below. He grabbed hold of his black T-shirt in the nick of time.

'Tell me,' Devereau snarled. 'Tell me who sent you.'

The man didn't answer. Instead he reached round to his back and produced a sharp-bladed knife. He obviously wasn't the brightest tool in the shed. He brandished the tip of the blade at Devereau's torso and instinctively Devereau released his hold on the man's T-shirt. A second later the man toppled backwards. His skull smashed open right next to the shiny shoes of Police Constable Fred Hackert, who was waiting below.

Chapter Eleven

'Not even one night in your new home, Mr Webb,' DS Grace commented, 'and already someone has tried to kill you.'

Devereau shrugged easily. 'What can I say? I'm a wanted man.' He raised his eyebrows pointedly at Scarlett who was standing less than five metres away with an irritated expression on her face. The second gunman she'd been running down had escaped by performing a well-timed kamikaze leap in front of a double-decker bus. He'd avoided being hit and, as the bus driver slammed to an emergency stop, he'd scrambled away before Scarlett could grab him. From her annoyed stance, she was taking his escape personally.

'Old enemies from your gang-running days?' Grace enquired.

Devereau scratched his chin. 'Actually,' he said, 'I'm certain they were supes.'

'Really,' Grace said flatly.

The lie slid easily off Devereau's tongue. 'I believe so.'

The detective took a step towards him, but if he was trying to be intimidating he failed massively. 'If they were supes, Mr Webb, our hands are tied. Regardless of that corpse lying directly opposite your home, we will be unable to investigate the shooting and it will become a supe matter.'

'Darn.' Devereau folded his fingers together. 'That's a real shame.'

Fred's voice piped up. 'DC Bellamy would—'

DS Grace's face contorted. 'I don't care would DC Bellamy would do. This is what *I'm* doing.' He glared at Devereau as if this were all his fault. 'Can you categorically state that your house was shot at by supernatural beings?'

Devereau smiled pleasantly. 'I can.'

'Supes wouldn't use guns!' Fred snapped.

'Lord Fairfax did.' Devereau was referring to the dead alpha of the Fairfax clan who'd run amok recently and employed a gang to perform a heist against the Talismanic Bank. Fred flinched in response.

Scarlett unfolded her arms and walked over to him. 'PC Hackert,' she said softly, 'I saw the attackers with my own eyes. I'm sure they were supes.' She lied with admirable smoothness. 'Humans just don't move that way.'

Fred couldn't stop himself from turning bright red. Devereau was starting to see why the one-fanged vampire was called Scarlett: it was certainly a reaction she seemed to provoke in others. Probably him, too.

Despite the young police constable's obvious embarrassment, he held his ground. 'What kind of supes? Vampires? Werewolves? Others?' Fred motioned towards the dead body of the fallen gunman. 'Because that guy looks human to me.'

'You know that you can't judge a person by their appearance alone, Fred,' Scarlett said. 'You can't always tell a supe from their looks. In fact, to do so would be extraordinarily prejudicial and I would expect far better from you.'

Something flashed in his eyes. Whether he fancied himself in love with Scarlett or not, Fred Hackert was about to explode with anger.

Fortunately for all of them, Detective Sergeant Grace was oblivious to the undercurrents of emotion and he blustered ahead. 'We need access to your property, Mr Webb. It's an active crime scene that needs to be examined before we leave.'

DS Grace seemed to think Devereau had been born yesterday, but it wasn't the first time the Shepherd's intelligence had been underestimated and he doubted it would be the last. 'Access denied. It's a supe property in a supe neighbourhood and you have no jurisdiction beyond that which I allow you.' He grinned. 'And you know what they say, DS Grace.'

'What?' Grace snapped.

'The law is the law.'

Grace's expression soured. 'Very well.' He turned on his heel. 'We're done here.'

Fred wasn't giving in quite so easily. 'But—'

'PC Hackert.' Scarlett crooked her finger and beckoned him over. Her head dipped towards his and she murmured something. Even with his enhanced hearing, Devereau struggled to make out her out words – then he felt ashamed for trying to eavesdrop and walked away.

'Mr Webb,' Grace called from his car. 'If that dead body turns out to be human, you know I'll be back.'

Devereau waved a hand. 'I'd expect nothing less, detective.' He nodded in an elaborate show of mock respect and headed into his bullet-ridden house.

Dr Yara and Martina were in one of the back bedrooms, well away from any open windows.

'It's alright,' Devereau said. 'The police are leaving.'

'Polis is not coming in here?' Dr Yara's eyes were wide. Martina, in contrast, simply looked defeated.

'Nope.' He managed a genuine smile. 'They'll probably be back, but we've gained a reprieve for now. It's the best we can ask for.'

'Is safe here?'

Devereau's smile vanished. 'No. It's not.'

Scarlett's heels clicked as she strode into the room, phone in hand. 'It will be fine.' She pointed at Devereau. 'You can't be seen running away with your tail between your legs. You're too new and your reputation is too shaky.' She pointed at Martina. 'And your life is in danger if you stay here.'

'Her life is in danger wherever she is,' Devereau retorted.

'True,' Scarlett conceded. 'That's why you're lucky you met me.' She held up her phone. 'I've called in a few favours. This street will be safe, at least for the next few days. Supes look after supes. I've strongly suggested that, as you're a lone werewolf potentially with a lot of power, we would do well to stay on your good side.'

Devereau stiffened. 'Did you—?'

'No. Everyone thinks that you're the one in danger. Not her.' Martina flinched.

'I've not told a soul about her existence,' Scarlett continued. Her expression tightened. 'But someone has.' She gave Devereau a meaningful look. 'Someone knew she was here.'

Dr Yara drew her shoulders back. 'I tell no one!' she declared defensively.

'I know you didn't. And neither did I,' Devereau murmured. He looked at Martina. 'So either someone tracked us from Goodman's Alley back to here—'

'I'd have noticed if that were the case,' Scarlett said.

'Or,' Devereau said, 'Martina told someone where she is.'

Scarlett sniffed. 'I told you she was a liability.'

Martina snarled, picked herself up in one fluid movement and threw herself at Scarlett, her fingers curved as if she wanted to gouge out the vampire's eyes. Devereau only just caught her by the waist in time and hauled her back. At least she'd remained in human form.

'Well, I suppose we know she's finally exhausted her wolf and we're safe for a few hours,' Scarlett said without blinking. Her tone was dry.

'This isn't the time for games, Scarlett,' Devereau said.

'Good,' she replied, 'because I'm done playing.'

They all stared at each other. 'There is one person who can answer our questions,' Devereau said finally. 'Though he might not be feeling very chatty right now. He's lost rather a lot of blood.'

Scarlett smiled humourlessly. 'What are we waiting for? Let's get that prick in here.'

***

The police had finally departed and night was drawing in, but Devereau was still nervous that someone would notice what he was up to. His twitchy neighbours had no doubt watched every moment of the unfolding action in the street earlier and, even though he'd yet to meet a single one of them, he was certain that they all despised him. He couldn't blame them – after all, he'd brought a gunfight to their doorsteps.

He had no idea why none of them had told the coppers about the unconscious bloke he'd shoved behind the gate. Someone must have seen what he'd done. Maybe they disliked the police even more than they disliked him. Devereau didn't have time to question their motives; there were far more important matters to worry about.

Waiting until the street was clear, he crossed the road and opened the rickety gate. It creaked loudly in protest. The gunman was lying just beyond it; he'd managed to prop himself up against a wall but otherwise hadn't moved. One hand was clamped to his neck, covering the single fanged wound from Scarlett, but his balaclava remained over his face and hid his features. Even with the dark woollen mask, Devereau could see that man's eyes were closed.

'Rise and shine, fucker,' Devereau muttered.

The man didn't stir though Devereau was sure that he'd heard him and was feigning unconsciousness. He walked over and nudged him with the toe of his shoe. Still nothing. He pulled off the balaclava and examined the slack face beneath. Clean shaven and young; Devereau estimated he was no older than twenty-one or twenty-two. He poked him in the cheek but the man didn't react.

With no other course of action open to him, Devereau bent down and scooped the man up in a fireman's lift. The bastard couldn't pretend to be comatose forever.

After carrying him into his house, Devereau dropped him onto the bare floorboards in the living room. There was a nail sticking out which caught the man's shoulder as he fell. His features spasmed in pain although he managed to avoid grunting aloud. Definitely not unconscious, then.

Devereau smiled and stepped back. 'How much blood did you take?' he asked Scarlett, who was watching the proceedings from the corner.

'Enough to keep him weak as a kitten for the next few hours. Not enough to do him any real damage.' She ran her tongue over her lips. 'Not unless I drink from him again.'

Dr Yara appeared in the doorway. 'He is now vampire?'

Scarlett shook her head. 'You have to drink vampire blood immediately after being bitten for that to happen.' She sent Devereau a sidelong look. 'And, like the werewolves, we're only permitted to turn a small number of very willing people. There are strict rules.'

He was getting incredibly tired of hearing about these rules. 'Mmm-hmm. Do these rules extend to killing humans who try to kill you first?'

She smirked. 'Not if no one finds out.'

Dr Yara looked alarmed at the prospect but Devereau put his finger to his lips. 'We'll have to dispose of his body without anyone noticing.'

'Cut him up,' Scarlett suggested. 'Then you can fit him neatly into a bag and dump him in the Thames.' She pursed her lips. 'Or give him an acid bath. It's up to you, really. Cutting him up will be messy but getting hold of acid at this hour won't be easy.'

Devereau scratched his chin. 'In that case,' he said, 'let's—' He didn't get the chance to finish his sentence. The man groaned loudly and opened his eyes. Devereau smiled. That had been far too easy. Whoever this guy was, he wasn't as tough as his compatriot on the roof had been.

'Don't hurt me.'

'Why not?' Devereau enquired. 'You tried to kill us. An eye for an eye is only fair.'

The man swallowed, his Adam's apple jerking visibly in his throat. 'Not you,' he said. 'We weren't trying to kill you. We only wanted the girl. We were after the girl.'

'Oh, well that's alright, then.' Devereau spread his arms wide in a dramatic, conciliatory gesture. 'If I'd known you only wanted to kill defenceless children, I wouldn't have got in the way. Brats, the lot of them. We're better off without them.'

The man stared at him as if he were unsure if Devereau were being serious or not. Weak *and* stupid. That was a dangerous combination.

'How did you know she was here?' Scarlett asked. 'Who told you about this address?'

'No one.'

With deliberate movements, she sauntered over to him then knelt and gazed at the wound on his neck. It was healing surprisingly quickly but it was still crusted with blood. Scarlett grazed it with the tip of her index finger. 'No prizes for guessing what I'm thinking,' she said huskily.

'Stop it!' The man threw up his arms to hold her off. 'I'm not lying! Nobody told us where she was because they didn't have to!' He pulled up the sleeve of his black shirt and showed them his watch. Its smart screen blinked at them. 'She's been tagged. All we have to do is follow the signal.'

Devereau leaned across and ripped the watch off his arm. Fuck. There was a tiny map displayed on the screen with a blinking green dot indicating how close Martina was. 'You tagged her? You mean like GPS?'

'Sort of, yeah.'

'Like she's some kind of animal?'

'She *is* an animal.'

Devereau's hands curled into tight fists. 'She's a kid.'

'Maybe. But she's no innocent,' the man croaked. 'She's killed people. I've seen her do it.'

'Uh huh.' Devereau glared, his eyebrow twitching furiously. 'You stood by and allowed a child to commit murder through no fault of her own?'

The man paled. 'She's a monster.'

Devereau grimaced, bent down and smashed his fist into the man's face. The man gave a single brief groan before his body went limp.

Scarlett gazed down at him. 'He's not faking this time,' she said. 'He's out for the count.' She glanced at Devereau. 'That wasn't a particularly smart thing to do.'

He shook his hand and flexed his fingers. He still didn't really understand his werewolf strength. 'No,' he said shortly, 'it wasn't.' He met her eyes. 'But it felt fucking good.'

Scarlett simply tutted. 'Wolves,' she said with a roll of her eyes. 'Deep down you're all the damned same.'

Chapter Twelve

With the gunman unconscious, it was time to explore other avenues of investigation. Unfortunately, Devereau's reluctance to leave the house was growing.

He was experiencing a combination of invincibility, anger and bloodlust that made him want to stand up and fight any and all comers. A damned army could come after him if they wanted to – but he wasn't about to put Dr Yara or Martina in harm's way. An hour ago, they'd been a whisker away from death. He couldn't allow that to happen again.

'I'm telling you it will be fine,' Scarlett said. 'At the moment, this is the safest damned street in London. Nobody will dare attack it again.' She leaned out of the window and let out a low whistle, which was immediately answered by several other whistles.

'I still don't like it,' Devereau growled. 'You're asking me to put Yara and Martina's lives in the hands of strangers.'

'You're a supe now, Devereau. Things aren't the same as they were before. The whole of Lisson Grove and Soho might hate you for how you became a wolf, but it doesn't change the bottom line. You're one of us. If someone attacked the clans, the vampires would offer their help in a heartbeat and vice-versa. It's the same for the Others.' She nodded out at the darkness. 'In fact, as well as vampires you'll find four gremlins, three pixies and two ghouls out there.'

'And a partridge in a pear tree?'

She didn't smile. 'You can trust them. Besides, they're not just here for you. This is a supe street in a supe area, and they're looking after everyone who lives on it.'

'Until,' he pointed out, 'they discover that as well as looking after this street, they're also guarding an illegally turned werewolf girl who's wanted for murder.'

'They won't find that out if she stays inside where she's supposed to.' Scarlett placed a hand on his arm. 'It's too dangerous to move her at the moment. Dr Yara thinks that the tracker was placed in her arm – she has a scar there. It's going to take a few hours to remove it safely. And even if the doctor gets rid the tracker, someone could see Martina and recognise her for what she is…'

'I know all that,' he snapped. He pulled his arm away.

Scarlett didn't flinch. 'It's going to get worse,' she said softly. 'The closer you get to the full moon, the harder it will be for you to control yourself. And the harder it will be for her. If you can't get a grip on your rage, you're going to end up causing far more problems than you'll ever solve. You don't have a clan to fall back on for advice and support.' She paused. 'But that doesn't mean you're alone.'

He bit back his angry reply. 'You're putting a lot on the line by helping us. Why bother?'

'What can I say?' Scarlett smiled disarmingly. 'Sometimes my good side gets the better of me.'

For a moment, Devereau didn't speak, then he rammed his hands into pockets. 'What did you say to the copper earlier? Fred? What did you tell him to get him to calm down and walk away?'

'I told him the truth,' she said simply. 'First of all that he could trust me to deal with matters appropriately and that I knew what I was doing. And secondly that he couldn't hold our fling against me. I reminded him that I'd made him no promises, that we had fun together and it was good while it lasted, but we weren't compatible in the long run.'

'And he was satisfied with that?'

She shrugged. 'For now. Deep down, he knows he deserves better than the likes of me. He deserves a nice, normal, human woman.'

'And me?' Devereau asked, unable to help himself. 'What do I deserve?'

A tiny smile curved her lips. 'That remains to be seen.'

There was a sudden knock on the door, causing them to stiffen. Devereau frowned and flung open the door open to glare at the dark-haired vampire waiting on the doorstep. 'A group of humans has just arrived,' she said. 'They say they're friends of yours.'

Devereau's eyebrows snapped together. He leaned out and saw a familiar-looking car at the end of the road. Three straight-backed vampires were barring its way. He watched for a moment or two then he stepped outside and walked over to them. As he approached, Gaz rolled down the window. 'Hi, boss.'

'What are you doing here?'

'It was on the police radios.' He waved an arm towards the house. 'About the shooting.'

Devereau's mouth tightened. He glanced at the three other people crammed into the car. None of them had approved of his decision to become a werewolf; they hadn't dared say anything out loud but they'd shown it in their every tone and twitch. 'So?'

'So,' Gaz said, avoiding looking at the vampires, 'we thought

---

we'd come and help out. Keep an eye on your new place for a bit. Just in case.'

'We don't work together any more.' It was hard to keep the bitterness out of his voice.

Gaz shrugged. 'That's as may be, boss, but you made us who we are. We owe you.' He lifted up his chin, displaying the faintest touch of defiance – and guilt. 'We still owe you.'

Devereau looked into Gaz's eyes. His old friend was scared but resolute. He nodded. 'It's better for you if you don't go into the house. Dr Yara is there but the rest of you need to stay outside. Yara is … busy,' he finished. 'And one of the bastards who attacked the house is handcuffed to a radiator. It's better if you don't go near him.'

'Okay.' Gaz's demeanour was unquestioning. 'We won't go in.'

Devereau wasn't done yet. 'And there are supes out here who are guarding both the house and the street. You'll have to share the air with them.'

Gaz swallowed but didn't step down. 'No problem, boss.'

Devereau certainly hoped not.

There was a warm breath against his neck. 'Happy now?' Scarlett asked, her voice low.

'I suppose so,' Devereau said grudgingly. He lifted his head. 'Thank you,' he said, directing his words at the supes and the humans. 'The people in every house on this street will sleep easier knowing you are all here. And your presence will free me up so I can go after the pricks who did this.'

'I'll help.' Scarlett hooked her arm through his. 'You might need the back-up.'

Gaz's eyes were wide as saucers as he goggled at Scarlett then glanced at his former boss. The power of speech seemed to have momentarily left him. The vampires remained impassive, though Devereau thought he noticed a knowing smirk on the face of the three-foot-high gremlin on the pavement opposite.

All he could do was nod. 'All right then,' he said. 'Let's go.'

***

'So what's the plan?' Scarlett asked. 'Where are we heading to first?'

Devereau checked the time on the dashboard. It was already gone nine o'clock; other than night-shift workers, anyone sane would have left work by now. 'Canary Wharf,' he said. 'One of the victims from Goodman's Alley worked there – a financial law solicitor called David Bernard. If we're lucky, the police won't have investigated his workplace yet. We might find something useful there. There was no reason for a stuffed suit like Bernard to be hanging around Goodman's Alley in the middle of the day.'

Scarlett's brow creased thoughtfully. 'Was he an unlucky victim in the wrong place at the wrong time? Or did sweet little Martina target him deliberately?'

Devereau gave her a long look. 'If he was targeted, it's hardly Martina's fault.'

'I appreciate that,' Scarlett said, 'and I believe you're right. But you need to remember that the gun-toting idiot back there was right, too. Martina's not a complete innocent and, regardless of her motives, she's holding back a considerable amount of information.'

'She's terrified. And traumatised.'

'I'm not disagreeing with you, Devereau. I'm just saying that you shouldn't be blinkered where Martina is concerned.'

For several seconds neither of them spoke then Scarlett put the car into gear. 'Canary Wharf?'

He clipped in his seatbelt. 'Yeah.'

She revved the engine and took off.

For the first few minutes, the silence between them was awkward. Devereau stared out of the window and Scarlett fiddled with the radio, trying station after station and eventually giving up when she couldn't find any music that she liked.

Rather than let the silence continue, Devereau turned away from the scenery and examined her. No matter what happened, she never seemed to have a single hair out of place. 'How long have you been a vampire?' he asked.

Scarlett gasped in mock horror. 'A gentleman should never ask a lady's age.' He gave her an exasperated look and she chuckled. 'About fifty years,' she told him. 'I was turned back in 1972 when I was twenty-four years old.'

She could pass for about thirty. He tried to imagine what it would be like to experience time differently and enjoy a longer life. It wasn't easy. 'Do you mind me asking why you chose this life?'

'No,' she answered easily. 'Plenty of people do. There's no simple answer. Don't get me wrong – nobody pushed me into it. I *wanted* to become a vampire and I have no regrets, but I didn't choose to change because I hated my family or I suffered a traumatic experience or I thought it would be cool to drink blood and spend the rest of my life partying. Neither did it solve all my problems. Before I was turned, it felt like something was missing from my life and sometimes I think that's not changed. There's still a hole inside of me.' A fleeting expression of melancholy flashed across her face.

'I get that,' Devereau said quietly. 'Sometimes I feel that way too.'

'Is that why you turned to a life of crime?'

He hesitated. 'Believe it or not, when I was a kid I wanted to be a farmer.'

'With a snarl, snarl here and a snarl, snarl there?'

'E-I-E-I-O.' Devereau smiled. 'Not quite what I had in mind. No, I liked the idea of doing something useful. Growing things. Feeding people. Providing a proper service.'

Scarlett leaned across until her shoulder brushed his. 'Good for you,' she murmured. 'When I was a kid, my burning desire was to be a queen.'

'With a shiny tiara and a pretty dress?'

'Less Cinderella,' she said, 'and more Boudicca.'

'Fair enough.' Devereau nodded. 'Play your cards right, Boudicca, and one day I'll show you my sword.' He winked and Scarlett burst out laughing.

'Oh, Devereau. It's only a matter of time.'

***

As expected, Canary Wharf was quiet. There were lights on in some of the office buildings but they were few and far between. That didn't mean there weren't security systems to deal with, but Devereau felt reasonably confident that they'd gain entrance to David Bernard's office without being noticed.

Scarlett had other ideas, however. After parking in an empty carpark nearby, they walked to the foot of the shiny building where Bernard had worked. She took one look at the bored-looking security guard behind the desk and strolled straight through the main doors. Devereau faltered briefly before following her.

'We're closed,' the guard said in an almost robotic voice. Then he looked up and his mouth fell open when he saw Scarlett. 'Hello.'

'Hellooo,' she purred in response. She sauntered up to him, her hips swaying exaggeratedly. She glanced at his name tag, reached across the counter and took his hand. 'Jonathan Lee. My friend and I need access to the fifteenth floor. We're going to look around for a little while and you're going to let us.'

'I...' The security guard swallowed. Devereau looked on, fascinated. 'I can't do that.'

'Of course you can.' Scarlett reached out and drew the tip of her finger down the side of his face. 'But you're not going to tell anyone we were here. We're like ghosts.'

'I…' He swallowed again. 'Okay.' He opened a drawer and fumbled inside. 'Here,' he handed over a key card, 'you'll need this for the lift but I can't help you with opening up any office doors. I don't have access to them.'

'Thank you so much. You're a darling. We'll worry about the doors.' Scarlett pulled back and, without a backward glance, walked towards the bank of lifts, before pressing the keycard against the black box set into the wall.

Devereau snapped his mouth shut and strode after her. 'You just did something to that guy.'

'Mmm.'

'Did you compel him? Like werewolves do?'

'Sort of. It's little more than a trick, to be honest. We can use touch to encourage certain humans to do our will. It's not an exact science and it doesn't always work, but when it does,' she smiled in satisfaction, 'it's very useful.'

Devereau stared at her. 'Can I do that?' He considered the possibilities. 'Can I compel humans?'

'No. Your powers only work on werewolves. And only on werewolves who are weaker than you.' She raised an eyebrow. 'Don't be too disappointed. I suspect most werewolves are weaker than you, despite your lack of experience.'

There was a cough from behind them and they turned to see the security guard. He was holding out a scrap of paper to Scarlett and he had a hopeful look in his eyes. 'Would you like my phone number?'

Scarlett rolled her eyes and turned away. 'No.'

Devereau snatched the paper out of his hands. 'Thank you.' You never knew what might come in useful in the future.

Scarlett gave him a strange look but he simply smiled. Then there was a ding and they stepped into the lift.

Chapter Thirteen

The fifteenth floor of David Bernard's office block was as silent as the grave. It must cost a pretty penny to rent even a square foot of space in this place, Devereau mused as he looked at the plush grey carpet and pristine blank walls. He could almost smell the money that had been sunk into those walls. Even so, it was little more than a featureless, characterless office; he'd take a life of crime any day over spending time in the prison that this office space provided.

He and Scarlett moved down the hallway until they came to a closed oak door with David Bernard's gold-embossed name plate.

'Whoever he was,' Scarlett murmured, 'he was clearly as dodgy as they come.'

'What makes you say that?' Devereau asked, kneeling down to examine the door lock.

'A well-heeled solicitor who specialises in finance but doesn't have the backing of a large firm? This sort of operation deals with clients who don't want to draw attention to themselves.'

He suspected that she was right. He reached into his pocket and located the tiny lockpick on his key ring. 'This won't take long.'

'We could just break the door down.'

Devereau inserted the pick into the keyhole and twisted deftly. 'We could,' he answered, 'but we don't want to advertise that we've been here.' He stood up as the door swung smoothly open. 'And my method is just as fast as a sharp kick.'

'Something tells me this isn't your first time breaking and entering,' she said drily.

'Funnily enough, it's not.' He offered her an arch smile before crossing the threshold into Bernard's office. The lights flicked on automatically.

The first room was small, with a single desk in front of the doorway. There was another door to the right. 'He has his own secretary,' Devereau murmured. 'I wonder if she knows that he's dead.'

Scarlett examined the desk. 'What makes you think the secretary's female?'

'The smell,' he said. He reached across and opened one of the drawers to reveal a small glass bottle of perfume. 'Chanel's finest. Whoever lives at 12 Goodman's Alley also wears this scent. It might be a coincidence – or it might not be.'

Scarlett acknowledged his discovery with a nod, then she frowned. 'Other than that bottle, the office is remarkably impersonal.'

Devereau took a pad of Post-it notes from the drawer and flicked through them. Several contained doodles of smiley faces but there were no helpful notes to tell them where the secretary might be or what involved David Bernard with a child wolf.

He showed the doodles to Scarlett and she shrugged. 'A few random doodles aren't much to go on. There are no photo frames, no identifying features.' She glanced at the stationery holder. 'Even the pens are generic. There's nothing branded.'

Devereau felt his left eyebrow spasm. 'Because when your clients are dangerous,' he said, 'you don't want them to know any more about you than is absolutely necessary.'

They exchanged a grim look then Scarlett swivelled towards the second door. It opened into a far larger room. It had the same grey carpet and similar office furniture but it was much grander. Various certificates lined the walls and Devereau peered at them; they included a university degree from Cambridge and an embossed document from the Solicitors' Regulation Authority. There were other showy pieces of paper that Bernard had felt the need to display, either because he'd wanted to prove that he was qualified or he enjoyed showing off.

Scarlett sat down at Bernard's desk. There was no computer so presumably he used a laptop, which he carried to and from the office. She rifled through the tray of papers on his desk then started opening the drawers.

Devereau went to the large bookcase and examined the array of legal titles lined up in alphabetical order. Unfortunately, there wasn't a single John Grisham novel in sight. 'I'm beginning to think coming here was a waste of time,' he remarked.

'Not entirely.' He glanced round. Scarlett was holding a small golden object between her thumb and forefinger. Devereau squinted; the symbol on it looked familiar. He took Dr Yara's drawing of Martina's brand from his pocket and compared the two. 'They're exactly the same,' he bit out. 'David Bernard was no random victim.'

Scarlett's mouth thinned. 'Looks like an evil conspiracy.' She tossed him the object. 'Feels like an evil conspiracy.'

Devereau turned it over in his hands. It was definitely made of gold and appeared to be some sort of pin, judging by the catch on it. 'Must be an evil conspiracy,' he murmured. And something icy cold and very angry crystallised deep inside him.

***

They searched the rest of David Bernard's office but there was nothing incriminating in it. The man had clearly taken pains to hide any important files.

'We could find his address and pay his home a visit,' Scarlett mused. 'Who knows what we might uncover? But the police will already have been there. Whether or not they consider Bernard to be nothing more than a victim, they'll have still done a search and taken his laptop. And if he didn't live alone, we're liable to run into his family – and they definitely won't take kindly to a vampire and a werewolf knocking on their door asking questions.'

'Agreed,' Devereau said. 'We don't want to draw any more attention to ourselves than we have to, not when we have Martina's safety to consider.' He tapped his mouth thoughtfully. 'The secretary is the key. Whoever she is, she's bound to know where all the dirty secrets are kept.' He glanced at Scarlett. 'Your new friend Jonathan downstairs might be able to help. He must have a list of everyone who uses this building.'

'Then let's go and ask him a few more questions.'

As they went back into the corridor, Devereau took care to lock the office door behind him before following Scarlett to the lifts.

'The more time I spend with you, Devereau,' she said, 'the more I realise you're nothing like I expected.'

'What did you expect?' he enquired.

'Someone more brash, I suppose. More cocky. Less … thoughtful.'

He watched her for a moment. 'You're the first vampire I've ever spent time with,' he said finally. 'And you're not what I expected, either.'

'Oh yes?' She smiled. 'In what way?'

'Well, for one thing you've not tried to drink my blood.'

Scarlett rolled her eyes. 'You should have learned by now that vampires have far greater self-control than werewolves. It's practically Supe 101.'

'I'm not so sure about that.'

She smirked and reached across to the press the call button.

Devereau grabbed her wrist. 'Don't,' he ordered.

'What is it?'

He pointed to the LED display above their heads. One of the lifts was already moving up towards them. Third floor. Fourth. Fifth.

'Do you think—?'

'At this time of night?' He nodded. 'Yes, I do.'

Without another word, they spun round and moved swiftly back down the corridor towards Bernard's office.

'There,' Scarlett said. 'Janitor's closet.'

Three seconds later they were crammed inside it, surrounded by cleaning equipment and the strong smell of bleach. Devereau pulled the door closed just as the lift pinged onto their floor. He left an inch-wide crack so he could peer out. Scarlett shimmied in front of him, ducking slightly so she could do the same.

A solitary figure stepped out of the lift and walked down the hallway towards them with silent but purposeful steps. Devereau didn't catch a glimpse of his face until the man was in front of David Bernard's door. White skin, pale watery blue eyes and a thick neck – he'd lay money that he was ex-military. It wasn't the guy's muscular build that gave him away, it was the self-possessed way that he moved.

Devereau and Scarlett watched, barely breathing, as the man paused in front of Bernard's office. He took a step back and kicked the door once, which was more than enough to splinter the frame and open it. He strode inside and disappeared from view.

'I guess he's not too fond of lockpicks,' Scarlett whispered, her words barely audible. 'What do you think? Do we confront him?'

It was tempting but Devereau decided against it. 'He's another thug for hire,' he murmured. 'We already have one of those. Let's see what he does first then follow him.'

Scarlett nodded and relaxed slightly against him. 'Is that a gun, Mr Webb?' she asked. 'Or are you just happy to be in this cupboard with me?'

'It's a mop handle,' he answered.

'Pity.'

He smiled in the darkness, then they settled back to wait.

It didn't take long. The man spent even less time inside Bernard's office than they had done. When he left, there was a dark frown on his face and a phone glued to his ear. 'There's no sign of her here,' he said. There was a beat. 'Yes, I'm sure.' Another beat. 'I'm heading back now.' He ended the call and stalked back down the corridor.

As soon as he'd disappeared into the lift, Scarlett stepped out of the janitor's closet. 'Interesting,' she murmured. She peered inside Bernard's office and clicked her tongue. 'Messy pup.'

Devereau followed suit. She was right; the man clearly didn't care about leaving a trail. He'd trashed the place: the secretary's desk had been overturned and in the second, larger room, the carefully arranged legal books were scattered across the floor. 'The plot thickens,' he muttered.

'Indeed.' Scarlett glanced at the lifts. 'Shall we?'

Devereau nodded. 'Let's go. We don't want him to get too far ahead of us.' He could already feel the adrenalin pumping through his body. They were getting close to finding out what all this was about. He just knew it. His wolf was twitching beneath his skin, insisting more and more strongly that it wanted to emerge.

As soon as the lift doors opened on the ground floor, Devereau knew something was wrong. Even if he'd still been human he would have smelled the cordite in the air. 'Shit.' He stared at the slumped body of Jonathan Lee, a man who'd done nothing other than be in the wrong place at the wrong time.

Devereau stalked over, even though he already knew what he would find. The security guard had a single bullet hole in his forehead and his eyes were wide and staring.

His jaw hardened. 'Why? Why do this? There were a million and one ways to get past a single security guard without resorting to murder. Killing him was wholly unnecessary.'

Scarlett maintained her distance. He wondered if the blood spatter bothered her given her vampiric nature, then he realised it was simpler than that. The guard's death scared her. Hell, it scared him too.

'Rampaging through Bernard's office like a hurricane was unnecessary too,' she said, her voice quiet but even. 'This is sending a message.' She met his eyes. 'The question is to whom?'

Devereau grimaced. 'This entire building must be riddled with CCTV and he wasn't wearing a mask. He must have been caught on camera. Why wouldn't he care about that?'

Scarlett pointed over his shoulder. 'Think again about those cameras.'

He turned, saw the sign on the far wall and read it aloud. *'Filming and photography are forbidden throughout this building.'* He glanced up. Scarlett was right; he couldn't see a single camera anywhere.

'The people who work here take their privacy very seriously,' Scarlett said. 'Which makes the late David Bernard even more interesting.'

Chapter Fourteen

They didn't waste any more time. The security guard's body would be discovered soon and calling the police would only complicate matters.

They jogged to the car park where Scarlett had left her car. They made it just in time. From an underground car park to their right, a small black vehicle appeared on its way out of Canary Wharf.

'That's our guy,' Scarlett said quietly.

Devereau nodded and ducked down to avoid the man noticing him as he drove past. Moments later they drove out of the car park on his tail. With the streets quiet at this time of night, it wouldn't be easy to follow him without being spotted so it was probably just as well that he had a decent head start.

They trailed him, occasionally dropping back when it was prudent to do so then speeding up when he appeared to be getting too far ahead. At no point did the man give any indication that he knew he was being followed. That's because he wasn't expecting to be, Devereau realised – he assumed his murderous activities had gone unnoticed. Did everyone involved in this mess possess the same over-confident arrogance? He hoped so because it would make it much more satisfying when he finally caught them and showed them the error of their ways.

'Penny for your thoughts,' Scarlett said when she stopped at a set of traffic lights a block behind the black car.

Devereau didn't take his eyes off the car ahead. He wasn't going to risk losing it in the maze of London streets. 'The people who're doing this don't fear being found out. Either they don't think they'll be caught, or they have confidence in their ability to escape if their crimes are discovered.'

'Surely that's the same for every criminal,' Scarlett said. 'Otherwise why would anyone commit any crime?'

He shook his head. 'It's a rare person who breaks the law and doesn't consider the potential consequences. It's basic common sense – risk versus reward. Committing a crime is a high-risk choice, and anyone with any sense considers the ramifications of that choice in a bid to avoid the worst-case scenario.'

Scarlett considered this for a moment. 'So essentially it's all about risk management.'

'It is if you're any good at what you do.'

She drummed her fingers on the steering wheel. When the lights changed to green, she released the handbrake and went in pursuit again. The black car turned right towards the outskirts of the city.

'Kill your lights,' Devereau said.

'That might make us more rather than less noticeable.'

'I know London. I'm certain there's nothing much beyond this road other than derelict wasteland and a few commercial buildings. There won't be any street lights, but headlights will stand out.'

Scarlett did as he suggested then also made the right turn. When she saw the dark street ahead, she gave Devereau a quick sidelong look of approval. 'Good call.' She slowed down further. 'There is something else that doesn't make sense, you know,' she said.

'What's that?'

'Motive. Why do this? Why turn a kid into a werewolf? Anyone who knows anything about wolves would know that it's more than just a bad idea – it's a terrible one. And why compound that crime with more evil deeds?'

'Not every crime has a motive,' Devereau answered. 'Sometimes people do things just because they can.'

'Do you think that's the case here?' She sounded sceptical.

'No, I don't.' He pointed ahead. 'Look. He's stopped.'

Scarlett pulled up and squinted through the windscreen. 'What is that? Is it a warehouse?'

'I think so.' Devereau bared his teeth in satisfaction. 'We've found the bastards' lair.'

***

They approached the warehouse silently on foot, skirting the edge of the road until the smooth tarmac turned into gravel ruts where they hopped onto the verge. Devereau fought the urge to change and bring his wolf to the fore. He needed to see inside that warehouse before he made any rash decisions.

It was a good thing that he was patient. When they were within fifty metres of the building, he heard the dim beat of music. This was more than a storage facility – it was a club. Probably an illegal one, at that.

'Look,' Scarlett whispered, jerking her head to the left of the building. Hidden from view from the road were dozens of cars.

Devereau let out a low whistle. 'Those are some expensive-looking beasts. Tesla. Ferrari. Maserati. It's a petrol-head's wet dream.'

'If you say so.'

'You're not a car fan?'

'As long my vehicle gets me where I need to go without breaking down, why would I care about how much donkey power it has?'

'Horse power,' he said automatically. Then he noticed Scarlett's smirk.

'Some men like it when I play dumb.'

'Some men are fucking stupid.'

She opened her mouth to say something else but was forestalled by the flash of headlights at the end of the road. She and Devereau exchanged glances then moved to the nearest row of parked cars. Scarlett rolled underneath a silver Porsche as Devereau slid beneath a chunky Rolls Royce.

The wheels of yet another expensive car rolled into the next parking space. The powerful engine was silenced and the driver's door opened. Devereau angled his head and watched as a pair of shiny black brogues appeared. The feet crunched on the gravel and walked to the rear passenger door. A chauffeur, he realised. A second pair of men's shoes emerged.

'Thank you, William.' The man had an English accent with the flat tones that belonged to only the very well-to-do; this was someone who had been educated at public school and whose idea of a good time was a dinner party with outside catering and solid-silver cutlery. The sort of man Devereau rarely came into contact with. 'From the number of cars, it appears that we're one of the last to arrive.'

A second voice, presumably belonging to William the chauffeur, spoke. 'It's a while yet before it will begin. Here. I have the invitation and the masks.'

'And the password?'

'*Actus non facit reum nisi mens sit rea.*'

'Of course.' There was a loud sniff. 'Stay close to me. I know there are already plenty of precautions in place but we're dealing with dangerous creatures here. I don't want to take any unnecessary risks.'

'Yes, sir.'

'Come on.'

Both pairs of feet moved away. Devereau strained his ears until he was sure that they'd walked to the warehouse entrance and vanished inside, then he rolled out and dusted himself down.

Scarlett did the same. She grinned at him, her single fang

gleaming in the dim moonlight and giving her a seductively dangerous look. 'Masks. Password.' She raised her eyebrows. 'Are you thinking what I'm thinking?'

It was both risky and rash, but that was why it might actually work. Devereau smiled back at her. 'Hell, yes.' As if on cue, another set of headlights appeared. 'Let's do this.'

This time they crouched between the cars rather laying on their bellies underneath them. They needed to move easily, and they needed the element of surprise. The car reversed into the spot opposite the Porsche. It couldn't have been more perfect if Devereau had planned it.

'When we move,' Scarlett said, 'it will need to be fast.'

'Yep.'

'The gravel will give us away and the last thing we need is for any screams to alert someone.'

'Yep.'

'And it would probably be a good idea if we didn't kill these folks.'

He gave her a long look. She shrugged. 'I thought it was worth saying.'

The car plunged into darkness as its engine and headlights flicked off. The front passenger's and the driver's doors opened simultaneously. One man and one woman. Ideal.

'You take her,' Devereau murmured. 'I'll take him. On a count of three, two … *go.*'

He threw himself forward, aware of the blur of movement to his right as Scarlett did the same. The man, was wearing an elaborate feathered mask that matched the black and white of his tuxedo. His mouth dropped open as Devereau crashed into him and sent him sprawling to the ground. Within a second, Devereau's hand clamped over the man's mouth. From the brief sounds of a struggle on the other side of the car, Scarlett had done much the same to the woman.

'Sorry about this,' Devereau said, looking into the man's blinking, terrified eyes. 'It's not personal.' He drew back his fist and rammed into the side of the man's head. His pupils widened fractionally with pain before the rest of his body registered what was happening and went limp.

Devereau stood up and glanced at Scarlett. She was on her knees with the woman in front of her, her fang firmly embedded in the side of the woman's neck.

'Probably a good idea if we don't kill these folks,' Devereau called out.

Scarlett pulled back, her lips glistening with blood. She smiled at him, pulled out a delicate lace handkerchief and wiped her mouth. Then she carefully removed the woman's sequined mask.

Devereau returned to his own victim and checked for a pulse. When he was satisfied that the man would wake up later with nothing more than an unsightly bruise and a bit of a headache, he peeled off the man's mask to reveal the slack face and ruddy jowls of a white bloke in his fifties.

Devereau glanced down at his clothes – a grubby T-shirt and pair of jeans that would benefit from a good wash – and undressed the man down to his underwear. He quickly donned the clothing. The tuxedo trousers were too short at the ankles and too large around the waist but they would do. Hopefully. He placed the mask over his face, grimacing as the feather trimmings tickled his cheek, then he picked up the unconscious body of the unlucky man and tossed him into the back seat of his car. Good enough. Scarlett hustled the woman into the seat alongside him and Devereau took the car keys and locked them in.

'With any luck,' Scarlett said, her purloined mask now covering her eyes and nose, 'they'll be out for a couple of hours. That should give us more than enough time.' She reached up to Devereau's hair and smoothed it down. 'I can't say that this a good look for you,' she murmured, 'but you'll do.'

'Yeah, yeah. Just remember to keep your mouth closed so that fang of yours is out of sight.'

She dipped into mock curtsey while Devereau drew out a shiny black card from the pocket of the tuxedo. On one side, there was a large number written in white: 324. Hmm. On the other side, in the centre of the card, there was the red embossed image of a wavy line intersecting the letter M. His eyebrow twitched. They were definitely in the right place. He waved the card at Scarlett. 'This must be our invitation.'

Her lips curved upwards. 'Come on then, darling.' She took his arm. 'Let's go get 'em.'

Chapter Fifteen

Devereau and Scarlett strolled towards the front of the warehouse, their body language casual and their steps unhurried. The entrance was a single wooden door that had been propped open, as ramshackle and unappealing as the rest of the building. If it hadn't been for the three broad-shouldered men standing outside and eyeing their every move, Devereau would have assumed he was in the wrong place.

Scarlett leaned across and planted a brief kiss on his cheek. Devereau curved his arm round her waist and drew her closer, and their heads dipped together as they laughed together at a fabricated joke. Smoke and mirrors and sleights of hand were tricks in which Devereau was well versed. He had to admit that he was enjoying these particular ones more than usual.

They were still draped round each other when they reached the three unmasked bouncers.

'Good evening,' Scarlett murmured with a slow languorous smile.

One of the men, a squat bloke with a bald head and pockmarked skin, gave her a piercing look. Devereau was certain that he'd identified her as a vampire and the game was up before they'd even started, but the sequined mask was doing its job. Scarlett's vampirically attractive features were invisible and anyway, the bouncer wasn't looking at her mouth. His narrow-eyed gaze was focussed on her chest. Devereau felt the stirrings of genuine annoyance.

'Good evening,' drawled one of the other men. 'Do you have an invitation?'

A faint furrow appeared on Devereau's brow as if he'd forgotten to bring it and he paused, then his face cleared. He slid his hand into his pocket, drew out the black card and handed it over. 'Oh yes. Here you go.'

The bouncer barely glanced at it. He raised his eyebrows and gave them a meaningful look.

Devereau was prepared. '*Actus non facit reum nisi mens sit rea.*'

The man who'd been staring at Scarlett's cleavage jerked up his head, suspicion clouding in his eyes.

'An act does not make anyone guilty unless there is a criminal intent or a guilty mind,' she murmured, remaining as close-lipped as she could.

The trio exchanged looks before the nearest bouncer stepped aside and gestured to the open door. 'Have a good night.'

Devereau smiled as he and Scarlett walked through the door. Behind him he heard one of the bouncers mutter to his buddies, 'Fucking public-school wankers. They've always got to show off.'

Leaning closer to Scarlett, Devereau raised a questioning eyebrow. 'You speak Latin?'

'I'm a vampire,' she purred. 'It's virtually my mother tongue.'

At his disbelieving look, she laughed. 'I went to grammar school in the sixties, Devereau. It was still on the curriculum. I guess my teacher was right – learning a dead language does occasionally prove useful.'

'*Iyay uessgay osay*,' he replied. 'Pig Latin. Courtesy of my big sister.'

Scarlett grinned.

They walked down a narrow corridor, old floorboards creaking under their feet. The music was getting louder. A door opened and a young woman wearing an old-fashioned maid's outfit came out curtseyed.

'Welcome, esteemed guests.' Her eyes were lowered in what Devereau supposed to be respect but looked more like forced submission. He felt a faint jab of familiar pain between his shoulder blades but managed a brief nod. Then he gazed at the scene in front of him.

Nobody wandering past outside could have ever guessed what was inside this warehouse. The interior of the warehouse wouldn't have looked out of place inside the Ritz Hotel. It wasn't a huge room – no doubt the rest of the warehouse was used for other purposes – but it was certainly grand.

There was a bar on the right with several mask-wearing bartenders. The bar top was made from burnished walnut, which caught the amber lights hanging overhead and gave off a warm, inviting feel. The glasses were polished to within an inch of their sparkly lives, and an ice sculpture that looked suspiciously like a rip-off of Rodin's *The Thinker* stood at the far end. Opulent fabrics draped the walls, adding to the luxurious atmosphere.

The floor was filled with groups of well-dressed people, all wearing masks to conceal their identity. The chatter was a muted hum compared to the beat of the music supplied by the DJ on the dais opposite the bar. There was a large space in front of the decks in which stood a lectern and a microphone. Devereau hoped sincerely that he wouldn't have to listen to any long-winded speeches.

'Close your mouth, Dev,' Scarlett murmured.

He snapped it shut just as a muscular, topless waiter appeared with a tray of impressive looking canapés. 'Would sir care for a caviar blini?'

'Sir would indeed,' Devereau replied, plucking one of the tiny pancakes from the silver platter. The waiter offered it to Scarlett but she shook her head and patted her stomach, as if the tiny mouthful might tip her non-existent diet over the edge.

The waiter nodded smoothly and moved away while Devereau frowned down at the poor excuse for food. 'What's this shiny stuff?' he enquired.

Scarlett peered over his shoulder. 'Gold leaf, I believe.'

'These folks aren't rich enough already? They have to *eat* gold as well?' He threw into his mouth. It was cloying and salty but not entirely unpleasant.

'They probably shit gold too,' she remarked, making him choke. A couple nearby wearing matching blue outfits looked over at him. Scarlett thumped him on the back and smiled at them before drawing him out of their line of sight. 'I don't see any sign of our murderous gunman from Canary Wharf,' she whispered. 'But there's a great deal of other weaponry on display here.'

Devereau swallowed the blini and followed her gaze. She was right: dotted around the room at strategic points were a number of solid men, including the bastard who'd put a bullet in Jonathan Lee's brain. He was wearing a mask now, but he was recognisable by his pale eyes and thick neck. Devereau tried not to glower at him and continued looking round. While all the men wore plain masks, none of them concealed the fact that they were armed to the hilt. He spotted several guns and more than one lethal-looking knife. These people weren't playing around.

'That doesn't bode well,' he muttered.

Scarlett agreed. 'Loud music, posh food and flowing drinks. But somehow I don't think that's why these people are here. They're waiting for something.'

Devereau caught sight of an elderly woman dripping in pearls who was checking her watch. 'It must be something to do with that stage where the DJ is.' He swivelled round. 'Maybe this is some weird sex party thing.'

'Maybe.' She sounded doubtful.

'Look.' He nudged Scarlett with his hip to direct her attention towards the far corner. 'There's another door. I bet it leads somewhere interesting.'

'We should check it out.'

He smiled grimly. 'Indeed.'

They started moving towards the unmarked door but before they got close to it the room was plunged into darkness and the music faded out. The door they were sneaking towards opened and several shadowy figures emerged.

Devereau strained his eyes but he couldn't make out the features of any of the people. They ascended the stage to the dais in single file. The DJ was already stepping down, her head bowed. There was a hush of anticipation across the entire room.

'Well,' Scarlett murmured, 'this is going to be interesting.'

There was a single cymbal clash and the dais was illuminated by a splash of bright light. Devereau squinted, blinking. Five people. His eyes narrowed. And two of them were unmasked and bound in heavy chains.

He felt Scarlett stiffen. 'Fuck,' she muttered in a low undertone. 'Fuck!'

The audience pressed forward and Devereau heard several muted whispers of appreciation. He gritted his teeth and continued to stare at the five people on the stage. Two of them were identikit versions of the bouncers outside; the only differences were that they were wearing black masks that covered their eyes and their noses and were carrying what appeared to be Tasers. The other masked man was about six feet tall, with dark hair. His mask was the same blood-red as the writing on Devereau's purloined invitation. He had a triumphant, almost predatory smile.

Devereau knew that Scarlett's reaction wasn't because of this bastard's air of superiority or because of the bouncers. Her hissed expletive was the result of seeing the two bound captives.

He reached across and placed a hand on her arm in a silent bid to keep her calm. She was trembling beneath his touch. Her rage was visceral and raw – like his own. She clutched his hand tightly and he squeezed hers in return. 'Wait,' he whispered. 'Just wait.'

'You know what they are, Devereau.'

He nodded curtly. 'I do. But we're surrounded by armed men and we still don't know what's going on here. Wait.' He gazed at the trussed-up figures, the pain between his shoulders increasing by the second.

There was one man and one woman. They looked young, perhaps in their early twenties, although that wasn't necessarily the case. The man was hollow cheeked, with thin arms and a scrawny body. His skin was remarkably pale and his dark eyes were dull, as if he were drugged, but his glazed eyes and thin features didn't detract from his appeal. Whoever he was, he was intensely good looking, exuding a sort of stoned sexuality that put Devereau in mind of the skinny male models who'd been so popular in the nineties. Those models hadn't possessed sharp white fangs, however.

The woman was about a foot shorter. Her eyes displayed the same lack of awareness but her strawberry-blonde hair was thick and gleaming. It matched the patches of fur that were visible across her bare arms and legs. Devereau glanced at her hands and noted the claws on the tips of her barely human fingers.

Something deep inside him roared viciously with anger. One male vampire. One female werewolf. And Devereau was holding a card that had a number displayed on it. He already knew what was about to happen and he could barely contain his wolf from bursting through and killing every single person in this damned room.

The tuxedo-ed man wearing the red mask stepped up to the microphone. He tapped it with the tip of his finger and the thud echoed round the room. He cleared his throat and his smile widened. 'Good evening, ladies and gentlemen. We are very pleased to welcome you to our little gathering this evening.'

Nobody clapped, nobody said a word, but everyone gazed at the man on the dais as if he were a god. The adulation scratched at Devereau's skin, digging into his flesh and tearing its way through his veins and arteries. Scarlett gripped his hand even tighter and he remembered to breathe again. He glanced towards her. Her mouth was pressed into a thin line but, when she felt his gaze, she opened it to form a single word, silently repeating his own advice back to him. *Wait.*

He nodded. Wait. It was all they could do for now.

'I know you were expecting someone else but unfortunately our usual master of ceremonies is indisposed at the moment, so you'll have to make do with my poor attempts instead.'

Devereau spotted several smiles of good-humoured acknowledgement. He wondered if the usual MC was indisposed because Martina had killed him.

'For those of you who don't know me,' the man continued, 'you can call me the Master.' Beneath his mask, his eyes glittered with malicious amusement. Devereau's jaw clenched as Scarlett's nails bit into his palm. 'But if that's too much of a mouthful, I also answer to Dom.' He grinned nastily. 'And boy, does Dom have some treats for you this evening.'

Devereau counted to ten in his head and looked round at the

---

security personnel. There were at least twelve armed men, not including the two on the stage and the bouncers outside. There was no way of telling how many others were beyond the closed door. And he wasn't factoring in the personal protection that the individual audience members had with them, such as William whose voice they'd heard outside. In his werewolf form, Devereau possessed more strength than several of them combined, and with Scarlett by his side that strength doubled. But he knew in his heart of hearts that, no matter how good they were, they'd never be a match for this many pricks with this many guns.

His impotence clawed at him, suffocating him. Devereau knew that if he lost his concentration for a second, he wouldn't be able to hold back his wolf. He had to maintain focus. There was no other choice.

On the dais, Dom's smile disappeared. 'Before we get underway, it would be remiss of me not to remind you of the rules. They are sacrosanct. Anyone who breaks a single one, in fact anyone who even *thinks* of breaking the rules, will face the harshest of consequences. It has happened before, and you know that our justice is swift and without mercy. It doesn't matter who you are or what power you might think you wield in the real world.' His voice grew louder. 'You do not breathe a single word to anyone about what has occurred within these four walls. Should you be fortunate enough to be one of tonight's lucky winners, you do not broadcast news of your winnings to anyone. In the unfortunate event that someone does discover your good fortune and you cannot deal with the results yourself, you must inform us immediately so we can take appropriate steps to minimise the fall-out.'

He smiled again, so suddenly and so darkly that Devereau felt his stomach clench in response. 'However if you *do* win, and if you *do* follow the rules, you will gain immense power and a level of protection that almost nobody else in this country enjoys.' His eyes gleamed. 'Good luck.' He beckoned behind him. The two other masked men grabbed hold of the vampire and pushed him forward.

Scarlett's body jerked but she remained in place. 'Devereau,' she hissed.

He gritted his teeth. 'I know.'

'This,' Dom said with a dramatic flourish, 'is Lucifer.' He patted the vampire on the shoulder. 'He was created five months ago and since then has proved to have both power and speed. He is also a fast learner.' He jerked his hand. A projector screen started to lower from the ceiling. 'Behold.'

The screen flickered to life. The video it displayed had a wobbly, home-made quality, which Devereau assumed was done on purpose to add authenticity. It showed a man walking down a quiet street. He wasn't wearing a mask but his head was angled away so his identity wasn't clear. A car, with its numberplate pixilated, pulled up alongside him. The couple next to Devereau held their breaths. A second later, the passenger door opened and the vampire sprang out. He threw himself at the man, his fangs latching onto his neck in the blink of an eye.

'Sixty seconds,' Dom declared. 'Sixty seconds is all it takes a truly motivated vampire to drain a human of their blood.' He jabbed at the drugged vamp next to him. 'And believe me, ladies and gentlemen, Lucifer is truly motivated.'

Devereau glanced at Scarlett again. She gave a tight nod, indicating that Dom wasn't lying. Out of the corner of his eye, he noted a woman a few metres away licking her lips. Sickened, he turned away.

On the screen, the hapless victim collapsed to the ground. There was a moment of stunned silence from the audience that quickly gave way to applause, a smattering at first that grew and grew until it included foot stamping and shouts of approval.

'We have to do something,' Scarlett said beneath the roar of the crowd.

'No chance,' Devereau muttered back. 'We'll be cut down in seconds. The smart thing to do is to wait and see how this plays out, then take our chance to free these two when there are fewer people around.'

'Tell that to yourself,' she said. 'I don't think that werewolf inside you is feeling quite so patient.'

He looked down and realised that his hand was covered in golden-tipped fur. Swallowing hard, he forced it to melt back into human skin just as Dom started speaking into the microphone again. The main lights flickered on, revealing the audience.

'I will start the bidding,' he intoned, 'at one million pounds.'

Almost immediately, twenty hands shot into the air, black cards waving towards the stage, their red numbers displayed.

'Two million,' Dom said. 'Three. Four.' He paused. 'Five.'

Some hands dropped. Others were raised.

'Ten!' yelled an American voice from the other side of the room.

'Twelve!' countered an Australian.

'Fifteen!' screamed a British woman.

Dom's grin was so wide it almost split his face in two.

———

Devereau spotted the three bouncers from outside; two had taken up position at the exit, effectively barring it, and the third was striding towards the dais and motioning to Dom.

'We've got a problem,' Devereau muttered as the MC bent down to listen to the bouncer. 'I think someone's found our unconscious couple outside.'

Dom straightened up as the vamp and the werewolf were dragged hurriedly backwards by the security men and hauled off the dais. 'I apologise for the interruption,' Dom said. 'It appears that we have a couple of intruders in our midst.'

Chapter Sixteen

Dom had barely finished his sentence when weapons were unholstered all around the room. Devereau noted several sharp gasps. His skin started to itch; the animal inside him wanted to be freed and its strength was growing with every second. Futile as it might be to try fighting their way out, it wouldn't be long before there was no choice.

'What?' Scarlett's voice rose above the clamour. Devereau turned to her, alarmed. So did many others. 'This is outrageous!' she shouted

A man standing just to the other side of her drew back his shoulders. 'She's right! You guaranteed our safety. There are supposed to be checks!'

'Who is it?' yelled a woman from further away. 'Who isn't supposed to be here?'

Two men at the front of the crowd turned and started pushing their way towards the barricaded exit. 'Let us out!' one demanded. 'We're not staying a second longer!'

'Ladies and gentlemen!' Dom bellowed. 'Stay calm! If you allow us to check everyone's identities, we will resolve this matter swiftly. As a result, you'll even get to witness Lucifer in action. Stay where you are and—'

'I'm not removing my mask,' Scarlett shouted.

'Yeah!' There were yells of agreement. One of the men by the door tried to push past the bouncers. They both pointed their guns in his face and he responded by drawing out his own weapon.

All hell broke loose. People surged for the door, pushing towards it. On the stage, Dom dropped his hands.

The captive vampire and werewolf were no longer in sight. Devereau spotted the far door closing and sucked in a breath. Scarlett had seen it too. Together they moved against the crowd, heading deeper inside the building rather than trying to escape.

'This is our shot,' Scarlett muttered. 'Come on.'

The shouts of the frustrated would-be bidders were getting louder. One of the security men raised his gun and fired at the ceiling. There were a few screams, but his action only served to rile the others. Someone threw a glass at the bouncers that shattered against the wall above their heads. Another shot was fired – this time Devereau couldn't tell where it was from or whether anyone had been hit. He didn't care if they had been.

Holding Scarlett's hand, he heaved himself through the last of the panicking crowd and ran after Dom, who was fleeing through the rear door.

'Don't change!' Scarlett yelled at him. 'Not yet! Not until there's no other choice!'

Devereau gritted his teeth. That was easy for her to say but he could already feel the growls rumbling deep inside his chest. He tamped them down –just – and lunged for the door. Then they were through and sprinting down a wide corridor.

There were several doors leading off it. As he passed by one of the open ones, Devereau glimpsed seven foot-high cages inside the room. He could smell blood, both old and new, overlaid with the scent of despair. Something inside him snapped. His growls changed to snarls, and he felt his teeth lengthening and his bones snapping.

Scarlett sprang in front of him and forced him to skid to an ungainly halt. 'No.' Her voice was quiet but forceful. 'You will *not* change. We can't afford for these bastards to know who is after them. Right now our supernatural status is our only element of surprise. Change now and we lose that.'

Devereau's jaws snapped but Scarlett's expression didn't change. She reached out and placed her hand across his still-human chest. Her touch was warm and soothing, and it did the trick. The animal inside him subsided and he gasped. 'Sorry.'

'Don't be sorry.' She spun round and started running again. 'Move.'

He watched her retreating back for one long second then he shook himself and took off after her.

There was a storeroom filled with crates of champagne. There was a kitchen with hastily abandoned canapés scattered across a stainless-steel workbench. There was a meeting room with a long table. But there were no people.

Devereau closed his eyes and blocked his other senses. He heard the clang of a door somewhere to the left. He swerved that way and located another corridor. 'Here!' he yelled over his shoulder to Scarlett.

He picked up speed, throwing himself forward with every ounce of energy his pathetic human legs could offer. He felt a brief rush of cold air and realised there was a fire exit ahead of him that lay slightly ajar. Dom had gone this way – and that meant the captive

---

vamp and wolf had, too.

Devereau flung himself through it.

No sooner had he stepped onto the weed-strewn gravel path outside than the shooting started. Something slammed into his shoulder, its velocity knocking him backwards. That was just as well because otherwise the second shot would have smashed into his skull.

There was a squeal of tyres as four separate vehicles revved their engines and started to pull away. There was yet another shot that caught him in his leg. He yelled in pain and then Scarlett's hands were behind him, pulling him back to the relative safety of the warehouse.

Devereau could hear more shots being fired on the other side of the building. There were screams and car horns and a lot of shouting. He blinked as the initial agony of the bullet wounds faded into numbness as his adrenalin took over.

Scarlett yanked his jacket down from his shoulder. 'You're in luck,' she said darkly. 'It's a normal bullet. If you'd transformed into a wolf, you might not have been so lucky. They might have taken the time to find some more appropriate ammunition.' She moved down to his leg and grunted in approval. 'If these bullets had been silver, you wouldn't be doing so well, even though both wounds are clean and the bullets have exited.'

'I … don't … feel,' he managed, 'that … I'm … doing … well.'

She rolled her eyes. 'Devereau Webb, you are still a moany bastard.' Her mouth twisted and she raised her head and listened for a moment. 'They've gone,' she muttered. 'They've escaped.'

Devereau struggled up. 'Then let's go after them.'

'You can barely walk,' she pointed out, stepping back from his wounded leg. 'And even if you could, by the time we get to our car they'll be miles away. By the sounds of things, there's a riot going on out there.'

'That was you,' he whispered. 'If you hadn't shouted out when you did and stirred everyone else up…' His voice faltered. 'Dom and his goons, whoever they are, aren't running from *us*. They're running from all those rich bastards who are upset that their evening was ruined.'

Scarlett met his eyes. 'Never underestimate the feelings of entitlement that rich bastards possess.'

'Noted.' He gazed at her. 'Thank you.'

'For what?'

'All of it.'

She leaned down and brushed her mouth against his cheek. 'You're welcome. But you might still die from your wounds.'

Devereau managed a smile. 'Unlikely.'

Scarlett smiled back. 'Fortunately I've got something that might help with the bleeding.' Her head dipped down and she licked him delicately.

Devereau shuddered.

'Does it hurt?' she asked, glancing up.

'No,' he answered honestly. It tingled. It made his blood sing and his stomach churn. It definitely didn't hurt.

She returned her tongue to his wound. 'Don't worry,' she murmured, her breath hot against his skin. 'Next time I'll use whipped cream instead.'

It didn't take her long to complete her ministrations. By the time she was done, there were no longer screams or shouts or shots. No doubt everyone had skedaddled back to the safety of their own homes.

Devereau checked his wounds. He shouldn't have been surprised to see how quickly they were healing but he was.

'Combination of werewolf immunities and vampire saliva,' Scarlett said. 'Sometimes it's good to be a supe.'

Devereau grunted. 'Not always.' He looked towards the depths of the warehouse. 'We should do a search. There's bound to be something that will lead us back to this Dom prick. If we can find him, we can find the wolf and vampire and help them. They shouldn't spend a second longer in shackles.'

To his surprise, Scarlett shook her head. 'No. This has gone beyond our capabilities. It was beyond us the moment we saw what was really going on here. We'll head straight back to Heart and inform Lord Horvath. He can contact the clan alphas then we can form an army of our own.' Her voice hardened to steel. 'We won't let these bastards get away a second time. We'll force that fucker back at your place to talk as well. He must know all about these … *auctions*.' She almost spat the last word, her disgust palpable.

Devereau was silent for a moment. 'There's still Martina to consider,' he said finally.

Scarlett sighed. 'Realistically, you were never going to keep her existence hidden for long. I'm sorry for her, truly I am, but every clan werewolf out there will tell you that she's too dangerous to have around. And all of this is too big for the two of us to deal with alone.'

He looked into her eyes. 'Alright. Drop me at Lisson Grove and I'll approach the clan alphas myself. You can go onto Soho and speak to your Lord.' His tone was shorter than he intended. 'Then we can meet up back at my place and get that gunman to talk. Maybe Martina will open up as well and tell us what she knows before anyone decides she's too much of a liability to exist.'

Scarlett sucked in a breath. 'Devereau,' she said, 'if there was any other way…'

He glanced away. 'I know.' He checked his watch. 'Come on. Let's get going. We've wasted enough time here already.'

***

Scarlett dropped him directly outside Lady Sullivan's mansion. 'Are you sure you want to do this yourself?' she asked. 'I'll understand if you don't want to speak to the alphas personally. Lord Horvath will be happy do it for you.'

'Are you suggesting that I'm scared?'

'No – although it wouldn't do you any harm to be cautious. The alphas are leaders of their clans for a reason, Devereau. They didn't get that status by smiling prettily and remembering people's birthdays.'

'They didn't intimidate me before I was a wolf and they certainly don't intimidate me now. Besides, I'm part of this community whether anyone likes it or not. It's time I stepped up to the plate and proved it.'

'Good.' Without smiling, she reached across and put her hand over his. 'This is the right thing to do. It's not just about Martina any more. There might be others who are being held captive – and we certainly can't allow a group of humans to control us. Any of us.'

He managed a nod. 'I know.' He unclipped his seatbelt and climbed out of the car. 'Let's talk soon.'

Scarlett acknowledged him with a wave of her hand. She didn't, however, make any move to drive off. Devereau shoved his hands into pockets, ignoring the dull throb of pain in his shoulder and his leg. His bullet wounds hadn't been serious but, even so, they were healing extraordinarily quickly. When he walked up the stone steps to the Sullivan front door, he didn't even limp. Impressive, indeed. Although it was only when the door opened and a man in his fifties peered out that Devereau heard Scarlett drive away.

'Yes?' the man asked, his expression cold.

'I'm Devereau Webb.'

'I know that.' He sniffed. Then with heavy reluctance he added, 'My name is Robert.'

Devereau glanced at the Robert's attire, noting the tag on his arm that indicated he was a beta wolf and therefore one of Lady Sullivan's right-hand werewolves. 'I came to apologise to Lady Sullivan.'

Robert glowered at him. 'Regardless of your lifestyle and the dubious company you keep, it is almost midnight. Lady Sullivan does not take visitors at this hour.'

'I understand that. She's getting on a bit and probably needs a good night's sleep.'

Sparks of fury lit Robert's face. 'Why you little upstart…! And what is this we've been hearing about a shoot-out at your house? If you think that you can waltz into our part of town and bring your nasty criminal element with you then…'

'Then what?' Devereau enquired mildly.

'Then you can fuck right off.'

'Huh.' He shrugged. 'Alright then.' He turned on his heel and descended to the pavement. He smiled to himself. And then he started to run.

Chapter Seventeen

There were more of his old crew hanging around on his new street than he'd expected. He might have been touched had he not known they were there out of fear of, rather than respect for, him. They were clearly wary of the supes who were still dotted around at Scarlett's behest. None of his people were anywhere near them, and vice-versa.

He was tempted to let them off the hook and tell them all to go home, but their presence served a purpose. He considered the angles, made a decision then strode up to Gloria, a platinum blonde who took no shit from anyone. She was watching him very carefully.

'Hi, Glory,' Devereau said softly. 'Thank you for doing this.'

'I'm only here because of who you were, not what you are now. I don't hold no truck with supes. It ain't natural.' She paused to glare at a gremlin who was perched on the roof of a van nearby before looking back at Devereau. 'No offence, like.'

He didn't have time to take offence and neither was he a delicate flower. He'd heard far worse. 'Is Gaz still here?'

'He's having a kip in a car at the end of the street. Shall I wake him up?'

'Yeah. Tell him to come to the house as soon as he can.'

'You gonna eat him?' she asked.

He gave her a long look. 'No.'

Her expression didn't change. 'I was making a joke.'

'Oh.' He shrugged. 'Okay.'

Gloria folded her arms and tapped her foot until Devereau forced a laugh. She finally nodded, satisfied that he'd acknowledged her attempt at humour. 'Five minutes,' she promised.

'Thank you.' He gave a brisk nod then strode over to two mean-looking pixies who were watching his every move. 'You're doing a good job, fellas,' he said. 'I appreciate it. I'm heading inside to get cleaned up. More vamps are probably on their way. I have a feeling this night is far from over.'

They frowned at him, mirror images of each other. 'You Devereau Webb?' one of them asked.

'Yeah.'

'Were you really bitten four times before you turned?'

'Yeah.'

They exchanged glances. 'It's been a long while since the clans had someone with that much strength,' the first speaker said.

'It's about time though,' said the other. 'Those furry bastards have been fucking up a lot lately.'

His buddy snorted and gestured towards Devereau. 'This one's house was shot up the day he moved in. I don't think he's going to be anyone's hero any time soon.'

Unfortunately, Devereau thought, the little pixie was right, especially given what had just occurred in that hellhole of a warehouse and what was going to happen over the next few hours. 'Well anyway,' he murmured, 'thanks for keeping an eye out. I owe you for this. If you ever need a favour, just let me know.'

The pixies nudged each other. 'Hear that? Maybe he is a hero after all.'

'I'm not,' Devereau said hastily. 'But I know how to pay my debts.' He moved off to his battered house before they could say anything else.

Everything was very quiet and very still. Devereau paused, genuinely appreciating a moment of peace, then he turned the doorknob and walked in. Inside there was the same aura of serenity. Unfortunately, he was certain it was only the calm before the storm.

First he checked on the man chained to the radiator. He'd regained consciousness and, from the marks around his wrists, had been making futile attempts to free himself. Devereau wagged a warning finger at him and he cowered in response. The bravado he'd displayed earlier had all but disappeared.

'Now, now,' Devereau chided. 'You wouldn't want to do anything to make me more angry than I already am. You were lucky that the worst you received last time was a punch – I am a werewolf, after all. When my animal takes over, anything is possible. You've seen what the girl upstairs is capable of. Imagine what I can do.'

The man flinched. Devereau shrugged; he didn't feel a jot of sympathy for the bastard.

He found Dr Yara and Martina upstairs, curled up together on a narrow single bed. Martina's arm was tightly bandaged. Devereau hoped that meant what he thought it did.

Yara opened her eyes as soon as he entered the room, extricated herself from Martina and sat up. 'She has nightmares,' she explained. She tilted her head up at Devereau. 'Is problem?'

'Yes. Did you manage to remove the tracker?'

She nodded. 'Yes. Was not so difficult.'

He had the feeling that meant it had been very difficult indeed. 'Thank you,' he said. 'That's a huge help because now we need to leave without anyone noticing.'

Concern lit her face. 'Is dangerous?'

'For Martina it is. You should go back home. I'll keep her safe. You've done more than enough.'

Dr Yara's eyes darkened. 'I stay with you.'

'I don't want you to get hurt.'

'I stay.'

Devereau sighed. 'Okay.' He glanced down at Martina's small body. Her eyes remained closed but he knew from her breathing that she was awake and listening to every word. That was good. She might be a child but she deserved to know the truth about what was going on. 'People are going to come here. Strong people. They are going to try and take Martina away. Probably even kill her. They will think that she's too dangerous and that she can't control the werewolf inside her. The only way we can protect her is by getting out of here and hiding somewhere else.'

Dr Yara's eyes were saucer wide. 'Where?'

Devereau grimaced. 'I haven't worked that part out yet. I will, though.' He ran a hand through his hair. 'Has she said anything about what happened to her? About who hurt her or who she really is?'

Mutely, Dr Yara shook her head. Damn it.

'Okay. Gather up anything you think you might need. Especially the tranquilisers. I don't want to use them but I'm finding it difficult to control my wolf so for Martina, it must be excruciating. Meet me back downstairs as soon as you can.'

'Yes, Mr Webb.' Dr Yara was already on her feet and moving around the room, grabbing the neatly piled clothes and stuffing them into a bag. Devereau left her to it and headed back to the ground floor just in time to hear a knock from outside.

Gaz was shuffling his feet on the doorstep and yawning. 'What's up, boss?'

Devereau smiled slightly at his stifled yawn before he got down to business. 'I'm going to ask you for one final favour, Gaz,' he said. 'And then we're done.'

Gaz swallowed back his second yawn and stared. 'Done?'

'You've done more for me than anyone. If you ever need help of any sort you'd better come running or I will hunt you down and rip your arms off with my big wolfy teeth.'

Gaz's eyes widened.

'But,' Devereau continued, more gently this time, 'we belong in different worlds. It's taken me a while to see it and for that I'm sorry. Look after everyone at home for me. Remember everything we've learned along the way, and don't allow any of them to be reckless or stupid. We might be criminals but we still have morals. Right?'

Gaz's head dropped. 'Right,' he mumbled.

'It's better for all of us if we stay separate. Obviously I'll still be in touch with Tash and Alice, and I might even drop by to visit from time to time. But that's it. Everything else is history.'

'Yes, boss.'

Devereau smiled. 'I'm not your boss. Not now.'

Gaz straightened up. 'Okay.'

'You've got this. I believe in you.'

Gaz nodded and Devereau was sure he saw the glint of tears in his eyes, but he knew better than to comment on it.

'What is it?' Gaz asked. 'What's the last favour?' He drew in a breath and his next words came out in a rush. 'Because if it's anything dangerous, we might not be able to do it. I'm not going put people in danger.'

'Good for you,' Devereau said quietly. 'And no, it shouldn't be dangerous. All I need is for you and the others to stay here for the next few hours. Make it seem as if I'm holed up inside this house and refusing to come out. Don't get into a fight with anyone, especially if they rock up and demand to get inside to check on me. Delay them as long as you can, then pull back and head home as fast as your feet will carry you. The longer everyone thinks I'm in here, the better.'

'Where will you be?'

'I don't know yet. And even if I did, it's safer if you don't know.'

Gaz bit his lip.

'If anything does happen to me, get blitzed at my wake and move on. My decisions are my own. Don't seek revenge. Don't go antagonising any supes or any humans. Don't try to find out what happened to me. You have a life to live. Anything that happens to me is on me. Got that?'

'Yes, boss.'

Devereau stared at him.

'I mean, yes,' Gaz amended.

Devereau smiled. 'You take care.' There was a thump behind him. He glanced over his shoulder to see Dr Yara at the foot of the stairs, her chin jutting out resolutely. Martina looked anxious and pale but she also had a look of steely-eyed determination.

'We're going to sneak out the back. I'll be seeing you, Gaz.' Devereau raised a hand in farewell and closed the door before he did anything daft like force his old sidekick into a hug. He turned.

———

'Alright, ladies. I'm going to grab our friend who's tied to the radiator and we'll be on our way. Follow me.'

***

They escaped through the dark undergrowth of the back garden without too much trouble. Devereau kept a tight hand on the pale-faced gunman but he was now completely cowed and still tied at the wrists, so he wasn't likely to try to escape. Devereau had also gagged him with one of Dr Yara's scarves just in case he tried shouting for help and drawing unwanted attention. He'd sing like a canary later though – Devereau would make sure of that.

Martina's trousers snagged on an old nail as they clambered over the fence and there was a loud ripping sound as she yanked them free, but other than that they managed to get several streets away without any ado. Luckily any werewolves who lived nearby weren't creatures of the night like the vampires. It made slipping away unnoticed far easier.

Devereau had been telling the truth to Gaz – he didn't have any particular destination in mind. Part of him thought it might be wise to get out of London altogether; the other part reckoned it would be easier to hide in the anonymity a big city. In the end, he decided that that running away didn't suit him. He'd never catch up with Dom and the other wankers behind all this if he skittered away like a mouse. All he had to do was find a place where Yara and Martina could stay out of sight and they'd be sorted.

They marched three abreast down the street with the captive gunman stumbling behind them. It was only when Martina started to drag her feet that Devereau allowed them to slow down.

They were far enough away from both Lisson Grove and Soho that he could steal a car without it being immediately traced back to him. There was an estate car on the other side of the road that was so old he knew he could break into it easily. He pointed it out to Dr Yara. She clicked her tongue in disapproval but followed him with Martina and their captive.

Devereau tried the door. It was astonishing how many people forgot to lock their cars and it was always wise to check before forcing a door open. Unfortunately, the owner of this vehicle was smart and the door didn't budge. Before he could try anything else his phone started to ring. He pulled his mobile out of his pocket with his free hand and glanced at the screen. Three missed calls, all from Mrs Foster.

———

He frowned as the phone continued to ring. He debated with himself and then answered it. 'Hi Scarlett.'

She didn't waste time with pleasantries. 'Have you spoken to all the alphas? How did they take the news?'

'I spoke to some sniffy werewolf called Robert,' he answered, unwilling to lie to her outright.

'That's one of Lady Sullivan's betas.'

'I figured.'

'What about the others?'

'I haven't spoken to them yet.'

There was a beat of silence. 'Where are you now, Devereau?'

The best way to answer any question that you didn't want to answer was to ask a question. 'What about Lord Horvath? How did His Fanginess take the news?'

Scarlett hissed. 'He's not here. He's gone up country to deal with something else.'

What a shame. 'Oh dear,' Devereau murmured.

'It doesn't matter,' she continued briskly. 'I've gathered up plenty of the others. I'm heading to your place to get hold of your prisoner so we can question him. The rest are heading back to the warehouse to investigate it inch by inch. Tell the clans to meet them there.'

Devereau didn't answer. The silence stretched out painfully.

Eventually Scarlett spoke again. 'I was afraid of this.' She sighed with grim resignation. 'You haven't told the alphas what's going on, have you? Are you back at your house? Is Martina with you?' She hesitated. 'Devereau, are you being a fuckwit and doing something really stupid?'

The smallest smile curved his lips. 'Scarlett,' he said, 'you knew deep down I was going to do something really stupid. And you wouldn't have let me go off alone to do it if you didn't approve, even though you can't say so aloud.'

'The next time I see you, Devereau Webb, I'm going to slap you so hard…'

'I'm already looking forward to it. Take care, Scarlett.' He ended the call.

Before Scarlett could call back and berate him again, he hit Mrs Foster's number. To his surprise, she answered on the third ring. Despite the late hour, the headteacher didn't sound tired at all. 'Mr Webb. I was hoping you would call me back.'

'You have news for me?'

'I do. I've managed to locate the girl's identity. I know who she is.'

Devereau sucked in a breath and glanced at Martina. She was staring at the ground. His fingers tightened round the phone.

'Go on.'

'Her name is Angelica Crystal. She's from Bromley. Her father is her sole guardian as her mother is deceased. He's a businessman who runs some kind of import company. She's not been reported missing, but she's been absent from her school for three weeks and they're concerned. They've contacted her father several times and he's not responded. Social services haven't had any luck in getting hold of him either.'

'Angelica,' Devereau whispered. As soon as he said her name, her head whipped up. He couldn't mistake the sudden terror written across her face. The bound gunman also stared at him, his baleful expression clear despite the night gloom. 'Thank you for this, Mrs Foster,' Devereau said more loudly. 'I think that, given the circumstances, it would be wise if you keep the information about her to yourself for now. I'll take care of things from here.'

'I don't think so, Mr Webb. You've involved me now by divulging what's happened to this girl. I completely agree that it would be sensible not to approach either her father or the police until you're sure exactly what has happened, but you can't seriously expect me just to forget about her.'

Devereau turned and walked a few metres away. He kept his voice low. 'Right now she's both dangerous and in danger. It's safer for you if you forget you ever heard of her.'

'I can't do that. Where is she at the moment? I can't imagine that she's in an appropriate environment for a child. You need a responsible adult who's going to look after her properly.'

'I *am* a responsible adult.' Some of the time, anyway. 'And I've got help. In fact—' He broke off as he thought of something. 'Mrs Foster,' he said suddenly. 'How many bedrooms do you have?'

Chapter Eighteen

It was after three in the morning when they reached the detached house with its pristine front garden and smart red-brick facade. Martina was curled up gently snoring in the back seat of the stolen car, while Dr Yara stared out of the window, agog at the vision of London's suburbia. It was a far cry from the tower block where she lived, and it was certainly different to the ramshackle terraced house which Devereau now rented. For one thing, there weren't any visible bullet holes.

'We can trust her? This teacher?'

Devereau's eyes flitted round the quiet street, piercing dark bushes and examining shadowy corners. 'We have to,' he said simply. 'But wait here in the car for a few minutes first.' He paused. 'Just in case.' They were already risking far too much to take any foolhardy chances.

He opened the car door and stepped out, tilting his head for a moment to listen. From the end of the cul-de-sac there was a rustle and he stiffened, watching as the leaves on a bush quivered. A fox padded out, its nose raised as it too sniffed the air. Its head twisted towards him and it froze, staring at him. The fox knew instinctively that he was a dangerous predator who was to be avoided at all costs. It remained stock still for several seconds before bolting across the road and disappearing into the shadows of another garden.

'You don't concern me,' Devereau whispered after it.

He turned on his heel and examined the rest of the area. All of the houses, bar Mrs Foster's, were in darkness. He suspected that the people who lived here were the sort who ensured they had security lighting at their front and back doors. There were certainly enough Neighbourhood Watch signs to give any burglar pause. Rather than upsetting him, however, their presence comforted him. Nosy neighbours meant there would be less chance that strangers could slide in without being noticed.

Satisfied that the street was devoid of watchers, he returned his attention to Mrs Foster's home. The curtains were drawn but it was obvious from the weak glow that there was a light on downstairs. He couldn't make out any movement from inside but that was to be expected. Stepping forward on the balls of his feet, he walked across the dew-laden grass where his footsteps would be muffled. He ducked low beneath the window and listened again; there was no sound other than the hushed murmur of classical music.

Abandoning the front of the house, he checked the rear. Mrs Foster appeared to have a penchant for ugly gnomes: they were dotted all over the back garden. Several of them looked remarkably evil and he glared at one that seemed to be giving him the eye.

Satisfied that all was quiet, he went to the back door and tapped gently on the glass. Within moments, Mrs Foster appeared, a belted dressing gown wrapped tightly round her body. White-faced, she peered out before registering his features and relaxing. 'You're alone?' she asked as she opened the door.

'I'd like to check your house first,' he said. 'It's not that I don't trust you but…' He shrugged and amended his words. 'It's that I don't trust you.'

Fortunately, she didn't seem offended. 'That's wise, Mr Webb. I'm still wondering whether I can trust *you*. This is my home. And you're a werewolf.'

'Before I was a werewolf, I was a crime lord,' he said. 'A small fact that you were aware of and which never bothered you.'

Mrs Foster's brow creased. 'Oh, I beg to differ, Mr Webb. You were no crime lord – a crime squire at best, if we're being honest.' Devereau raised an eyebrow and she smiled. 'I have a nephew who works for you. Or at least he used to work for you.'

He had no idea who she was talking about. 'It doesn't bother you that I led a family member of yours into a life of crime?'

'It was a year of his life at best. Ian was always a troubled lad, despite our best efforts. He worked for you for ten months and then you booted him out and sent him on his way to university.'

'Ian Tanner,' Devereau said slowly. 'He went off to do electrical engineering.'

She nodded. 'He graduated last year.' She looked at him levelly. 'Let's be clear, I do not approve of what your organisation does but you sorted out Ian. He still speaks very highly of you.'

'Even though I'm now a werewolf?'

'Even now.' She gazed at him assessingly. She might be in a dressing gown but she still cut a formidable figure. 'Tell me what it means to be a werewolf.'

He crossed his arms in exasperation. 'I'm sure you've read plenty on the subject in the past few days.'

'I want to hear it from you.' She fixed him with a glare.

'I left school at fourteen,' he said. 'I was expelled and I never bothered going back. I don't think I can explain it eloquently enough for your purposes.'

'I doubt that very much, Mr Webb. I think you're more than eloquent enough for the both of us. I might be a school teacher but I'm not naïve enough to think that intelligence only begins at the classroom door.' She waved at him impatiently. 'Speak. And be quick. You're letting in a draught.'

He didn't appear to have much choice. He shifted his weight from foot to foot. 'I have power,' he said finally. 'When I change, I can feel it in every sinew, in every vein and in every bone of my body. I'm hyper-aware of everything and there's almost nothing or no one that I don't think I can kill. When I'm a wolf, I can *smell* what people feel. Their emotions seep through their pores with such strong scents that I'm amazed I never noticed them before. There's a man tied up in the boot of my stolen car right now and, even though he's metres away and I'm like this,' he gestured at his human form, 'I can still smell his terror.'

Mrs Foster's hand rose to her throat in horror. 'What do I smell like?'

'Confusion,' he said. 'Fear. Wariness. Worry.' He tilted his head. 'And garlic.'

She gave him a puzzled look before her expression cleared. 'Oh. I had chicken Kiev for dinner.' She swallowed. 'Why is there a man in your boot?'

'He tried to kill Angelica Crystal, and I think he might have some answers about what's happened to her and who is responsible.'

'Will you torture him?' Her voice was steady despite the loaded question.

Devereau didn't lie. 'I will do what it takes to get the information I need from him.'

Mrs Foster didn't blink. 'Have you ever killed anyone, Mr Webb?'

He thought of the man from the roof who'd fallen next to PC Hackert's shiny shoes. 'I have,' he said quietly, and with considerable shame. 'Not as a wolf but as a man.' He didn't attempt to explain that it had been self-defence, or that the man had been trying to kill him. He'd done what he'd done and he would own up to it. 'I won't hurt you, Mrs Foster. I won't hurt Angelica Crystal. I can't say more than that.'

She gazed into his eyes then stepped aside and gestured him indoors. Devereau jerked in surprise. 'You told me the truth, Mr Webb. I can ask for nothing more.'

'You have to be sure.'

———

She nodded. 'I am.'
He didn't smile. 'Then call me Devereau.'
She held out her hand. He took it.
'I'm Rachel,' she said softly.

***

He didn't take long checking Rachel Foster's home. Nobody else was there. 'Your husband?' he asked.

'My wife passed away last year,' Rachel said.

Devereau winced. 'I didn't know,' he said. 'I'm sorry.'

'That I had a wife? Or that she's dead?'

'Both.' He put his hands in his pockets in a vain attempt to avoid the sting of discomfort from showing in his body language.

'I try to keep my professional and personal lives separate,' Rachel said. 'I was more successful than I realised.' She gave a slight smile, although it lacked humour. 'Madeleine had cancer. It still feels very raw.'

Alice's face flashed into his mind. 'I'm truly sorry.'

'I know.' She sighed. 'Everyone always is. When I heard about Alice's leukaemia...' She didn't finish her sentence.

'She was lucky.' He looked down. 'We all were.'

'I'm glad.' Rachel sounded as if she meant it. 'Listen, about the library. I'm truly sorry for what happened.'

Devereau growled, 'I don't care about the damned library.'

'Fair enough. I just want you to know that it wasn't my decision. We all have to answer to other people.'

'I don't answer to anyone.'

She laughed. 'Of course you do. You've got a young girl waiting out there and probably an entire community of werewolves somewhere, too. Where is Angelica anyway?'

Devereau rubbed the back of his neck. 'I'll go and fetch her.' He went back to the front of her house and nodded at Dr Yara, who was still in the passenger seat of the car. She opened the door and peered at him. 'Is alright?'

'Yes.'

Dr Yara sniffed. 'Good.'

From the back, Angelica stirred. 'We're here?' she asked sleepily.

'We are.' Devereau smiled at her. 'You'll be safe here.'

She didn't flinch. 'I won't be safe anywhere.'

He had no response for that.

———

The three of them walked to the front door where Rachel was waiting. She smiled with far more warmth than he'd seen before. 'Hi, Angelica. I'm Rachel. It's lovely to meet you.'

'Martina.'

Rachel started. 'Pardon?'

'My name is Martina.' There was a mutinous tilt to her chin. 'It means little warrior. I don't want to be Angelica again. *He* called me Angelica all the time and now I don't want that name.'

Devereau, Dr Yara and Rachel exchanged looks.

'Who is he?' Devereau asked.

Martina stubbornly pinned her mouth shut and shook her head. It was clear she wasn't going to talk.

Rachel recovered first. 'Then Martina it is,' she said cheerfully. 'Are you hungry? I know it's the middle of the night but I can get you a snack, if you like.' Martina shook her head. 'Then let me show you to your room. I've made up a bed for you.' She glanced at Dr Yara and Devereau. 'There's a room for the two of you as well, if you don't mind sharing.'

'Dr Yara can take it,' Devereau said. 'I have a few things I need to deal with.'

Both women looked at him.

'Yes,' Rachel murmured. 'I suppose you do.'

Yara gave him a disapproving frown that Devereau pretended not to see. 'Call me if there's any hint of trouble,' he said.

'We'll be fine.'

He sincerely hoped so. He nodded once and left.

***

This wasn't something he particularly wanted to do but he was going to do it anyway. Steeling himself, he drove the car until it was several miles away from Rachel Foster's house, then found a quiet spot on the edge of some playing fields and pulled up. He walked round and opened the boot. To the gunman's credit, he'd stayed quiet throughout the journey but he let out a terrified squeak when he saw Devereau gazing down at him.

Devereau reached down and removed the gag. 'You can scream now if you want,' he said conversationally. 'Nobody will hear you if you do.' He wasn't entirely sure that was true but it sounded good. The key to success here was brutal confidence, the more brutal the better. He'd had plenty of practice in the past – and now he was a werewolf he had even more tricks up his sleeve. 'What's your name?' His tone was mild.

The man hesitated. 'Morty,' he quavered. 'What do you want?'

Devereau grinned nastily. 'To have a little fun.' He grabbed Morty's shirt and hauled him up, dragging him out of the boot and depositing him unceremoniously on the ground. 'Take a look around.'

His captive lifted up his head and gazed round. 'Wh – what? There's nothing here.'

'Exactly.' Devereau licked his lips. 'I'll give you a twenty-second head start.'

'Huh?'

Devereau smirked and finally allowed the werewolf inside him to take over. Within moments, his hands and feet changed to heavy paws. His body grew and altered. The release was almost orgasmic. He shook out his fur and drew his lips over his sharp lupine teeth.

And that was when the man in front of him started to run.

Devereau watched. For someone who'd lost a lot of blood and had recently spent a considerable amount of time unconscious, Morty was putting on a good show. He sprinted away, zigzagging across the first field. Unfortunately, it was often used for amateur rugby matches and the ground was uneven, with divots and holes and bumps that would make even the best runner struggle. He'd barely managed thirty metres before the toe of his shoe caught in a rut. Momentum flung him forward and he landed spread-eagled on the ground.

Devereau winced. Even from this distance it looked as if the runaway had twisted his ankle badly. He waited another beat – and then he leapt after his prey.

Morty cried out but he was only wasting energy. Devereau's paws thundered across the uneven ground, his four-footed gait giving him greater speed and stability. In seconds he'd reached him. That was too fast – he wanted to play a little with his food.

Morty tried to scramble to his feet as Devereau circled him. Every time he tried to push forward and get away, Devereau lunged at him, his jaws snapping. Once. Twice. Three times. When biting at air grew dull, he allowed his canines to scrape Morty's skin. It wasn't even enough to draw blood but it still caused the frightened wee shite to screech, 'No! No! Please!'

There was something oddly pleasing about the tremor in his voice. Fear was quite an aphrodisiac, Devereau decided. He growled in satisfaction and nipped him again. This time he was rewarded with a howl.

'I'm sorry, alright? I'm sorry! I was only doing what I was told to! I shouldn't have gone to your house. I shouldn't have tried to shoot you or that kid. I won't do it again.' Morty fell forward onto his hands and knees, his fingers digging into the wet dirt. The salty scent of tears filled the air around him. 'Please. I can help you. I'll tell you everything I know. I told you about the tracker in the kid's body but I can tell you a whole lot more. I know it all. I know everything! I'll talk. I'll talk. I'll talk!' His words ran together, his breath ragged and his tone a high-pitched whine.

Devereau narrowed his eyes and then, with considerable effort, transformed himself again. 'I thought you'd never offer,' he said. He folded his arms across his bare chest, ignoring the fact that he was now stark bollock naked. 'So talk.'

Chapter Nineteen

They returned to the car. Devereau pulled on the pair of trousers and fresh shirt that Dr Yara had packed and left in the boot for him while the pathetic excuse for a gunman waited miserably. Devereau was rather hoping he'd attempt to run off again. He'd never quite appreciated the joy of the chase before now. Sadly, Morty simply perched on the car bonnet until Devereau was ready. Oh well. You couldn't have everything.

'Begin.'

Morty wrapped his arms round himself like a small child. It was an odd look for such a muscle-bound adult. 'I've been working for a company called Matelot for about twelve months. They're the ones who sent me to your place. I only got the job because my old sergeant put in a good word for me. At first I thought it was going to be a normal security gig.' He dropped his head. 'I was wrong.'

'Aw, diddums,' Devereau said. 'Didn't you get a job description first?'

'It's not my fucking fault! I needed the money!'

'I bet they pay you pretty well. It would have to be good money to be prepared to put bullets in the skull of a twelve-year-old girl.'

Morty's bottom lip jutted out. 'If she'd done what she was told, she'd have been fine. It's her fault things ended up this way.'

Unbelievable. Devereau had heard some outlandish examples of victim blaming in his time, but this took the damned biscuit. But he couldn't afford to lose his temper and smack the guy in the head again, so he folded his arms and ignored the stabbing pain between his shoulder blades. 'Let's stick to the subject, shall we?' he said grimly. 'Continue.'

Morty swallowed. 'Don't pretend like you're some kind of saint. I know who you are. I know what you've done.'

There was nothing in Devereau's past that compared to this bastard's deeds but he managed not to rise to the bait. 'I'm not the one in danger of getting my flesh ripped to pieces. Keep talking.'

There was an audible sigh. 'Fine. At first I was just helping with the regular shipments, nothing out of the ordinary. Containers came in, usually filled with shite like cheap T-shirts and cuddly toys, and I made sure the contents got to the right places for the right prices.'

Fair enough – except there weren't any mass-produced teddy bears anywhere in the world that needed armed guards to protect them. 'Drugs?' Devereau asked.

'Yeah. MDMA, heroin, that kind of thing. If Matelot had continued along those lines everything would have been fine, but they decided they wanted to diversify and make more money.'

'Sure,' Devereau said sarcastically. 'Because throwing addictive shite out onto the streets is a real community service kind of thing.'

He received a baleful glance. 'Do you want to hear this or not?'

'Go on, then. Tell me about Matelot. Who's in charge?'

Morty shrugged. 'I have no clue.'

With deliberately casual movements, Devereau unfolded his arms. He reached forward, grabbed the man's ear and twisted it hard.

'Ow! Fuck off! If I tell you, he'll kill me!'

'If you don't tell me, I'll eat you. It's quite the conundrum,' Devereau said easily. 'If I were you, I'd focus on the more immediate threat. Who's your boss? Who runs Matelot?'

Morty was pale and shaking. Devereau reached for his ear again and he flailed backwards. His words came out in a rush. 'Alright! Alright! It's a man called Dominic Phillips. He runs Matelot.'

'Dominic Phillips?' The man nodded. 'Dom, for short? About six feet tall? Dark hair?' Enjoys wearing masks and prancing around on a stage?

The response was surly. 'That's him.'

'What's he like?'

'He's a sadist. Thinks very highly of himself. Went to some posh school with a special tie that he still wears when he wants to show off. He knows a lot of people in high places and seems to think that makes him better than everyone else.'

'You don't like him.'

'I don't like rich boys who think they're better than I am.'

'But,' Devereau murmured, 'you don't mind working for them.'

'I told you, I needed the fucking money.' Morty sighed dramatically as if he were nothing more than a poor innocent who'd been pulled, protesting, into a life of crime. 'Besides, things weren't that bad until Germany. Dom was born with a silver spoon in his mouth but he's still a smart guy with a lot of power. There are advantages to working for someone like that. Until Germany, I was enjoying it but that was when the shit really hit the fan.'

Devereau eyed him. 'What happened in Germany?'

'We were in Berlin about eight months ago. There was some kind of big deal going down. I was there with a few others. We were supposed to keep our mouths shut and just look menacing. I was packing heat, of course, but we weren't expecting much to happen.'

Packing heat? This idiot seemed to think he was an American gangster in a film with more car chases than sensible dialogue. Devereau had encountered plenty of halfwits like this before; even so, his faith in humanity sank every time he met another one.

'Anyway, Dom wasn't happy with the product. He weighed it and said he was being short changed – he pulled that sort of crap all the time. More often than not it worked and the other guys would toss in an extra bag to show they could be trusted. This time, instead of backing down, they attacked.' Morty shook his head. 'I'd never seen anything like it. There were only three of them but they moved faster than lightning. I got off a few shots. If those guys had been normal they'd have been dead on the floor, and we'd have had the drugs and the money. Instead, we barely made it out of there alive.'

'Let me guess,' Devereau said, 'they were supes.'

'Two of them were. The other guy must have been human. He stood and watched them almost annihilate us. I don't know what happened after that except that there were a lot of mysterious meetings. Three weeks later we were told that we were going to start dealing in a different product.'

Devereau gave him a sickened look. 'People, you mean.'

'Monsters,' Morty corrected. 'Not people.'

Devereau shook his head in disgust. So Dominic Phillips had realised that Matelot, whether they had guns with them or not, couldn't match up against supernatural creatures. The only way to compete was to match the strength of their competitors. He probably couldn't get hold of any supes who would willingly work for him so he went a different route – one that was far, far worse.

'We found out where the Germans were hiding and took them on.' There was a nauseating pride in Morty's voice. 'We were on them long before they knew what was happening, and we had orders to incapacitate rather than kill them. In the end there were only four of them – two humans, one vamp, one werewolf. Once Dom had established what they were, the humans were killed and the supes were taken. I don't know where to, but six weeks later we suddenly had some vampires and werewolves of our own. And when other people saw how much power we had, they wanted it for themselves. It turns out dealing in power is a lot more lucrative than dealing in dope.' He grimaced slightly. 'There's a bit of a catch, though. It's not always easy finding people who are willing to be turned into monsters.'

'So,' Devereau said, his voice dangerously quiet, 'you started to force people.'

'Not me.' Morty held up his hands. 'That wasn't my job. I wouldn't do that!'

'Yeah. You're a real saint.'

'I don't know where Dom got the people from, alright? Not from this country. You don't shit where you eat, do you? Besides, we knew that if the supes here cottoned on to what we were doing, there'd be trouble.' He pulled a face. 'Nobody wanted to go up against Lord Horvath and the wolf clans.'

'You're a despicable excuse for a human being,' Devereau said. He lowered his face to the man's, his features twisted into a snarl. 'So instead of shipping illegal drugs, Matelot started bringing in illegal supes. You are trafficking people.'

'We're probably doing them a favour! They've got better lives now than they had before!'

Devereau's hands clenched into fists. He doubted that very much.

'They get sold to rich pricks who use them for protection or intimidation or whatever weird shit they happen to be into at the time.' Morty's desperate attempts to justify what Matelot were up to were disgusting. 'It's not a bad gig.'

Devereau thought about the glazed look in the eyes of the vamp and wolf he'd seen at the auction. 'Except the people you're talking about are controlled through drugs, manipulation and threats to their families. Am I right?'

'I wouldn't know about any of that!'

Devereau hissed quietly. 'And the girl? What about her? How did she get involved?'

Morty's gaze dropped. 'Her father worked with Matelot. What happened was his own fault. Word was he was skimming off the top and thought nobody would notice. Dom found out and decided to make sure that nobody tried anything like that again.'

Something hardened inside Devereau. 'I bet I can guess. Dominic Phillips nabbed his daughter and forced her to become a wolf.'

'Yeah. He thought he could kill two birds with one stone. Turn someone that young and have more control over them in the future. He could make that kid his own creature and get his revenge on her father at the same time. Except it went wrong.'

No wonder Martina had refused to say a word about who she was or what had happened to her: she thought she would be putting her father in danger. Devereau had a feeling he knew what had happened but he asked anyway. 'How? How did it go wrong?'

'The kid's father wasn't happy and he started to cause more problems. And the kid wasn't as compliant as Dom thought she would be, so he decided to give her a bit of a nudge. Prove to her that there would be consequences if she didn't do what they wanted. He had her dad roughed up while she was forced to watch. Dom said he'd kill him if she ever revealed who or what she was. He made it clear that she had to do everything they told her to, then he smacked her around a bit too so the orders really sank in.'

Morty looked at Devereau and finally registered the ice-cold fury reflecting back at him. 'But I didn't hurt her! It was Dom, not me. None of this is my fault!'

'Yeah,' Devereau said sarcastically. Images of all the different ways he could kill this bastard and get away with it flashed through his mind. 'You're truly a blameless innocent.' He shook his head in disgust. 'So I assume this little show took place at Goodman's Alley. That's why there were three different types of spilled blood but only two bodies. The girl was supposed to be under control but instead she flipped, transformed and killed two men. The rest of the blood belonged to her father.' Devereau paused. 'Is he still alive?'

'When his kid went nuts, he managed to escape. So did Dom, me and a couple of others.'

Martina's dad ran away from his daughter instead of trying to help her. Devereau's opinion of him wasn't improving – but that was nothing compared to what he thought of Dominic Phillips. 'So you don't know where he is now?'

Morty's eyes shifted. 'Dom has him.'

Pain jabbed between Devereau's shoulders. No doubt the sadistic bastard was holding Martina's father as leverage against her. No matter where Martina was, Dom could use her father to stop her from talking. He breathed in deeply. Manipulating a child in this manner was beyond the fucking pale.

But something didn't quite add up.

'Why Goodman's Alley?' Devereau asked. He knew Dom had a perfectly serviceable warehouse where anything untoward would go unnoticed. Goodman's Alley was in a heavily populated area of the city; it didn't make sense to go to a place where they could be both seen and heard. 'Why go to that house?'

'The secretary.'

Devereau stared. 'You mean David Bernard's secretary.' He thought about the information he'd gleaned from Supe Squad. 'Is her name Marsha Kennard?'

Morty looked at him suspiciously. 'You're very well informed.

David Bernard did a bunch of legal stuff for Matelot. He wanted to get involved with some of the more unsavoury shite but he was worried about his secretary. She didn't approve of Matelot and started to complain. She said that she'd contact the police if he didn't drop Matelot as a client. Dom took the kid to her house on Goodman's Alley to force her to toe the line and make her do as she was told. Either Dom was going to kill her father, or the kid was going to kill the secretary.'

Nausea rose up from Devereau's gullet. He swallowed back the bitter bile. 'Is she dead? Is Marsha Kennard dead?'

'Nah.' The man shrugged. 'She escaped when the kid freaked. I don't know where she went. Nobody does.'

So that's who the macabre, bloodied message had been for at Bernard's office building. The secretary had run away from Goodman's Alley and was now in hiding, while Matelot were deep into damage limitation and desperate to keep their activities secret. The only way they could do that was by tracking down and eliminating everyone involved. The dead security guard and the devastation at Marsha Kennard's office was a result of Dominic Phillips' attempts to intimidate her.

Devereau shook his head. The lengths to which some bastards would go in order to make money were horrifying. He might be no angel but he had nothing on these fuckers.

All the pieces were starting to slide together. Dominic Phillips, and by extension Matelot, had turned Martina into a werewolf because they thought they could use her as some kind of weapon. When Martina lost control of her wolf, however, they realised that she was more of a liability than an asset. Dom, despite his masks and posh ties and extensive contacts, must have been shitting himself. If the clans and the vamps found out what his company was up to, all bets were off. That was why he'd ordered his men to locate Martina via her tracker and kill her.

Now all Devereau had to do to restore peace to the world was to get hold of Marsha Kennard and rescue Martina's dad. Once that happened Matelot, whoever the fuck they thought they were, were finished. And Dominic Phillips wouldn't last another night. 'Where is he?' he growled. 'Where can I find Phillips?'

'There's a warehouse down by the river. He usually hangs out there.' Morty's eyes dropped. 'You're turning furry again.' He sounded scared.

Devereau slowly raised his hand and inspected the claws emerging from beneath his fingernails then he leaned across and raked one across the man's cheek. 'Where else? Where does Dominic Phillips live?'

'I … I don't know! I only know the main warehouse! I can give you directions. It's not that far. I don't know any other places!'

Devereau watched him through slitted eyes. Morty was too frightened to be doing anything other than telling the truth. Shame.

'You're not going to win against them, you know,' Morty continued shakily. 'You might think Matelot is a two-bit organisation that's got bigger ambition than capability, and you might think they're already on the ropes. Hell,' he shrugged, 'if you're lucky, you might bring down the company. But you're never going to beat Dom. I might not like the guy much but he's a lot stronger and a lot smarter than anyone else. He's got contingency plans upon contingency plans, and he's more ruthless than you can imagine.'

'Yeah, yeah,' Devereau said. Whatever. It might be a cliché but the bigger they were, the fucking harder they fell. And he was going to enjoy making Dominic Phillips – and anyone else who worked for his bastard company – fall from the greatest height possible.

'For example,' the man continued, 'every building under Matelot's control here and in Europe is prepped for infiltration. If there's a whisper that any place might be compromised, they're rigged to go boom. The kind of person who thinks of that sort of detail is the kind of bloke who's thought of everything.'

Devereau's head whipped towards him. 'What did you say?'

Despite his continuing terror, there was a faint mocking curl to Morty's mouth. 'Dominic Phillips thinks of everything. *Everything*. And he has balls of steel. He'd probably take out all of Soho, Lisson Grove and every vamp and wolf there if he thought he could get away with it.' He laughed. 'And the rest of the country would probably cheer him on.'

Devereau stared at him, then he pulled out his phone and turned it on. He found the number he needed, his stomach clenching as he called it. It rang and rang and rang – and each time it did, Devereau felt even sicker. 'Pick up,' he muttered. 'Bloody pick up.'

Finally there was a click. 'You hung up on me.' Scarlett's voice was cool. 'And you lied to me.'

'Where are you?'

'I'm not in the mood to tell you right now.'

'Where the fuck are you?'

The urgency in his tone must have registered. 'I'm back at the warehouse,' she said. 'There's not much here—'

'Get out,' he said. 'Get everybody out of there *now*.' There was a single beat of silence.

Scarlett wasn't stupid; without asking any more questions, she drew in a breath and then he heard her roar, 'Evacuate!'

Devereau kept the phone pressed to his ear. He could hear scuffles, the sound of running feet and several shouts in the background. A door banged. 'Scarlett,' he said. 'Scarlett?'

'I'm here,' she answered. 'There's—' There was a deafening crash and the phone went dead.

Morty looked at him. 'Told you,' he said simply.

Something inside Devereau snapped. He reached and grabbed the gunman by the shoulders and heaved him up to his feet.

'You p-p-promised! You said that if I told you what I knew, you'd let me go!'

'No,' Devereau bit out. 'I did not say that.'

Morty's face whitened. 'Please.'

Devereau released him and stepped back. 'Get out of here,' he hissed. 'Find Dominic Phillips and whoever the fuck else works at Matelot and tell them that The Shepherd is coming after them.' He hawked up a ball of phlegm and spat it on the ground as if the action would add weight to his words and cement his vow. 'And make sure Dom knows that next time I won't show any mercy.'

A moment later, Devereau was back in the car and speeding away.

Chapter Twenty

The glow of fire was visible from at least half a mile away. By the time Devereau arrived, his foot to the floor of the car the entire way, dawn was breaking over the horizon. Ambulances, fire engines and police cars surrounded the area, their flashing lights combining with the rising sun and the spitting fire to create a kaleidoscope of sinister colour. It didn't help that a strong wind had picked up and was blowing the flames in the wrong direction, along with a fog of thick ash.

Unable to get down the gravel road, he parked further away and ran the rest of the distance. Several uniformed idiots tried to stop him but he ignored them. It was only when he drew close to the warehouse, scanned the small crowd of grim-faced vampires and spotted Scarlett that he slowed and remembered to breathe. He ran a relieved hand through his hair then strode up to her.

She turned as he approached. 'Why, Devereau Webb,' she drawled. 'Anyone would think you were worried about me.'

There was a black smudge of soot down one side of her face and he could smell the acrid tinge of burned hair. He suspected that Scarlett's escape from the warehouse had been far narrower than her calm demeanour suggested. 'That's because I *was* worried,' he said.

She smiled slightly, showing her single fang. 'The building must have been wired but we got out. All of us. And that's thanks to you.'

He inclined his head. 'I'm pleased to hear it. I'll accept your undying gratitude later.' Scarlett snorted. 'And,' he added, 'I apologise for hanging up on you earlier. But I didn't lie.'

Her smile vanished. 'You lied in all but words, Devereau.'

'You knew all along what I was going to do.'

She opened her mouth to argue then her eyes flickered at something over his shoulder and she frowned. Devereau turned to see DS Grace striding towards them. 'Why am I not surprised to see you here, Mr Webb?' drawled the detective.

Devereau smiled pleasantly. 'I don't know, DS Grace.'

'What did you have to do with this explosion? Are you involved? It's obviously got something to do with supes or there wouldn't be so many of you here.'

'I didn't show up until well after it went up,' Devereau said. 'As I'm sure plenty of witnesses will attest.'

'You seem to have a habit of turning up to crimes just after they've occurred.'

'I always had a good sense of timing.'

DS Grace glowered. 'You might change your mind about that when you're doing time.'

Devereau raised his eyebrows. 'Pardon?'

'The preliminary work has come back on the dead body we recovered outside your house. The man who was shooting at you, who you pushed off a roof and subsequently killed, is human.' Grace smirked in a practised manner; Devereau was sure it was an expression he had perfected over time in a mirror. 'Which means I'm taking you in for questioning.'

It was Scarlett, not Devereau, who started to protest. 'You can't do that. He's a supe and is subject to supe justice.'

'He killed a human being.'

'It doesn't matter.'

DS Grace sniffed. 'We'll see about that. Every human life matters.'

Scarlett started to move towards the detective but Devereau shook his head. 'It's fine. I'll deal with this. Stay here and see if you can find out anything about the warehouse.'

Grace interrupted. 'She will do no such thing. This warehouse has nothing to do with you supes. Anyone who is not human will leave the area immediately.' His words took on a supercilious edge. 'Unless you want to join Mr Webb in custody.' He produced a set of handcuffs. 'There's plenty more where these came from.'

Scarlett gazed at the dangling cuffs and raised an eyebrow. 'Oh my.' She offered the detective a slow smile and his cheeks reddened. 'Well, DS Grace,' she drawled, 'in that case, you'd better arrest me too. After all, I've been with Devereau almost all the way, so I must be as guilty as he is.'

That clearly wasn't the response Grace had been expecting. 'You've not killed anyone.'

Her eyes danced. 'How do you know?'

DS Grace swallowed and Devereau almost smiled. It was one thing to arrest a lone werewolf who had no support network but it was quite another to arrest a vampire who had Lord Horvath at her back. Not to mention at least a dozen other vampires behind her who were glaring with growing fury. Grace had backed himself into a corner, however, and had no choice but to follow through.

Devereau relaxed his shoulders and held out his wrists. 'The law is the law, detective.'

Grace frowned, shook his head in exasperation and snapped the handcuffs over Devereau's wrists. 'I'm going to get to the bottom of this, you know.'

'I'd expect nothing less from the Metropolitan Police,' Scarlett murmured. Then she winked and held out her hands.

***

They weren't driven to Supe Squad as Devereau had expected because apparently there weren't any suitable cells there. Instead, he and Scarlett were taken to a large, boxy building on the fringes of the city. Detective Sergeant Owen Grace was probably under the delusion that locking them up as far away as possible from Soho and Lisson Grove would give him an advantage. For a career police officer, he still had a lot to learn.

He also seemed to think that throwing them into tiny separate cells and leaving them to cool their heels for several hours would soften them up for interrogation. But it was hardly Devereau's first time inside a police cell and, despite his new incarnation as a werewolf, he doubted it would be his last. He stretched out on the narrow bed and immediately went to sleep. He suspected Scarlett was doing the same. After all, it had been a long night.

The sliver of cold sunlight shining against the far wall from the boxed-off window was in the opposite corner of the room by the time Devereau woke up. Even within these four walls he could smell rain approaching, and it didn't sound as if the wind from earlier had subsided. He stretched lazily and scratched himself, wondering what the coppers would think if he exploded into a werewolf right now. He wondered what Martina was doing, if she was managing to maintain control of herself, and he sat up.

A voice drifted towards him from further down the hallway. 'You're awake then.'

Scarlett. He breathed out. 'How can you tell?'

'I have excellent hearing. Not as good as you, of course, but good enough. How could you sleep? My cell stinks so strongly of wee that my eyes are stinging. And I'm beginning to get hungry. Someone shoved a tray through about half an hour ago and there was nothing on it apart from a bottle of lukewarm pig's blood. Clearly none of these fuckers has ever met a vampire before. I wouldn't drink that if the Queen herself demanded it of me.'

Devereau smiled as his gaze landed on the floor in front of his door. There wasn't a tray there, or any bottles of dubious blood, but there was a tin of dog food. Somebody somewhere probably thought they were being funny. It wasn't even good dog food, it looked like bargain basement shite that contained no meat and a lot of sawdust.

Devereau picked up the tin and rolled it from hand to hand. It was a remarkably foolish joke. If he chose the right angle, he could launch it at the head of the next person who opened the door and kill them. He tutted and set it on the floor. 'Scarlett,' he called softly, 'I need to know.'

'Red thong,' she called back. 'With a cute lace trim.'

Devereau blinked and Scarlett's laughter rolled towards him. 'Have I actually managed to make you lost for words?'

He licked his lips. 'Scarlett…'

'I haven't told anyone about her.'

That wasn't the answer he'd been expecting. But it was very, very welcome news. 'Thank you,' he said.

'You're racking up a lot of owed favours, Devereau. I've been entertaining myself by imagining all the ways that you can repay me.'

'Quiet down there!' an authoritative voice shouted.

'Or what?' Scarlett called back. 'You'll arrest us for talking?'

Devereau smirked but he quickly smoothed his expression when someone thumped on his door and then unlocked it.

'You're up, Mr Webb,' said a uniformed PC. 'And your solicitor is here.'

His solicitor? He'd not called anyone, although he'd been offered the opportunity to do so. Perhaps Scarlett had hired someone for him. That would mean yet another favour he owed her. Happy days.

He nodded at the officer as if he'd expected nothing else and followed her down the corridor to Interview Room Three. Someone was already seated at the small wooden table. Devereau eyed the three-foot high man with his folds of slate-grey skin, pointed ears and immaculately tailored navy-blue suit. 'You're a gremlin.'

'Score one to the criminal werewolf.' The gremlin paused. '*Alleged* criminal werewolf.' He gestured at the chair beside him. 'Take a seat, Mr Webb. We've been granted a few minutes to discuss matters before your interview begins. My name is Phileas Carmichael, Esquire. I have been appointed on your behalf.'

'By who?'

'Whom.'

Devereau gave him a long look. The gremlin simply smiled. 'Millicent Thompson.'

'*Whom* is that?'

'Who,' Carmichael corrected automatically. Then he appeared to realise that Devereau was teasing and clicked his tongue. 'Miss Thompson is, I believe, your pixie next-door neighbour.'

'My neighbour?' Devereau's disbelief was palpable. One of the curtain twitchers? It barely seemed credible.

Carmichael shrugged. 'What can I say? You seem to have made an impression.' He pointed at the chair again. 'Come, come. We need to move quickly on this.'

Devereau sat down. 'It's very good of Miss Thompson, whoever she is, to send you but I really don't need a lawyer.'

Carmichael bent down and picked up his briefcase, placing it on the table in front of them. He clicked it open, drew out a pair of half-moon spectacles and carefully put them on. Devereau wasn't sure if the gremlin had even heard him. The small man seemed to possess incredibly selective hearing.

'Now,' he intoned, 'first of all, we need to challenge your presence here. While the police are certainly permitted to question supernatural creatures, making an arrest is a very unusual step and rarely allowed without first speaking to the supe leaders, which Detective Sergeant Grace hasn't done. I'm inclined to think that he doesn't know what he's doing. Unfortunately that may prove detrimental as far as you are concerned. He's an unknown quantity, which makes predicting what he's going to do rather hard.'

'That's not a problem,' Devereau said.

Again, Phileas Carmichael chose not to hear him. 'If DS Grace has read the legal statutes correctly, he will make a case against you and present it to the Clans, demanding that they take appropriate action. If it is proven to their satisfaction that you have committed murder against a human being, they can either have you killed or they can make arrangements for you to be incarcerated in the Clink.'

'Have me killed?' Devereau's jaw dropped. 'What?'

'Supe justice tends to be faster and stricter than that which humans enjoy,' Carmichael explained. 'Obviously the Clink is the better option. It's essentially a prison run by supes for supes. Most of the detainees have committed petty crimes and are not detained for long periods.' He paused to slide his spectacles up his nose. 'There is a third possibility.'

Devereau folded his arms. 'I have the feeling I'm not going to like this either.'

'Probably not,' the gremlin agreed cheerfully. 'There is the likelihood that the clans will disown you and refuse to deal with you further. It rarely happens, in fact the last time was more than sixty years ago. In your case, however, I believe it is possible.'

'No matter what the clans think, I'm still a supe,' Devereau said. He was part of the supernatural community and there were currently all manner of magical beings outside his new house to prove it.

'Yes, but you're also a werewolf,' Carmichael returned. 'If the wolves won't take responsibility for you, neither will anyone else. The alternative is—'

'A specially designated institution run by humans where I'm likely to go slowly insane. I've heard about it already.' Devereau grimaced. 'It's just as well that I've not actually broken any laws.' Then he amended himself. 'At least not recently.'

'DS Grace is alleging that you killed a human.'

'By accident – and that human was trying to kill me. He'd shot up my house. I was merely protecting myself. I'm sure my helpful new neighbour Millicent Thompson saw what happened and will provide a witness statement to that effect.'

Carmichael nodded slowly. 'Oh, she did. Unfortunately that's not the human whose murder is in question. Not any longer.'

Devereau's brows snapped together. 'Then who?'

Carmichael consulted his notes. 'A man called Jonathan Lee.'

'Jonathan Lee? But—'

'He was shot dead at a building in Canary Wharf. You and Scarlett Cook were caught on CCTV camera at a car park close to the building. The timing matches the estimated time of death.'

'That's circumstantial at best, and incredibly flimsy evidence.'

'True,' Carmichael agreed. 'The fact that the police discovered Jonathan Lee's phone number in your wallet when they checked you in this morning is also circumstantial. But,' he added, 'it doesn't look good.'

Oh. Devereau sighed. He'd forgotten about that.

Chapter Twenty-One

Detective Sergeant Owen Grace chose to take the interview on his own. He was the only Supernatural Squad detective available given DC Emma Bellamy's absence. Devereau was surprised but far from unhappy about it.

'You've not had anything to eat or drink since you were brought in, Mr Webb,' Grace said solicitously. 'I can arrange for some food to be brought to you, if you require.'

Devereau sniffed loudly. 'Actually, someone left some food in my cell while I was sleeping.'

A flicker of surprise lit Grace's face. 'Oh? That's good.'

'Yes,' Devereau continued. 'It was a tin of dog food.'

Phileas Carmichael stiffened. '*What?*'

Devereau glanced at his solicitor. 'Tripe flavour, I believe.'

'I am horrified, DS Grace!' Carmichael said. 'Horrified! You are treating my client as if he's some kind of dumb animal. I'd have expected far better than this from the Metropolitan Police. I can assure you that I will be making a formal complaint. This is an abuse that cannot go unchecked.'

To DS Grace's credit, he looked incredibly uncomfortable. 'I'm sure it was a misunderstanding. I apologise, Mr Webb. That should not have happened.'

'It most definitely should not!' Carmichael spluttered. 'It proves that the police force is already prejudiced against my client. He cannot possibly receive fair treatment when this sort of thing is likely to occur.'

Grace shifted in his chair. 'It won't happen again.'

'It had better not!'

This was already going well. Devereau leaned back. 'I would quite like a coffee, if that's possible.'

'I'm not sure that's wise, Mr Webb,' Carmichael said. 'There's the very strong likelihood that one of these so-called protectors of the peace will spit in it.'

Grace jumped up to his feet. 'That won't happen. I'll fetch you a coffee myself.' He stalked out of the room at great speed.

Carmichael turned to Devereau and gave him an approving nod. 'Excellent stuff,' he murmured. 'It won't do much about the murder charge, of course, but it will create sympathy for you if there's ever a court case.'

If there was one thing Devereau knew, it was that this would *never* end up in court.

DS Grace returned with a polystyrene cup. Steam rose up from its surface and it actually smelled like half-decent stuff. Given the polystyrene, Devereau considered making a comment about the Met's lack of environmental concern but decided he'd probably already done enough. He inclined his head. 'Thank you.'

'No problem, Mr Webb.' Grace glanced at Phileas Carmichael. 'Let's get started, shall we?' At the solicitor's nod, he leaned across and pressed a button on the tape recorder. 'Wednesday, June thirtieth. Four thirty-two pm. Present are myself, Detective Sergeant Owen Grace, Devereau Webb, and his solicitor, Phileas Carmichael. Please state your names for the tape.'

Devereau resisted the urge to put on a funny voice. 'Devereau Webb.'

'Phileas Carmichael.' The gremlin gave Grace a hard look. 'Esquire.'

'Thank you,' Grace said without flinching. He turned to Devereau. 'Mr Webb, let's begin with the events from two days ago. You moved into a new property on Dalkeith Road, did you not?'

'I did,' Devereau replied pleasantly. 'I was forced to move by your good self. You told me that if I did not do so then I would be imprisoned.'

DS Grace glared at him. 'Indeed. Because the law states that all supernatural beings must reside within a specific area, namely within a fixed radius of Soho and Lisson Grove. You are a supernatural being, are you not?'

'Yes.'

'Detective Sergeant,' Carmichael said, 'we are all more than aware that my client is a werewolf. There really is no need to belabour the point.'

Grace didn't react. 'Mr Webb,' he said, 'a few hours after you moved in, you decided to go to Goodman's Alley in Whitechapel.'

'Is that a question?' Devereau enquired.

'Yes,' Grace snapped. 'Were you there?'

Devereau nodded. 'I was.'

'There was a serious incident at 12 Goodman's Alley at the time. Two human beings were murdered there. Subsequent pathology has indicated that they were murdered by a werewolf. Did you kill those two human beings, Mr Webb?'

'I did not.'

'Then why were you near Goodman's Alley?'

'I heard that there was a crime involving a werewolf and I wanted to see what was going on.' Devereau smiled. 'Curiosity is not a crime.'

Grace gazed at him levelly. 'Do you know who killed those two humans?'

Devereau's left eyebrow twitched. He drew in a breath and answered, 'Yes.'

Both Owen Grace and Phileas Carmichael jerked in shock. Neither of them had been expecting that answer. Surprisingly, it was Grace who recovered first. 'Who?' he asked. 'Who did it?'

Carmichael shook himself. 'I require some time alone with my client!'

'You just had time alone with your client, Mr Carmichael. You don't need any more.' Grace stared at Devereau. 'Who killed them?'

'DS Grace! I demand to speak to my client alone!' Carmichael jabbed his thumb at Devereau. 'Don't you say another word!'

Devereau shrugged at Grace. 'On advice of counsel—' he started.

'Fine,' Grace snapped. 'You've got three minutes.' He thumped off the tape recorder and marched out of the room.

As soon as the door closed, Devereau glanced at the gremlin. Carmichael didn't say anything. He didn't even look at his client.

'Do you have something to say?' Devereau asked.

Carmichael held up his hand, indicating silence. Another few seconds passed then he raised his head and began to speak in a calm, level tone. 'You know what that was, Mr Webb? That was me counting to ten in my head. If I hadn't done that, I would be more than likely to end up in prison myself for committing aggravated assault. The reason being that,' his voice suddenly rose to a high-pitched screech, 'I am your fucking lawyer! I am the one to whom you tell relevant information! If you have knowledge of a fucking murder, then you fucking tell me and then I can make a fucking deal with the fucking police to get you the fuck out of here!' His nostrils flared and his body quivered.

'Are you alright there, Phileas?' Devereau enquired. He nudged the cup of coffee towards him. 'Would you like a drink?'

The gremlin ignored it. 'Tell me about Goodman's Alley.'

'You're my lawyer, right?'

'Yes.'

'That means client confidentiality?'

'Yes.'

'It doesn't matter who hired you or who is paying your bill? You

———

won't repeat what I tell you?'

'I won't breathe a word unless you say otherwise, Mr Webb.' Carmichael was starting to calm down. 'What do you know about those two murders?'

'I'll tell you and Grace at the same time. I want you to hear it together.'

Carmichael shook his head. 'No. If you have information on another crime, we can use that to help with Jonathan Lee's murder.'

Devereau's expression was implacable. 'I didn't murder Jonathan Lee.'

Carmichael waved his hands. 'That's not actually relevant.'

'I don't need to make a deal,' Devereau said. 'But I do need to speak to you and Grace together.'

Carmichael sighed heavily. 'Mr Webb, I can't possibly act effectively as your solicitor unless you take my advice.'

'That's alright, Philly.' Devereau clapped him on the shoulder. 'I won't hold what happens against you. Let's get Grace back in here.'

***

The tape was started again. DS Grace was licking his lips in anticipation, his eagerness at potentially solving two crimes in one day getting the better of him. 'Well, Mr Webb?'

Devereau linked his hands together. 'As I was saying, I heard that something was going down at Goodman's Alley and that it involved a werewolf. I decided to investigate. I sneaked into the house in question before armed police entered it. When I was there, I discovered the two corpses. I also discovered a twelve-year-old female werewolf who was very much alive.'

Grace's jaw dropped and Carmichael blanched in horror. Devereau didn't miss a beat. 'I should add that this girl is not a naturally born werewolf. She was born human.' He met Grace's eyes, making sure that the detective understood the full importance of that detail. From the detective's suddenly pallor, it was clear that he did.

Devereau nodded and continued. 'With the help of Miss Scarlett Cook, I investigated further. The female werewolf, the *child*, had been transformed against her will as an act of retribution against her father. This transformation was conducted by a shadowy human organisation that's been forcing people from other countries to become vampires and werewolves. They are then auctioned off to the highest bidder for whatever sick purposes the buyers have in mind. I don't know how many victims there are, but I'm assuming several.'

'Oh my God,' Carmichael whispered.

Devereau nodded grimly and continued. 'David Bernard, one of the humans found dead at Goodman's Alley, did financial work for this organisation.' He wasn't prepared to yield the names of either Matelot or Dominic Phillips; if Grace had all the pieces of the puzzle, he might decide to do something stupid and take care of matters himself. That would inevitably result in the detective's death and, more to the point, disaster for the rest of them.

'Bernard was at the flat to witness the werewolf child's father being tortured in front of her. As I'm sure you're already aware, the flat belongs to his secretary, Marsha Kennard. The child was ordered to kill Ms Kennard to save her own father but instead she lost control and her wolf took over. She attacked Bernard and killed him and one of his companions instead. It wasn't a planned move on her part – I'm told such loss of control is typical in an unnaturally created adolescent werewolf. She couldn't help herself and she's not responsible for her actions.'

Devereau paused and raised his eyebrows meaningfully to ensure that Grace understood. 'In the ensuing chaos, various people escaped including the leader of the organisation, the girl's father and Marsha Kennard.'

'Fucking hell,' Grace blurted out before he could stop himself.

'Indeed,' Devereau agreed. He stared at the pale-faced detective. 'I don't suppose you've located Ms Kennard?'

Grace shook his head. 'Our working assumption is that *you're* involved in her disappearance.'

Devereau's eyebrow twitched in irritation. 'I am not. I've never met the woman.' He did his best to tamp down his annoyance. He was fairly sure that Dominic Phillips had already disposed of Kennard. Her body could be floating down the Thames right now for all any of them knew.

'How is Jonathan Lee linked to all this?' Grace asked, clearly trying to regain control of the interview. 'We know he worked in the building where Bernard and Marsha Kennard were based. He must be part of it too.' His tone was still heavy with accusation.

'My best guess,' Devereau said evenly, 'is that the unfortunate Mr Lee was shot dead in the hope that the news of his death would reach Marsha Kennard and she would panic. This organisation is desperate to contain the chaos that they've created and no doubt want to get rid of both Kennard and the werewolf child without further delay. They attacked my house because the girl was there. They want to kill her to keep her existence – and their activities – secret. Hence the rather dramatic shoot-out that resulted in the death of yet another human.'

DS Grace opened his mouth then closed it. A moment later he opened it again. 'I should go and get someone else to hear this,' he said shakily. 'If you're telling the truth, Mr Webb, it's clearly above my pay grade.'

'Oh,' Devereau murmured, 'I can assure you that it's the truth. But you can't get anyone else, not unless you want things to become far, far worse than they already are.'

Grace shook his head. 'I don't understand. How can they become worse?'

Devereau glanced at Carmichael. 'Phileas?'

The solicitor swallowed. 'Supes have been living on a knife edge for years,' he said, his words barely audible. 'If word of this gets out to the supe community, it will be the tinder to a powder keg that's been waiting to go off for a very long time. Every supe in this city is forced to live under the strictest of conditions. We deal with prejudice on a daily basis, but we get on with it because we are afforded certain legal protections that make life in this country bearable. Mr Webb's existence aside, the creation of new werewolves and vampires is carefully monitored to follow the letter of the law and maintain population numbers. When the clans discover that *humans* are illegally turning people into wolves and selling them off as slaves…' He exhaled. 'Well, let's just say that you can't expect peace to reign as a result. And that's before the vampires get involved.'

'The vampires are already involved,' Devereau said casually. His tone did nothing to reassure DS Grace. 'I imagine there are fanged folks scurrying all over London looking for the bastards behind this. When they find them, you can expect fireworks. And, let's be clear, detective, I'm not talking about the celebratory kind of fireworks.'

Grace ran a shaky hand through his hair. 'They can use this as a reason to ignore the population limitation laws and turn as many people as they want. They'll claim precedent. And they'll blame humans for setting that precedent.'

'Yup.' Devereau smiled humourlessly. 'And how do you think the humans will react when they find out that children are being forcibly transformed into killers? They'll blame the supes. The supes will blame the humans. Frankly, if you tell other people what's been going on under the noses of the Metropolitan Police, word will get out within hours and the entire city will be rioting by the end of the week.'

'If the vampires already know what's going on—'

'I can handle the vampires,' Devereau interrupted. He hoped that Scarlett could, anyway. 'You need to handle the humans. And that means ensuring that nobody finds out what is going on.'

'I can't keep something like this to myself,' Grace whispered. He was fumbling. Under any other circumstances, Devereau would have enjoyed this.

'Then,' he said, 'if the prospect of London burning isn't enough to sway you, let me give you another reason to stay quiet. The girl. The werewolf child. I know where she is.'

'She killed two people,' Grace muttered. 'Child or not, we have to bring her in and charge her.'

'What she did wasn't her fault. She couldn't control herself – there's no way she could have. To be honest, it's a miracle she didn't escape onto the street and kill more people. She was pumped full of lycanthropic magic that, mixed with her hormones, sent her crazy. And then her father was tortured in front of her.'

'But—'

Phileas Carmichael straightened up. His initial shock at Devereau's revelations had worn off and he'd reverted to pragmatic law professional. 'It's highly illegal for children to be turned,' he said.

Grace snapped. 'I know that.'

'In the unfortunate and rare event that it does occur,' the solicitor continued, 'there's really only one course of action to be taken.'

The blood drained from Grace's face. 'The clans will kill her.'

'It's the law,' Carmichael said.

'And the law is—' Devereau added.

'Shut *up*, Mr Webb.' Grace shuddered. 'This girl didn't choose to be turned into a werewolf. She might be dangerous and she might deserve to be charged with what she's done, but she doesn't deserve death.'

'No, she doesn't.' Devereau leaned forward. 'But your job states that you have to find her and turn her over to the clans. They won't want to kill her but legally they'll have no choice. So if you pursue this matter, DS Grace, her blood will be on your hands.' He paused. 'Twelve years old. She's a slip of a thing.'

Grace put his head in his hands. 'How do I know you're telling the truth? Where's your actual proof?'

'The warehouse that blew up is where the slave auction was taking place. I'm sure you can sift through the debris and find evidence to back me up. And if you really want me to, I'll take you to meet the girl in person. She'll confirm what I've told you. She might also flip and go crazy again and kill you by accident but,' Devereau shrugged, 'then you'll be sure of the truth.'

Grace raised his head. He looked defeated. He reached for the tape recorder and turned it off once more. 'I don't know what to do with all this information.'

'I understand,' Devereau said. 'Fortunately, I do.'

Chapter Twenty-Two

Scarlett gave him a long look. 'I can't believe that you persuaded Owen Grace to let us go and to keep his mouth shut.'

'He's out of his depth but he believes in his job. He told me the first time we met that he wants to protect people. Detective Sergeant Grace believes wholeheartedly that his job is to look after innocents. Right now, he agrees that includes Martina and allowing me to continue alone is the best way to keep her safe.'

Devereau met her eyes and added more quietly, 'I suspect, however, that once he's had a chance to sleep on things he'll change his mind. We need to ensure that we put a stop to Matelot and Dominic Phillips once and for all before that happens.'

She raised an eyebrow. 'We?'

'You might not have told the other vampires about Martina, but you've told them about the auction and what we discovered at the warehouse. I know your loyalties lie with your own kind, but if you can give me forty-eight hours I can sort this out on my own. You said yourself that Horvath isn't in the city at the moment, so you're not going against his wishes by helping me. The man isn't even here.'

Scarlett's lips pressed together. 'There's a fabulous new invention that you might have heard of recently. It's called a telephone. It allows you to speak to people over great distances.'

'Scarlett...'

She sighed. 'Fortunately for you, I've not spoken to him. He's not answering his phone and he's out of contact. Technically that means I'm in charge. But Lord Horvath aside, there are more than a thousand vampires in London. They can help in ways you can't even imagine. *We* can help. Not with Martina, of course, but with Matelot.'

Devereau shook his head. 'I'm not trying to be the big hero here, or to pretend that I'm invincible and better than the rest of you. The explosives at the warehouse proved that Dominic Phillips is a canny bastard who thinks ahead and plans for every eventuality. We know he's desperate to keep his activities hidden. If he realises that every vampire in town knows what he's been up to, we won't see him for dust. He'll leave London at high speed – and probably under a false identity – and we'll never see him again. But you can bet that he'll start again wherever he ends up. He thinks he's onto too much of a good thing to stop turning people into supes and enslaving them. The best way to stop him permanently isn't to use an army that will scare him off, it's to use one person who can sneak under the radar and bring him down before he realises what's happening.'

Scarlett folded her arms. She wasn't happy but she knew he was right. 'Two people,' Scarlett she said finally. 'Two heads are better than one. We can track down Phillips together.'

'I don't want you to get into trouble with your Lord.'

Scarlett frowned. 'I am a loyal London vampire but I'm also my own person. I can hold the vamps back for a short time at least, and I'll deal with the fall-out from Lord Horvath when he returns. But even if we track down Dom Phillips, it's not going to solve the problem of what to do with Martina. She's still an illegal werewolf. It's going to be years before she can control herself, and the full moon is within touching distance. You can't pretend she doesn't exist and that she's not a danger. Sooner or later, everyone will find out about her and then nobody will be able to help her.'

'I have a certain gremlin lawyer who's looking into matters involving Martina. There has to be some way to help her.'

Scarlett tutted. 'You barely know the girl. She's hardly spoken to you.'

'You're helping her almost as much as I am,' Devereau pointed out. 'And you're risking more than I am because of who you are.'

'I'm a sucker for damaged creatures,' she retorted. 'What's your excuse?'

'Well,' he murmured, 'if nothing else, it gives me a reason to spend more time with you.'

Scarlett reached out and trailed her fingers across his collarbone and down the centre of his chest. Devereau shivered. 'You don't need an excuse for that.' She leaned across, brushing her mouth across his with such a light touch that Devereau wasn't even sure it had happened. 'How are we going to find Dominic Phillips?'

'We have Martina,' he said simply, 'she'll tell us.'

'She's not told us anything so far.'

'She will now,' Devereau said.

'Why would she?'

He shrugged. 'Because she has to.'

***

Tempting as it was, Devereau didn't want to risk stealing another car and incurring DS Grace's wrath; he'd already pushed the detective to his limits. Neither did he think it was a good idea for Scarlett to arrange for a vamp car. They couldn't risk any nosey buggers following them to see what they were up to. In the end, they grabbed an Uber.

For the first time since he'd become a werewolf, Devereau found himself confronted with someone who couldn't give a hoot about what he was.

'Please,' the driver said, 'help yourself to any tissues or boiled sweets or bottled water.'

'Thank you,' Scarlett said.

'What kind of music would you like to listen to during your journey?'

'Whatever you enjoy will be fine.'

The driver beamed happily. He glanced at them in the rear-view mirror. 'You two are very much in love.' Devereau stiffened but the man continued blithely, 'I can tell these things from the way you are acting. Look at how you are sitting.'

There was at least a foot between them.

'And,' the driver said, 'the look in your eyes is one that I know very well. My wife and I have been together for twelve years and I love her more now than I did on our wedding day.' He gave Devereau a knowing glance. 'You'll be the same. I feel it in my bones.'

Devereau sneaked a look at Scarlett. From what he knew of her, lasting relationships of any kind were not even remotely her thing, but he couldn't let such an obvious opportunity pass. He reached across, took hold of her hand and raised it to his lips. 'Oh, I can well believe that,' he murmured. He kissed her hand and then drew slow circles in the centre of her palm with his index finger. Gratifyingly, she smiled in response, then she one-upped him by leaning towards him and putting her hand on his thigh.

'We're so much in love,' she drawled. Her hand moved higher. '*So* very much. Between you and me,' she said to the driver, 'I think he's going to pop the question any day now.' Her fingernails dug suddenly into the flesh at the top of his leg and he sucked in a breath.

'Well,' Devereau said. 'There's no time like the present.' He turned to Scarlett. 'My darling. Will you marry me?'

'Oh, I will.'

'You will make some beautiful children,' the driver declared in delight.

Devereau's grin widened. 'We certainly will. And,' he added, 'I'm really looking forward to having Scarlett at home all the time. I know she's going to love keeping house.'

———

'Ironing is my life,' Scarlett said. 'There's nothing more satisfying than making sure my man is out and about in crisply starched shirts.'

The driver smiled until his eyes flicked to Devereau's shirt. After being worn for several hours on a hard prison cell bed, it was creased and grubby. It was about as far from crisp starch as an over-ripe banana.

'You're making fun of me.' The man didn't seem particularly put out. 'But I will have the last laugh. The two of you are destined to be together. I'm sure of it. We all deserve such happiness.' He pulled up outside Mrs Foster's house. 'Have a good day now. Stay dry. There is a storm coming soon. And don't forget to give me a good rating!'

They got out. 'Well, husband-to-be,' Scarlett said, gazing at the house, 'everything looks quiet enough. Hopefully our ferocious little charge hasn't killed Dr Yara and this teacher woman yet.' She wagged her finger at him. 'Because if she has, you're cleaning up the blood. I expect you to pull your weight around the home.' Their eyes met and her voice changed. 'That's not as funny as it sounded in my head. You realise that there might well be carnage inside?'

'It will be fine.' Devereau wished he felt as confident as he sounded. He drew back his shoulders and walked up to the front door. Then he rang the doorbell and crossed his fingers.

***

'Everything is great,' Rachel Foster said. 'Tickety-boo. We were a bit worried about where you were and why you were gone for so long, but there have been no problems here.'

Devereau glanced down at the carpet. There were several fragments of white porcelain lying by his feet.

'I dropped cup,' Dr Yara said. 'I am very clumsy woman.'

'Surgeons don't tend to be clumsy, do they?' Scarlett asked, picking up two broken pieces of wood from a nearby table.

'That's a craft project,' Rachel said. 'I'm making stakes.' She made a stabbing motion with her hand, gesturing towards Scarlett's heart.

Scarlett looked at Devereau. 'She's spicy,' she commented. 'I like her.'

Devereau sighed. 'What happened?'

Yara and Rachel exchanged glances of mutual resignation.

'Martina, she grow more anxious. You were not here. This place is new. She start to panic and,' Dr Yara shrugged, 'she lose control.'

Fuck.

'It's really not that bad,' Rachel said. 'We dealt with it.' She turned her head slightly. As she did so, her hair fell to one side, revealing a long scratch down the side of her neck. It looked painfully deep.

'I'm sorry,' Devereau murmured.

Rachel straightened her back and gave him an imperious look. 'There is nothing to apologise for.'

'Martina is in no danger from me,' he said, realising why the women were trying to pretend that everything was fine. 'It doesn't matter what she does. She's not responsible for her actions when she turns into a wolf. I can assure you that I'm not going to hurt her.'

Scarlett crossed her arms. 'You might not have any choice,' she said softly.

Devereau glowered at her. That sort of comment wasn't helpful. 'Where is she?'

'Dr Yara shot her with a tranquiliser then we managed to get her into the garden and barricade her in the garden shed.'

'Martina is locked in your shed?'

Rachel shrugged helplessly. 'It's the best we could do. We had to reinforce the door to keep her inside. As far as I can tell, she's still in her wolf body. She's beginning to come round – I've heard a few whines. And I'm not sure it's safe out there. The wind is getting stronger as we speak.'

Dr Yara bit her lip. 'I cannot sedate her again. Is too dangerous. All those drugs…' She shook her head. 'Is not good. Too much and her kidneys suffer. Her liver too.'

Devereau exhaled. 'Okay,' he said. 'Okay. We were never going to be able to rely on tranquilisers as a long-term measure. And you're right, we can't keep her locked up in a garden shed. There has to be another way.'

Scarlett opened her mouth to speak but Devereau frowned at her. 'Not that way.' She closed her mouth again.

'What do we do, Mr Webb?' Dr Yara asked. 'You are wolf, too. You must have idea.'

Rachel gazed at him with anxiously. 'She's a child. No matter what she's capable of, we can't keep her locked up. It isn't right. We're denying her every essence of freedom and life and … and … and … happiness. It isn't right,' she repeated.

Devereau stilled.

'What is it?' Scarlett asked.

'Happiness,' he said. 'The Uber driver said it. Rachel said it. It's what we all strive for, right?'

She pursed her lips. 'That and good sex.'

'Good sex leads to happiness, dear, that's the whole point.' Rachel's eyes focussed on Devereau. 'What are you thinking?'

'I have an idea,' he said.

Chapter Twenty-Three

'For the record,' Scarlett said, 'I think this is a very bad idea. And you do remember that we're trying to stop an international trafficking ring before you get thrown back in jail and charged with various counts of murder because you're the easiest person to blame?'

Devereau smiled at her. 'What's the worst thing about being a supe?'

'All the restrictions,' she answered back instantly. 'We're treated as a sub-species because we're a little bit different.'

Rachel snorted. 'A lot different.'

Devereau held up his hands. 'We chafe under the supe laws because they give us less freedom. What's the worst thing about what we discovered at the warehouse?'

Scarlett's lip curled. 'The slaves, of course.'

'Their freedom was taken away from them. Their choice was taken away from them. And so was their happiness.'

'Those two people we saw are still slaves, Devereau. And there are probably plenty more like them. We haven't helped any of them.'

'Yet,' he answered. 'We haven't helped them *yet*. We will. Right now, we have to focus on Martina. We help her, we help everyone else. And this is the way to help her.'

'You might end up getting somebody killed.'

He gestured to the shadowy trees in front of them. Their branches were swaying in the wind but they provided some shelter from the worst of the elements. 'We're on the outskirts of the city. It's dark, and there's nobody else around. It will be fine.'

'I'll remind of you that statement later.'

He nodded at her. 'I'll take full responsibility if anything goes wrong.' He tilted back his head and looked at the moon hanging in the night sky and so very nearly full. Then he walked round to the back of Rachel's car.

Martina was curled up in the back, her yellow wolf eyes narrowed at him. There was no mistaking her vicious intent. All her instincts was telling her to kill him, Scarlett and anyone else who got in her way.

Devereau was starting to understand why his own people had been so terrified of him. A werewolf – even a twelve-year-old

werewolf who was tied down and suffering the effects of a sedative –
was incredibly intimidating.

He tapped on the glass. Martina didn't move. He crouched down
until he was face to face with her. 'I'm going to let you out in a
moment,' he said, speaking loudly enough for his voice to carry
through the window. 'And then we'll see what you're really capable
of.'

She was in wolf form but she could still communicate. At his
words, her hackles rose on the back of her neck and her mouth drew
back in a tiny snarl. Right now she was far more wolf than girl, but
she understood what he was saying. She recognised that she was
being challenged – and she was more than ready to meet that
challenge.

Devereau turned to Scarlett. 'It's probably wise if you're well
out of the way.'

She snorted. 'I can look after myself.' All the same, she moved
back out of Martina's line of sight. 'You know,' she called to him
from the darkness, 'you're in more danger than I am. Her animal
recognises your animal and wants to destroy it.'

'Well,' Devereau said under his breath, 'I'd better be damned
careful.' He reached for the door and opened it.

Martina launched herself forward, a ball of flying fur. At the last
second, before her teeth sank into his flesh, she was forcibly halted.
The rope holding her in place strained with the tension.

Devereau clicked his tongue. 'Now, now,' he chided. He
stretched his fingers out to the knotted rope. Despite his confidence
in the face of Scarlett's doubt, he wasn't sure this was going to work
but he had to try. He drew in a breath and untied the knot. 'Now you
can go,' he whispered.

This time Martina didn't move. She glowered at him but her
suspicion at his actions led her to stay where she was. Devereau took
a step back, then another and another. When he was two metres from
the rear of the car, Martina reacted.

She leapt out and planted all four paws on the ground. Her ears
were back, flat against her head, and there was a ridge of fur raised
along her spine. She huffed out a breath and it clouded in the cool
night air.

Devereau stared her down. 'Wait,' he commanded, the
compulsion threading through his voice.

Martina growled.

Devereau said it again. 'Wait.'

Martina's body quivered. Her yellow eyes spat promises of

blood and vengeance. She bared her teeth, showing him that she'd killed before and she was ready to do so again. He could smell her fear but underlying it was something else. It took him a moment identify it: power. What he smelled was her power. She shook out her fur and tensed, the muscles in her haunches bunching together. Then she flew towards him.

Devereau ducked in the nick of time as Martina's wolf sailed over his body. He felt the soft edges of her fur brush against the back of his neck. A split second later she was gone, disappearing into the night.

'Well, that didn't work,' Scarlett said conversationally from somewhere behind a tree to his right.

Devereau flashed her grin. 'Wait,' he said a final time. And then he allowed his wolf to burst free and took off after Martina.

The wind whipped at his fur as he bounded into the darkness, leaving the small car park and Scarlett behind. The night called to him and the air itself seemed to be alive with a myriad of scents and sounds. He could hear the distant motorway and the odd passing car to the east. Water in the wide river was burbling over stones and reeds to the west. His nostrils prickled as a badger nosed its way out of its den and an owl swooped overhead in search of tasty prey. And yes, his damned balls were itching again.

He picked up speed, running harder and weaving in and out of trees. His paws barely made a mark on the soft, grass-covered ground. Devereau's blood sang. This. This was what it meant to be a wolf.

A flicker of movement caught his keen eye. He thundered forward on Martina's tail, but he didn't need to see her to know that he was gaining on her. She was too young, and she didn't possess his strength and speed. But this wasn't like it had been with the gunman when he'd sent him running across the playing fields; this wasn't about catching her or bringing her down. It was about allowing her the freedom her werewolf required.

Up ahead she changed course and turned left. Initially, he adjusted his trajectory and prepared to follow but then he realised what she was doing and slowed his speed. Smart. She'd worked out that she couldn't outrun him so she was using a different tactic.

He slowed to a walk, keeping his nose raised so he didn't lose her scent. He needn't have worried; Martina had circled round and was now behind him. She wasn't running away. She'd decided that she wasn't going to be prey. She had decided that she far preferred being the predator.

———

Even though he'd been expecting it, he still felt a jolt when he heard the sudden rush of air as she threw herself forward. Her body landed on top of his, her claws raking through his thick fur to his skin. Her jaws opened wide then snapped down, sinking into the scruff of his neck. He felt a brief surge of pain. He shook himself and she tumbled to the ground, but he'd been careful and barely winded her.

He dipped his head and gave her the tiniest nip on the shoulder. Then he licked the same spot and pulled back to allow her to spring up again.

Martina faced him and he met her lupine eyes with his own. This time something was different. Her hackles were still raised, but they were less pronounced than before and her ears were more pointed.

Devereau hadn't been a werewolf for long. He hadn't experienced a full moon yet and he didn't have a clan to teach him what was what, but somehow he knew. He dropped his head slightly and lowered the front part of his body. It wasn't submission – it was play.

Martina stared. Perhaps she didn't understand. Why would she? But then, with very slow and deliberate movements, she tilted her head to the side. A second later, she threw herself at him. This time her claws were sheathed.

He let her pounce and she landed on top of him again. This time he allowed her to remain where she was for several seconds before he shook her off. He batted her muzzle with his paw and her tongue lolled out of her mouth. He danced to the side and she danced after him. Then he spun round and took off once more, racing through the woods. He didn't attempt full pelt – he didn't want to lose her – but he maintained enough speed to test her and force her to exert herself. He ran around an oak, down a small dip, across a tiny stream and through a sparse thicket of bushes and branches. Martina was on his heels the whole way.

He reached a slope. Instead of powering up it, he dropped his speed so Martina could draw level with him. Together they raced upwards as the slope grew steeper. Exhilaration and joy spun through him. He pushed on and crested the hill, before finally coming to stop. Throwing back his head and seeing the moon again, pregnant and white and glowing, he opened his mouth and started to howl. A second later Martina joined him and their calls combined in a strange yet beautiful chorus. This world was theirs. He knew it like he knew his own name. This was happiness.

Suddenly, there was a rustle to the side and a musky scent filled the air. Badger, perhaps, or stoat. Martina's howl stopped abruptly and she twisted towards the source of the sound, ready to attack. Devereau didn't look at her; all he did was growl once. A heartbeat later her shoulders dropped in acquiescence, and in that moment he knew he had her.

*****

The wind was still gaining in strength, making the trees nearby rattle and shake with far more drama than before. Devereau was certain he heard a rumble of distant thunder. As their Uber driver had confidently stated, there was a storm approaching. The electricity in the air made his hackles to rise uncomfortably across his skin. From Martina's shudder and wary look up at the sky, she felt it too.

Scarlett draped a tartan blanket round the girl's shoulders and passed her a cup of hot chocolate from a thermos flask. Martina took a sip, curling her tiny fingers round the steaming cup, and gave Scarlett a wary look. 'Why do you only have one fang?' she asked baldly. 'Did they take it from you?'

To Scarlett's credit, she didn't flinch. 'Nobody took it from me. I lost it when I was trying to stop a bad man from doing bad things.'

Martina nodded as she absorbed this. 'I'm bad,' she said. 'I've done bad things.'

'You mean you've killed people.'

Devereau sucked in a breath but Scarlett threw him a warning glance.

Martina bit her lip. 'Yes,' she said quietly.

'What do you think would have happened if you hadn't killed them?' Scarlett asked conversationally.

'I…' Martina blinked, clearly startled by the question. 'I don't know.'

'Yes, you do.'

The child gulped down another mouthful of hot chocolate and, with shaky hands, placed the cup to one side. 'I think they'd have killed my dad,' she whispered. 'They kept hitting him. And … and…'

'You don't have to continue,' Devereau interrupted.

'Yes, you do,' Scarlett said. She looked at him. 'She needs to confront what she's done. It's the only way to move forward.'

'It wasn't her fault.'

'I know that and you know that,' Scarlett answered. 'Martina needs to know it too.'

There was another rumble of thunder and Devereau felt drops of rain. His mouth tightened and he looked away. Martina watched them both, wide-eyed.

'What do you think would have happened to you, Martina?' Scarlett asked softly.

Martina gave her head an almost imperceptible shake. 'They wanted me to kill a woman,' she whispered.

Scarlett nodded grimly. 'You asked about my fang. You asked if they'd taken it.'

Martina swallowed. 'That's what they did to Marcus. They tied him up and then used pliers and…' Her face paled. 'There was a lot of blood.'

'Marcus was a vampire?'

'Yes.'

'Why did they do that to him?'

Her head dropped. 'The Master said that the people who bought Marcus were afraid of him. They wanted a vampire, but not one that was dangerous.'

Scarlett turned her head, her eyes meeting Devereau's. Unspoken fury glittered in their dark depths but, when she spoke again to Martina, her voice remained soft. 'The Master?'

'Master Dom. He's the one who made me like this. He made that other wolf bite me. Three times.'

'Uh huh.' Scarlett pressed her lips together. 'Well, there are three things you need to know, Martina. First of all, nobody is allowed to force anyone to become a werewolf against their will. You did not choose to be a wolf. In fact, you couldn't have chosen to be a werewolf because you're not able to make that choice until you're an adult. Secondly, children who are turned into wolves can't control what happens when they turn. Frankly, it's a miracle that you managed to hold back until they hurt your dad in front of you. That's an incredible amount of self-control.'

'But the Master said there were lots of young werewolves. Lots of children like me. He said they can control themselves so I should be able to as well.'

'The werewolves he's talking about were born that way. Their bodies are prepared to cope with what happens to them. Yours isn't. What do you think happens if you poke a hornet's nest?'

Martina stared at her. 'They sting you.'

'And why would they do that?'

'They're upset. They're protecting themselves from you.'

'Yes.' Scarlett's gaze intensified. 'Whose fault is it if you poke a hornet's nest and you get stung?'

'Yours,' Martina whispered.

'Exactly.' Scarlett gave a satisfied nod.

Martina thought about this for a moment. 'What's the third thing?' she asked finally. 'You said there were three things I needed to know. That's only two.'

'Devereau?' Scarlett questioned.

He lifted his chin. 'The sort of people who defang a vampire, who turn people into werewolves and vampires against their will and force them to kill others, who also sell those people to make a profit and kill anyone who gets in their way, those sorts of people don't deserve to live. It shouldn't be up to you to kill them, Martina. That's not your responsibility. But there was nobody to help you. You were alone and they gave you no choice.'

Martina sniffed and a single tear rolled down her cheek. She brushed it away furiously. 'It's their fault,' she said. 'They did this. The Master did this.'

'That's right.' Scarlett sat down and put an arm round her shoulder. 'None of this is on you.'

Devereau knelt down in front of Martina. 'Why didn't you tell us about any of this before?' His voice was gentle rather than accusatory, but she still flinched.

'Because I'm not the only one. And the Master said that if we tried to escape, or if we tried to tell anyone what was going on that … that … that he'd hurt those who were left behind.' Her words dropped to a whisper. 'He's not a nice man. And if he has my dad—' She couldn't complete the sentence.

Devereau took her hands and squeezed them. 'Listen to me. You're not alone. I'm going to find your dad. And I'm going to stop Dominic Phillips from doing anything like this ever again. You can trust me. You know you can.'

'Okay.' Her voice was small.

'I mean it, Martina.'

She bit her lip. 'But what happens if I lose control again? What happens if I kill someone else?'

Scarlett leaned across. 'You won't.'

'Why not?' Martina asked.

She smiled at Devereau. 'Because that man over there is the alpha wolf. And he won't let you.'

Chapter Twenty-Four

'We have a problem,' Devereau said to Rachel Foster and Dr Yara when they returned to the house. It was raining harder now and there were several clatters outside as the wind grabbed empty rubbish bins and loose tiles and sent them flying down the street.

'I can't possibly imagine what that might be,' Rachel replied, watching Martina with her mouth half open. The girl's entire demeanour had altered. There was no longer the sense that she remained on a knife edge between pure violence and sheer despair. Instead, despite the growing storm outside, her eyes were glowing and she was more relaxed where before there had only been restlessness. Her anxiety about her father and the deeds she'd inadvertently committed hadn't disappeared, but when she looked at Devereau she trusted him to sort all this out.

He prayed that he'd live up to his promises.

Martina bit into an apple and tucked one leg underneath her. 'I don't know where Matelot are,' she said baldly. 'And I don't know where the Mas … I mean,' she amended, 'where Dominic Phillips is. Whenever we went anywhere, I was blindfolded.'

'These guys really don't take any chances,' Rachel said.

'They are shipping company, yes?' Dr Yara gazed round. 'We go to port and we find their ship. Then we find them. Then we end this.'

'Except,' Scarlett said, 'either they're very good at covering their tracks or they don't have any ships here at the moment. We did a search and I called a couple of guys I know who work at the Port of London. There's no sign of any boat belonging to Matelot at any of the wharves or terminals. If they have any ships here, they're registered under a different name.'

'And there are no obvious London-based addresses for either Phillips or Matelot,' Devereau added grimly. 'Not that we can find without a warrant. We could approach DS Grace and ask him to do a search for us, but that's a dangerous route. We got round him once but I'm not convinced we'll manage to do it again.'

Rachel tapped her mouth. 'You think that the secretary escaped when everything went to hell at Goodman's Alley, right? This Marsha Kennard woman?'

Martina was pale but her chin was firm. 'Yes, I think so. It was all a bit blurry. I only remember flashes after I … changed. I think that's what happened.'

'And,' Rachel said gently, 'your father is injured.'

Martina nodded. 'But that happened before. He was beaten up.' She swallowed but her voice didn't waver. 'It was really bad. They hit his legs and I think maybe one got broken. I heard a crack. And his nose was broken too. There was a lot of blood.'

Devereau gazed at her. 'We'll do whatever we can to find him and help him.'

Martina didn't look away. 'I know.'

'So,' Rachel said, 'we're assuming that Martina's dad is still being held by Matelot but that Marsha Kennard got away and is holed up somewhere out of sight. Matelot is looking for her and they've got a head start on us. Let's not forget that Dominic Phillips sent a gunman to wreck that office, even though David Bernard was already dead.'

Devereau twisted his mouth. 'Yes. Phillips was sending a sick message to Kennard.' He glanced at Martina but it was too late for sugar-coating; she understood the score. Hell, she'd already lived through it. 'If she shows her face, she'll end up with a bullet in her skull. Unfortunately it's probably only a matter of time before Matelot catches up to her.'

Rachel frowned. 'Marsha Kennard worked for a criminally negligent and powerful solicitor. She can't be an idiot. She knew enough to run away and hide when everything went tits up. She's not going to show her face again.'

Devereau stood up, walked to the window and gazed out at the quiet street for a moment before turning round again. 'It would be a suicidal move on her part.'

Scarlett jumped up. 'Turning over her office and murdering Jonathan Lee isn't going to make her call up Dominic Phillips and tell him where she is. He can't possibly think that. What if his so-called message wasn't to put her under pressure and cause her to panic? What if it was about something else?'

They all looked at each other.

'She know where bodies are buried,' Dr Yara said slowly.

Scarlett agreed. 'She was David Bernard's secretary and we know that Bernard was involved with Matelot right up to his grimy neck. Bernard and Phillips wanted her dead from the beginning for a reason. I'm betting there's more to it than her demands that Bernard drop Matelot.'

'Yes,' Devereau said, warming to the topic as he considered the ramifications. 'Yes. She's bound to know where Matelot's money came in from and went out to. The message was to make sure she keeps her mouth shut or more people will die.'

'If we find Marsha Kennard, I bet we find everything and everyone,' Scarlett said. 'She knows about Matelot. She can finger Dominic Phillips and probably provide enough evidence to put him away for life. I reckon that with her help we can find everyone who bought a vampire or a werewolf. Not only can we free them, we can make sure all those bastards pay for what they've done. We can also locate Dominic Phillips and help Martina's dad. Marsha Kennard is the key to everything.'

'But how you find someone who do not want to be found?' Dr Yara asked.

Rachel raised her eyebrows at Devereau. 'You must have contacts in the criminal world who can help.'

'Not for this kind of thing,' he answered. 'My social circle was somewhat different.' He ran a hand through his hair. 'We're going to have to go back to the beginning and return to the scene of the crime. Maybe we'll find something that the police missed.'

Scarlett smiled grimly. 'There's no time like the present.' She looked outside. As if in response to her words, there was a sudden loud rumble of thunder and a howl of wind that rattled Rachel's windows. 'Storm be damned.'

***

At four o'clock in the morning, the narrow streets around Goodman's Alley looked very sinister. Nobody was around and there was a distinct lack of decent street lighting. The wind was in a frenzy, whipping their hair and tugging at their clothes; within seconds of leaving the car, Scarlett and Devereau were soaking wet from the driving rain. There was little choice but to grin and bear it.

They hunched their shoulders and marched towards Goodman's Alley, leaving Rachel Foster's car in the same place where Devereau had parked his own vehicle the first time he'd been there. It had gone, doubtless impounded by the DS Grace and the damned police for no good reason other than to irritate him.

The only sign of life was a plump rat he spotted scurrying into a nearby drain seeking refuge from the storm. Scarlett and Devereau ducked under a covered walkway which offered a small degree of shelter and picked their way carefully towards Marsha Kennard's house.

'Did you know,' Scarlett said, raising her voice so that Devereau could hear her over the wind and rain, 'that after sex a male rat sings to himself? It's beyond normal hearing levels so I doubt that even a werewolf could tune in properly, but it's been scientifically proven.'

'Do you sing after sex, Scarlett?'

She shrugged. 'There's a first time for the everything.' She glanced around. 'What do you say? You, me, a stormy night and a bloody crime scene? It's quite a turn on.'

He gave her a long look and she grinned back. 'Let's find our own dirty rats first, shall we?' he said.

'If you insist.' Scarlett's smile vanished and her tone changed. 'I have to apologise to you, Devereau. I didn't think you'd manage to bring Martina round but your little jaunt in the woods really worked.'

'The joy of freedom isn't to be under-estimated.'

'Martina's not free. What you gave her tonight was little more than the illusion of freedom.'

He didn't disagree with her. 'Maybe that will be enough.'

'Maybe.' She touched his hand. 'But if it's not, don't beat yourself up too much. You've done more for her than anyone else. I do believe that deep down you're a good man, Devereau Webb.'

'I'll take that as a compliment.'

'You should.'

He stopped walking and glanced at her. 'You're a good woman. You've had plenty of opportunities to tell other people about her existence.'

Scarlett sighed. 'By staying quiet, I'm putting more lives at risk so I'm not convinced that makes me a good person at all. Regardless of what I said to Martina, I'm not sure that she'll be able to control her wolf.'

'Then why do it?' he asked. 'Why help her?'

'I'm not doing it for her.'

Devereau felt his breath catch. Sod the damned storm. He leaned forward and dipped his head. She tilted hers up. Then he shook himself and pulled back abruptly. 'Sorry,' he muttered.

Scarlet nodded. 'We have to find Marsha Kennard and all those rats first.'

'We do.'

She raised her hand and trailed it across the stubble on his jaw. 'Anticipation is so delicious, don't you think?' She flashed him another heart-stopping smile. 'Come on, then. Let's see what we can find.'

They emerged from the walkway into the pelting icy rain. The windows on the buildings around them were rattling from the force of the wind but they pushed on towards Goodman's Alley, their bodies not quite touching.

Devereau was painfully aware of Scarlett's proximity. He couldn't work her out. For all of her light-hearted gibes and saucy quips, there was a lot more going on beneath the surface – and he strongly suspected that, despite what she'd just said, she'd do everything she could to help Martina.

They stopped outside Marsha Kennard's small house. It was the first time Devereau had seen it from this angle. Unfortunately the bashed-in door and copious amounts of police tape detracted somewhat from its appearance. The dark skies and appalling weather only added to the desolate effect.

Scarlett wasted no time in ducking under the tape and sidling past the broken door. He followed her in. The escape from the storm was welcome but the interior of the house still smelled strongly of blood, even though it was no longer a fresh scent.

'How many different blood types can you pinpoint?' Devereau asked quietly, as if speaking normally was forbidden. He shook himself, sending a shower of droplets into the air.

'Three,' Scarlett said, squeezing water from her hair with a grimace. 'The same three I smelled on Martina the first day.'

She glanced into the first room. It was covered in smudges of fingerprint dust and appeared to have been ransacked. The police had been both messy and thorough. Searching the room would be a waste of time.

In silent agreement, they ascended the stairs. As much out of habit as anything else, Devereau took care not to touch the banister and leave traces of himself. 'You know,' he said, 'back when I used to break into houses, I went into one just like this. It was tall and narrow. Four storeys high, with wooden floors that creaked like an old man's bones. It shouldn't have mattered because the home owners were supposed to be away. They were posh types who went off on their yacht almost every weekend and—'

'Devereau,' Scarlett interrupted, 'are you telling me this because you're reminding me of your criminal past? Or are you telling yourself because you're nervous about walking into a house where a double murder has just taken place and you need to fill the silence?'

'I'm bricking it,' Devereau said starkly.

Scarlett laughed. 'In that case, continue.'

'Anyway, I headed up to the bedroom. That's usually where the good stuff is kept.'

'Jewels?'

'And then some. You wouldn't believe what people put under their mattresses for safekeeping.'

They reached the first floor. The smell of blood was getting stronger. Devereau spoke faster. 'So I walked into where the master bedroom should have been but there wasn't a bed in there. There were two large coffins, lying on the floor side by side, and inside each coffin was a body.'

'Corpses?' Scarlett recoiled.

'That's what I thought at first, but it was the middle of the night and the lord and lady of the house weren't away on their yacht.'

'They were inside the coffins?'

'Oh yes. And they were both alive. Just fast asleep. In their matching coffins.'

Scarlett reached the second-floor landing and turned to him. 'So what did you do?'

'Ran out of there as fast as my terrified thieving legs could carry me.'

She grinned. 'You know I'm a vampire.'

'Do you sleep in a coffin? Because I'm afraid that might be a deal breaker.'

'I don't. I have a very large, very comfortable bed. And one day,' she winked, 'you might even get to see it.'

He smiled at her.

'Do you feel better now after sharing that little story?' she asked.

He shook his head. 'No, not really.' He paused. 'But thanks for letting me babble on.' He pointed down the corridor. 'The room where I found Martina is this way.'

They walked into it together. The horrifying blood spatter had dried, and of course there were no longer any corpses, but the scent of death remained. The desolate atmosphere made Devereau shudder. Patches of fur broke out across his skin and he rubbed at his arms to force them down.

In contrast, Scarlett was completely business-like. She swivelled round, her eyes taking in all the details, then she walked to the corner where Devereau had found Martina.

'Martina was here.' She pointed to a bare patch lower down the wall. 'There's no blood at this spot.' She turned and examined the other marks. 'There was someone there, and there, and there.' She frowned at the far wall. 'And two people there.'

'That was where David Bernard and his accomplice died.'

'Hmm.' She didn't look at him. 'Let's try not forget that our little warrior killed two people with her bare claws.'

'They didn't give her any choice.'

'Hmm.'

Devereau gritted his teeth but held his tongue. There was no point in going over old ground.

Scarlett gazed down at the floor. 'Three people escaped through the door.'

'How can you tell?'

She pointed at a few small rust-coloured droplets. 'I'm a vampire,' she said lightly. 'The blood speaks to me.'

He stared at her.

'I'm kidding,' she said. 'I took an online course in blood spatter once upon a time.'

'Why would you do that?'

Scarlett shrugged absently. 'Call it professional interest – and a mistrust of the police. I'm a highly-placed vampire. I want to walk into a crime scene and understand what has happened without having to rely on prejudiced humans to make up a story that fits their own narrative.'

He continued to watch her. 'You don't trust anyone, do you?'

She gave a mild snort. 'Who do you trust, Devereau?'

Until recently, there had been hundreds of people that he'd trusted. He put his hands in his pockets and chose not to answer. Instead, he focused on the reason they were there. 'So Dominic Phillips, another man who was probably the gunman from my street and Marsha Kennard run out of the room when Martina transforms and attacks.'

He walked back into the corridor. Now that Scarlett had pointed them out, he could see tiny spots of old blood leading to the staircase. He almost smiled. He enjoyed the thought of Phillips fleeing for his life.

'Two headed for the stairs,' Scarlett said from behind him, 'while one ran into that room to the right.'

Devereau glanced over to where she was pointing. 'I came in that way. I climbed up and came in through the window.'

'Did you leave that way too?'

He nodded.

Scarlett pursed her lips. 'I reckon you weren't the only one. Kennard obviously didn't want to leave with Dominic Phillips. She was panicking but not stupid. If she'd tried exiting with him through the front door, he'd have grabbed her and forced her to go with him so he could kill her as soon as he got to a safe place. He wasn't alone, after all. He could have taken her easily.'

'So you think she escaped from the same open window that I did?' He grimaced. 'We have no reason to believe Marsha Kennard is anything other than human. I managed the climb, and I'd have managed it before I become a wolf, but I have a history of breaking into houses and clambering up walls. Marsha Kennard is a secretary who sits behind a desk all day.' He went into the room, strolled to the window and gazed down. 'It's quite a drop. For a human woman to fall that far without injury has to be nigh on impossible.'

'Perhaps,' Scarlett answered. 'But she didn't have much choice. It was either get nabbed by Phillips, be killed by Martina, or jump out of the window.'

'There was no sign of Kennard by the time I got here. And I don't see how she could have reached the ground without breaking her leg at least. Not unless she scales mountains in her free time.'

Scarlett tapped her mouth. 'So let's imagine then that she's not Spiderwoman and that she flung herself out of the window in a panic and was injured when she landed. She managed to scrabble away but she would be too scared to go to any hospital. The police would have found her if she'd been admitted as a patient.'

'She'd also be too afraid to contact family or friends for help. Anyone she got in touch with would automatically be at risk from Dominic Phillips and the dark arm of Matelot. If I were Marsha Kennard, I wouldn't want to put anyone else in danger.'

'If you were Marsha Kennard,' Scarlett said, 'I wouldn't want to wrap my thighs round your hips and slide down onto your thick, hard—'

He looked at her and she smirked, not bothering to finish her sentence. Devereau swallowed then cleared his throat. 'Marsha Kennard lives here,' he said. 'She knows the area. She probably feels safer here than anywhere else. Plus, it's very likely that she's both traumatised and injured. I bet she's somewhere nearby and hiding out until she recovers enough to escape properly. She won't contact the police because Dominic Phillips has already warned her that innocent lives are at stake if she does.'

They stared out of the window into the violent darkness.

'It's a plausible theory,' Scarlett said. 'But it doesn't help us track her down. Not unless your wolf senses are strong enough that you can smell days' old Chanel perfume lingering in the air and track her down that way.'

'Not outside, unfortunately, and certainly not in this weather.' Frustrated, he scanned the rows of barely visible houses. The pub he'd sneaked through was directly opposite. Then there was a house with plastic kids' toys in the garden, none of which looked as if they'd survive the blustery night, and next to that four flats stacked on top of each other. In the other direction, there were more flats, at the rear of which he knew was an ironmonger's shop, followed by a few more family homes. This was a high-density area of London. Marsha Kennard could have gone just about anywhere. He sighed deeply. And then a flash of lightning lit up the sky and the buildings beyond. His eye caught something and he stiffened.

'What is it?'

A slow smile spread across Devereau's face. 'I know where she is.'

Chapter Twenty-Five

Devereau and Scarlett wove in and out of muddy puddles in several gardens and backyards until they were standing at the foot of a tall house. Devereau counted twelve windows, all with darkened rooms beyond them.

'Here?' Scarlett whispered, her scepticism obvious.

Devereau nodded and pointed up to one of the windows. In the corner of the glass, just visible in the smoky condensation which coated the surface, someone had drawn a sad face.

Scarlett wrinkled her nose and blinked through the rain. 'I don't see—' Then her face cleared. 'Oh.'

'Marsha Kennard is a compulsive doodler. We didn't find much in her office but what we did find was a note pad with smiley faces drawn on it. She won't be feeling so smiley now.'

'It might not have been her who drew them.'

'It was.' Devereau exuded confidence. 'I'm sure of it.'

Scarlett didn't appear convinced. All the same, she stepped back and gestured to the back door. 'Go on then,' she murmured. 'Prove it.'

He grinned at her then shrugged off his jacket and wrapped it round his hand. He smashed a pane of glass in the door and reached in to unlock it. Scarlett winced at the noise. 'If she's in there and awake, she probably heard that even with the storm blowing out here.'

'I hope she did. I want her to know that we're coming.' He stepped through the door.

'You want her to attack us?'

'She's had enough heart-stopping surprises. Sometimes a little advance warning goes a long way.' He tipped his head back and called, 'Marsha!'

Scarlett rolled her eyes. 'If she tries to jump out of a window again, she might break her neck. And she'll end up very muddy and very wet.' Scarlett gestured down at her own bedraggled clothes. 'Like me.'

Devereau paid her no attention. 'Marsha! My name is Devereau Webb. I know who you're hiding from and why. I know what sort of man he is and what he tried to do to you.' His words echoed round the empty kitchen. Water dripped from his body and pooled on the tiled floor. 'I don't work for Dominic Phillips. If you've seen the news at all in the last few weeks you'll already know that. I've scarcely been off the front pages.'

Scarlett folded her arms and watched him.

'I'm a werewolf,' Devereau called. 'Just like the girl who was ordered to kill you at your house – but I'm in control of what I am. I'm trying to help the girl and I'm trying to find Dominic Phillips so I can stop him from the fucking evil shit he's pulling. I think you can help me. I *know* I can help you.' His voice rebounded. There wasn't so much as a whisper of an answer.

'If Marsha Kennard really is in here and we'd taken her by surprise, we'd have had a chance,' Scarlett said. 'Now we've no hope.'

Devereau glanced at her. 'That's where you're wrong,' he said calmly.

She tapped her foot. 'What makes you say that?'

'I've learned a little something about loneliness over the last few weeks,' he said softly. 'I know what it's like to feel like nobody's got your back and nobody cares. If you're not used to that sort of feeling, you'll do almost anything to get rid of it. You might even stroll into a vampire nightclub to find solace.'

Scarlett gazed at him without saying anything.

'Marsha is alone,' Devereau continued. 'Her life is in danger. She's probably wondered several times over the last couple of days whether it would be easier just to turn herself in so she can stop living in fear. That's probably why she drew the face on the window – part of her wants to be found. She knows she needs help to get out of this situation, but she's no idea where to get that help. I've seen plenty of people at rock bottom and the desperation they feel overtakes almost every other sensation. If we'd crept up on her, she'd have fought us like a cornered animal and she could have done herself and us some very real damage. Plus we'd never find Dominic Phillips, or help all those poor souls he's fucked over. We already know Marsha wants to do the right thing because that's how she got into this situation in the first place. If we can get her to trust us, we've got a chance.'

'You're pretty insightful for a werewolf,' Scarlett said.

He winked. 'And sinfully sexy too, right? It's almost unfair.'

She gave a small smile. 'I won't disagree there.' She touched his arm. 'And while I'm not sorry you walked into Heart, I am sorry you've felt lonely.'

There was a voice from the kitchen doorway. 'So am I.'

Scarlett and Devereau snapped round. In front of them was a

petite woman with a lined face and tired eyes. Outside there was yet another groan of thunder.

'Hi,' the woman said weakly. 'I'm Marsha.'

***

'This place belongs to my neighbours,' Marsha said. 'They're away on holiday and asked me to keep an eye on it. Houses around here often get burgled when their owners are away.'

'So I've heard,' Scarlett said smoothly, patting her face with the towel which Marsha had given her.

Devereau coughed. Truth be told, it was a very nice house and there was a plenty he could have taken from it. Once upon a time. 'What happened, Marsha?' he asked. 'How did you end up hiding here?'

She sighed and rubbed her ankle. 'I think you've worked out most of it already. My boss, David Bernard, did a lot of work for a lot of unsavoury customers.' She shrugged. 'But everyone's entitled to a lawyer and most of the stuff involved finding ways to avoid going to prison for tax evasion. When he got involved with Matelot, things became very different. Dominic Phillips wined and dined him. He spoke of a better world where supes worked for us instead of against us – and he flashed a great deal of cash. David isn't a bad guy,' she said. Her face clouded. '*Wasn't* a bad guy. Not really. But he was greedy. It didn't help that when he was younger he'd applied to be turned into a werewolf and had been declined.'

Devereau held the opinion that anyone who got into a business that made money from forcing vulnerable people to become supernatural beings and then selling them as slaves was a very bad person indeed. Wisely, he avoiding saying so to Marsha. 'He held a grudge?'

'Yeah.' Marsha looked down. 'It's not right, though. My cousin is a vampire and he's not evil. And he's not an animal. He's just a person.' She shook her head. 'David could never see that.'

'So he got involved with Dominic Phillips and Matelot? Forcing people to become supes against their will and then enslaving them?'

'Yes.' Her voice was barely audible. 'I told him it was wrong but he wouldn't listen. All he could see were pound signs. I said I'd go to the police if he didn't drop Matelot as a client, and a day later he showed up at my house unannounced.'

'And he wasn't alone?'

'No. Dominic Phillips was there, and a girl. And three other guys. I think one of them was the girl's father. He didn't look very … well.'

That was one way to describe someone who'd been beaten within an inch of his life.

'Phillips told the girl she had to turn into a wolf and kill me, so she turned,' Marsha continued. 'But she didn't go after me. First she tried to bite Phillips. He grabbed David and used him as a shield, so the girl ripped out David's throat. Phillips and another guy ran, and the girl lunged for the third man. I ran too and jumped out of the window.' She rubbed her ankle again. 'I think I broke something when I landed.' Judging by the swelling and the colour, she was right.

'Why didn't you go to the police straight away?' Scarlett asked. 'It could have solved a lot of problems.'

Marsha took a moment before answering. 'It took everything I had to get myself here. When I got inside, I passed out. My leg hurt so much and I was terrified. By the time I'd decided to get in touch with the police, I had a message on my phone.' She swallowed. 'Well, two photos anyway. One was of my office. The other was…' She couldn't finish.

'Jonathan Lee,' Devereau said grimly. 'The night security guard.'

Marsha bit her lip. 'Yes.' She wrung her hands. 'After that I didn't know what to do.'

'It's okay,' Devereau told her. 'We're here now. We'll help.'

There was no mistaking the relief on Marsha's face. 'Dominic Phillips is terrified of the clans or the vampires finding out what he's done. He knows he's no match for that many powerful supes. Now there's an army after him, he'll get what's coming for him.'

'The clans aren't involved,' Devereau said. 'It's only me and Scarlett.'

Marsha blinked. 'What?'

He shifted his weight. 'There are other considerations.'

She stared at him. 'Like what?'

'He means the girl,' Scarlett said cheerfully.

Marsha's mouth dropped open. 'The one who's a wolf? Who tried to murder me?'

'Technically she didn't try to murder you,' Devereau said. 'She saved you.'

'I don't think—'

'And whatever she did wasn't her fault. If the clans find out about her, they will kill her because of what she is. She doesn't deserve that. Nobody deserves that.'

'But – but – but—'

'I wholly agree,' Scarlett said. 'Unfortunately, it is what it is. Devereau is intractable about the girl.'

He gave her an irritated glance then turned back to Marsha. 'Dominic Phillips will get what he deserves, don't you worry about that. First, we need to know where we can find him and his clients who bought their own vampire or werewolf.'

Marsha stared at him, pale-faced. 'If I give you that information, I won't last the week. It's not just Dominic Phillips I have to worry about, it's every single person who bought from him.'

Devereau's expression remained unchanged. 'If you don't give us that information, you won't last the day.'

'Is that a threat?' she sounded shaky.

He sighed. 'You're not in danger from us – quite the opposite, in fact. We can protect you, Marsha.'

Scarlett agreed. 'I can arrange for you to be taken to Soho. You'll be surrounded by hundreds of vampires who will ensure nothing happens to you.'

'I thought it was only the two of you and the other supes weren't involved.'

Scarlett smiled faintly, flashing her single white fang. 'They'll look after you if I tell them to.'

Marsha considered this for a moment then lifted her chin defiantly. 'And what if I don't tell you what I know? What then?'

Devereau shrugged. 'That's your prerogative. We'll leave you here without harming a hair on your head.' He glanced at Scarlett. 'How long did it take us to find Ms Kennard once we started looking for her?'

Scarlett answered instantly. 'Oh, less than two hours, I reckon. Of course, Matelot doesn't have people as smart us, so it's taking them a bit longer. But I'm sure they'll find this place sooner or later.' She looked at Marsha impassively. 'We're not going to wait around for long. Either tell us what we need to know and we'll take you to Soho for your own safety or we walk.'

The diminutive secretary swallowed and flicked her eyes towards Devereau. If she was hoping for help from him, she was going to be sorely disappointed. He sympathized with Marsha Kennard but he wouldn't allow that sympathy to get in the way of what had to be done.

Marsha's shoulders dropped. 'I have a file with everything you need. It's got the names and addresses of all the people who bought vampires and werewolves, about twenty of them.'

'And Dominic Phillips? Where will we find him?'

'He has a warehouse. It's—'

Scarlett interrupted. 'We know about the warehouse. He's not there.'

Marsha blinked. 'Oh.' She put her hand to her mouth. 'Oh.'

Devereau's eyes narrowed. 'What does that mean?'

'Is the warehouse still there?' Marsha whispered.

'Most of it was blown up.'

She swallowed. 'In that case, he's probably already left the country. He's not going to hang around to be attacked by vengeful supes. When I first told David that I didn't like what was going on, he told me that I shouldn't worry because there were plans in place to keep everyone safe.'

'What kind of plans?'

'First, burn all the London operations to the ground. Second, get the hell away.'

'By plane?' Scarlett asked, her voice hard.

Devereau was still watching Marsha. 'No. Matelot is a shipping company,' he said slowly.

She looked down at her feet. 'Yes. He always keeps a ship ready to go. It's usually moored at Baron's Wharf where it's registered under a dummy company.'

'What's it called?' Devereau demanded. 'What's the damned ship called?'

Marsha dropped her head even further. '*Monster*,' she said. 'The ship's called *Monster*.'

Chapter Twenty-Six

Scarlett was speaking into her phone. Less than ten feet away, Devereau was doing the same, albeit talking to a different person.

'What happen?' Dr Yara asked. 'You find Marsha Kennard?'

'Yes, we found her.'

'And?'

'She thinks that Dominic Phillips will cut his losses and make a run for it. He has a boat at Baron's Wharf.' His lip curled and he felt the familiar twinge between his shoulder blades. 'It's called *Monster*, of all things.'

'Yes,' Dr Yara said. 'Because he is monster.'

Devereau smiled suddenly. 'Thank you, Yara.'

'What I do?'

'Everything,' he replied simply. 'You're amazing.'

'This is true. But you are also amazing. You help me before. Now you help Martina. You are not big bad wolf. You are good wolf. Good man.'

Devereau doubted that was true but it wasn't really the time to argue.

'Martina!' Dr Yara said. 'What you do here? Go back to bed!'

Devereau stiffened. 'Is everything alright?'

'Is fine. Is no problem. The storm wake her.'

'Dr Yara—'

'Is fine,' she said firmly. 'You go stop monster.'

He drew in a deep breath. 'I will. Stay safe.'

'Of course, Mr Webb.'

'It's Devereau.'

'Goodbye, Mr Webb.' Dr Yara ended the call.

Mildly vexed, Devereau shook his head and glanced at Scarlett. She slid her phone into her pocket. 'A car is coming for Marsha. She'll be looked after.' She pointed outside. The storm hadn't lessened; if anything, the wind was getting stronger. It was ripping through the streets outside as rain lashed against the windows in a furious, incessant attack. 'And the weather means that *Monster* hasn't left the wharf yet.'

Devereau's eyes flew to hers. 'You're sure?'

'I was just speaking to one of my Port of London contacts. Dominic Phillips must have taken too long to get his affairs in order and get to the boat. Now it's too late. The docks have been shut down for several hours. Nobody has been allowed to leave since early afternoon, no matter how much they yell and scream.'

The corners of his mouth curled into a smile. 'Let me guess,' he said. 'Our Dom is throwing a tantrum and demanding to be allowed to sail.'

'He's told the port officials that it's an emergency. Fortunately for us, human health and safety regulations don't care about his emergency. He's stuck on board his ship at Baron's Wharf as we speak.'

'We can do this.' A warm of glow of satisfaction spread through Devereau's chest. 'We can get him.'

Scarlett moved closer, stopping inches from his body. She tilted her head up. 'Yes. We can.' She reached up and entwined her fingers in his hair. Devereau groaned and lowered his mouth to hers in a long, deep kiss, his fingers moving to her waist to draw her closer. When she broke away, Scarlett's lips were parted and her cheeks were flushed. 'And,' she said softly, 'we will.'

Devereau savoured the heady taste that lingered on his tongue. 'Soon,' he promised. They knew he wasn't talking about Dominic Phillips.

From the doorway, Marsha coughed nervously. 'Is everything ready? Is it going to be okay?'

'We're good to go.'

She nodded at the file on the counter which contained the names and addresses of Dominic Phillips' clients. 'If any of those people get wind of what's going on before you get to them, they'll take measures to protect themselves. That sort of people always do. I should know – I've met plenty of them.'

'She has a point,' Scarlett said. 'They'll dispose of any evidence that shows they've been involved. And that means—'

'Killing the vamps and werewolves they bought from Phillips and getting rid of the bodies,' Devereau finished grimly.

'Twenty names,' Scarlett said. 'Twenty separate addresses. You might be desperate to keep Martina out of this, and you're probably right that we'll have more success against Phillips if only the two of us sneak up on him. We don't want a bloodbath on that damned boat. But we can't deal with everyone in that file on our own. All the vampires know about Matelot – there were enough of them at the warehouse to witness what was going on. They'll jump at the chance to bring those bastards down. I can send them to those addresses so nobody has chance to harm another enslaved supe while we go to *Monster* and take on Phillips.'

<hr>

'I'm sensing a but,' Devereau said.

Scarlett didn't miss a beat. 'But it's not only vampires who have been enslaved, Devereau – there are werewolves, too. That means you have to involve the clans whether you want to or not.'

His mouth tightened. 'I suggested to DS Grace that the clans wouldn't find out about any of this so that we could prevent future problems.'

Scarlett snorted. 'You don't give a shit about that detective, and the clans were always going to find out what's been happening. Even Grace knows that.'

Devereau was quiet. 'Involving the clans means risking Martina.'

She touched his shoulder. 'Which we both know is what really worries you. But right now we're the only supes who know she exists. Nobody else knows where she is. She's safe. The werewolves and vampires in captivity are not.'

Devereau folded his arms and looked away. 'Fine,' he said.

'It's the right thing to do.'

He knew that but it didn't make it any easier.

'It'll be better for you if you're the one to contact them. You might not be part of a clan but you are a werewolf. Show them that you know how to belong.' Scarlett raised her eyebrows meaningfully. 'In the long run, that could help Martina as well as you.'

He sighed. The clans weren't his enemies and, if he played this right, they could end up being his friends. Maybe.

He knew that Scarlett was right. The clans didn't know about Martina and there was no reason for them to find out about her; he could still protect her. He nodded. 'I'll make the calls.'

***

Devereau's ears were smarting from the tirades all three separate clan alphas had given him. He supposed he should be grateful that the Fairfax clan remained officially alpha-less until the next full moon because it was one less tongue lashing.

He understood that the rage Lady Sullivan, Lord McGuigan and Lady Carr were feeling wasn't directed at him; it was focussed entirely on the bastards who were behind all of this. That hadn't made the phone calls any easier, though. Devereau wasn't used to being shouted at; in fact, the last time anyone had tried he'd still been a teenager. Even then it had taken all his willpower to play nice.

173

'You know they're afraid of you,' Scarlett said.

He jerked. 'Pardon?'

'The clan alphas are terrified of what you're capable of. You've been a werewolf for less than a month and you're already almost as strong as they are. Plus you were bitten four times before you transformed. I've only ever heard of one werewolf that's happened to before. His name was Bradford Carr and, even though he died seventy years ago, the wolves still think of him as a hero.'

Devereau snorted. 'The clan alphas aren't prepared yet to admit what I might be capable of. And I'm reasonably certain there isn't a single werewolf on this planet who thinks that I'm heroic.'

'You're wrong,' she said softly. 'As far as Martina is concerned you're not just a hero, you're her saviour.'

Devereau looked out of the car window at the Port of London terminal at Baron's Wharf. The edge of *Monster*'s hull was visible to his right. The ship might be firmly anchored in a sheltered spot but it was swaying alarmingly in the wind. At least it had stopped raining. 'I've not saved anyone yet,' he said. 'Not properly.'

Scarlett grinned. 'Let's see if that's still true by the time the sun rises. Are we ready to go?'

He flashed her a mocking smile.

'Oh no.' Scarlett shook her head in alarm. 'Don't say it. Please don't say it.'

'I have to.'

'No, you don't. You really don't.' She clamped her hand over ears.

'Scarlett Cook,' Devereau said in a voice loud enough for her to hear him, 'I was born ready.'

Scarlett groaned. 'You said it.'

He smirked. 'I did.' He opened the car door and prepared to prove it.

His hair was still damp but it didn't stop the wind flicking it in all directions. Scarlett didn't fare much better; she'd tied her dark hair into a tight ponytail that was immediately picked up by a gust of wind. It smacked her wetly across the cheek. She rolled her eyes.

'At least we'll be safe from the elements once we're on the ship,' Devereau called.

'Assuming it doesn't sink,' she muttered. 'Come on.'

They stayed low to avoid anyone on board noticing their approach. It was wise to be cautious, although Devereau wasn't really worried. Anyone with half a brain would be inside where it was warm and dry. The steel containers dotted around the terminal made it easy for Devereau and Scarlett to stay concealed from all but the higher decks.

The size of the ship gave him momentary pause; it was larger than he'd expected and there would be a lot of ground to cover once they got inside. He felt a flicker of doubt; maybe limiting the boarding party to the two of them wasn't such a good idea. Then he quashed it. The fewer people who stormed *Monster*, the less chance there was for events to spin out of control and for the imprisoned vampires or werewolves to get hurt. An intelligent attack was going to win the day, not numbers.

They sneaked down a shadowed gap between two long blue containers, pressing against the rusted corners to peer out. Despite the howling wind, which didn't appear to have abated at all in the last hour, the ship was making its presence felt with loud creaks and groans as it shifted in the water. Lights flickered from above deck on the starboard side and more were visible from a few grimy potholes. *Monster* was certainly a far cry from the millionaire's yacht that Dominic Phillips could doubtless afford – but illegal goods, nasty drugs and live slaves with supernatural abilities wouldn't fit on a damned yacht.

A door opened on the top deck. Devereau stiffened and gestured to Scarlett. She nodded as a figure appeared. It looked like a man, although it was difficult to be sure from this distance. He was tightly wrapped in a long coat to shield him against the weather. The ship lurched and he staggered to one side and fell against the wall. He picked himself up, slipping and sliding as he regained his balance, before deciding that being out in the open was a bad plan. Seconds later, he disappeared back through the door. It was much more exposed on top of the ship than it was down here on solid ground.

'I hope you've got your sea legs,' Devereau said.

Scarlett grimaced. She was already looking rather green. 'Don't even joke about it.'

They slipped from their hiding place and crept through the remaining containers until they reached a crane standing near the centre of the ship. On a fine day it would be easy to climb up it, shimmy across and drop down onto the deck, but in these ridiculous winds such a feat would be far less simple. The crane heaved, rattled and jerked sharply. *Monster* wasn't an old building with handy footholds and crumbling stonework, though; if they wanted to get on board, they'd have to risk it.

Scarlett took the lead, climbing upwards with slow, steady steps. Devereau followed closely behind her. The cold metal was slick with icy rain, making it difficult to grip with either his hands or his feet, and he had to brace himself against both the swaying structure and the fierce wind. Wolves, he decided, were meant to roll around sunshine-filled fields. They were definitely not designed for this. And neither were humans. Every step was a battle and, when he had to clamber over onto the boom, the horizontal section of the crane, it became even harder.

Scarlett's kept her body low and slowly edged along. Devereau had little choice but to copy her. They made painstaking process; the further along the boom they moved, the more ferocious the wind became. His fingers were curled so tightly round the steel that they started cramping, and the combination of damp clothes and chilled gusts made his teeth chatter. This was not fun, not even slightly.

The crane had been pulled back from the ship, probably because of the storm, so when they reached the end of the boom they'd have to leap a fair distance to land on the deck. If the jump went badly, they'd end up in the water trapped between the steel hull and the harbour wall. If another strong gust of wind moved the ship, they'd be crushed. Devereau had a sudden grim image of his skull bursting like a watermelon.

Ahead of him, Scarlett muttered something but he couldn't hear her words. 'What was that?'

'I said,' she repeated, 'I can't believe I volunteered for this shit.' She shook her head and pushed herself up to a crouching position. Everything seemed to pause and even the wind appeared to take a breath. Then, timing her leap with the next strong gust, Scarlett threw herself off the tip of the boom.

Devereau's stomach lurched. Lightning flashed and for a moment she looked as if she were suspended in mid-air, her arms flung forward in a graceful, ballerina-like pose. Then she soared past the lethal sea break at the side of the ship and landed with an audible thud onto the deck below.

Alarmed, Devereau shuffled forward and peered over the edge of the crane down towards Scarlett's small body. He shouldn't have worried. She picked herself up, shook out her hair and gave him a wave as if to show that the entire manoeuvre had been a piece of cake.

Devereau swallowed. He wasn't particularly afraid of heights, or of the dark, or of crashing storms, but he didn't relish the prospect of leaping to his death. But Scarlett had done it and she was fine. All he had to do was match her prowess.

He brought his knees closer to his chest and managed – just – to move into a crouch. His hands gripped the steel edges of the boom on either side of his body so that he wasn't blown off before he could jump. He eyed the deck. It wasn't *that* far away. He could do this. He *had* to do this. On a count of three.

One.

Two.

Three.

He didn't move. The wind was getting stronger and seemed to be subtly shifting direction. He had to get a move on. If the wind changed much more, he wouldn't have the benefit of it behind him, propelling him forward. He gritted his teeth and steeled his stomach.

'Born ready,' he repeated to himself. 'Fucking born ready.' He heaved in a breath. And then he tried again.

One.

Two.

Three.

He released his hold on the crane and sailed into the air, his legs pumping to give him greater momentum. He was going to do it, it was going to be fine. Then he made the mistake of looking down. One glimpse of the dark oily water of the Thames and the heaving ship's hull next to it was enough to distract him. Shit.

He saw Scarlett's eyes widen in fear just as he started to plummet straight down.

There was no time to think. As the air rushed past him, he transformed from man into wolf. The burst of energy and whatever lycanthropic craziness occurred during the change was enough to propel him forward; instead of plunging into the dangerous icy water, his gigantic front paws slammed onto the edge of the ship's deck and immediately scrabbled for purchase. His hind paws couldn't get any traction against the ship's side but he held on with all his lupine might.

Within a single breath Scarlett was there, her eyes glowing red. She reached down and he felt her fingers pinch the scruff of his neck. She grunted and heaved, tugging at him with all her might. It was enough. He fell forward, landing on top of her. His heart was hammering against his chest and adrenalin was coursing through his veins, but he'd made it. His yellow wolf eyes met Scarlett's vampire ones.

'You're lucky I'm here,' she said, panting slightly. She extricated herself from underneath his furry form and managed a smile. 'Now the monsters are truly on *Monster*.'

Chapter Twenty-Seven

They walked the length of the deck, Scarlett on two legs and Devereau on four. She had to brace herself against the wind several times but Devereau discovered that his lower centre of gravity and four legs were more than enough to keep his balance despite the storm that continued to rage around them.

The ship swung violently from side to side, tipping first one way then another. This was definitely not a night to be on the open sea, much as Dominic Phillips might wish otherwise.

'Okay,' Scarlett said, once they'd analysed the scene. 'We have four possible entrances.' She pointed at the door nearest them. 'I reckon this one is our best bet. We're going to want to take out as many of Phillips' slimy, gun-toting bastards as we can before we confront him. The last thing we need is to kill him and find ourselves facing fifty more fuckers carrying guns. I'd like to leave this damned boat while I'm still breathing.'

Devereau nodded his heavy head. He didn't particularly care which entrance they used; his need for bloodthirsty justice was growing by the second. Every single person on board this ship would pay for what they'd done. He'd make sure of it.

Scarlett opened the door. 'Fur before fangs,' she murmured, her voice low. He widened his mouth in a wolfish grin and padded through ahead of her.

The first corridor was wider than Devereau had expected but his wolf form was so large that his fur still brushed against the walls on both sides. The salty sea scent was all-pervasive, though he caught an odd whiff of other smells such as old sweat and over-cooked cabbage. When he was about halfway down the corridor and passing a closed door, he caught the deeper aroma of coffee.

He paused then lifted a paw to indicate it to Scarlett. She grinned and nudged him forward so he was out of sight before moving in front of the door and smoothing back her wet, windswept hair. A moment later, she raised her fist and knocked.

'Yeah?' called out a bored voice. 'Is that you, Daz? Has the poker game started?'

Scarlett didn't answer. Instead, she adopted a seductive pose, jutting out one hip and tilting her head. The door finally opened and a ruddy-faced bloke peered out. When he caught sight of her, his jaw dropped.

'Hello,' she purred.

His cheeks, which were already red from his natural high colour, flushed even darker. 'H – hi,' he stammered.

Scarlett's tongue darted out tantalisingly, then she opened her lips and smiled. That was when the sailor clocked her fang. In an instant, he went from bright red to pure white.

He leapt back and tried to slam the door shut but he was too slow. Scarlett was already stepping into his room. Before Devereau could slide back to get a better view of what was happening, she'd taken hold of the man, her hands clamping him in a steel grip. 'You'll regret it if you scream,' she murmured.

All the man could manage was a squeak. When Devereau swung his shaggy head into the room and the man saw him, a tell-tale wet patch appeared at his groin, followed almost immediately by the rancid smell of urine.

'Dear me,' Scarlett tutted. She pressed the man's body against hers and slowly ran the fingers of her right hand through his hair.

'Are you from downstairs?' he quaked.

She smiled. 'No.' She stroked the side of his neck. He shuddered. 'How many of you on this ship work for Matelot?'

His bottom lip quivered. 'Don't hurt me.'

Devereau growled.

'Twenty-seven!' he answered quickly. 'There's twenty-seven!'

'How many are armed?'

He shook his head, panic making it hard for him to form coherent thoughts. 'About half, I think.'

'You think?' Scarlett prodded softly.

'I know! About half! I'm not one of them! I'm just an engineer! I'm...'

Scarlett dropped her head. Her fang pierced his skin just enough to draw blood. The man whimpered.

'How many slaves?' she asked.

'S-slaves?'

'Vampires. Werewolves. People in cages. Supernatural beings who've been forcibly imprisoned. How many people are on this ship who are like me?'

'I don't know. I haven't been down there. I don't know!'

Devereau opened his jaws and stared at him.

'Guess,' Scarlett said.

His shoulders slumped. 'Thirteen,' he whispered.

She smiled again. 'Good boy.' She dropped her head again and her fang slid into his flesh. The man's body juddered. Within

———

seconds, his eyes rolled back and he went limp. She let him fall to the floor.

Scarlett reached for a tissue on a cupboard nearby and dabbed the corner of her mouth. 'We're going to have to come up with another technique,' she commented. 'If I drink from every damn Matelot fucker on board this ship, I'll spend the next three days throwing up. I've already had double the blood this month that I usually take.'

Devereau licked his lips.

'Fair enough,' she said. 'The next one is yours.'

They continued along the corridor. The sea was still rocking the ship from side to side, making it difficult to move quickly. At the far end there was a staircase that seemed to lead down to the hold.

Devereau and Scarlett were still several metres away when they heard the clatter of ascending footsteps. A head appeared at the top of the stairs, followed by a lanky body. Perhaps this was Daz. He wasn't paying much attention to his surroundings; he took several steps before he raised his head and finally noticed the gigantic werewolf and fanged vampire blocking his path. He froze and stared at them, then threw back his head and prepared to bellow.

Devereau launched himself forward, his front paws slamming into the sailor's chest and winding him so he couldn't shout for help. The man fell backwards and Devereau straddled his body before raising his head and smashing it into the man's forehead.

'Mmm,' Scarlett said. 'A Glasgow kiss from a London wolf. How very incongruous.' She grabbed the man's feet and dragged his unconscious body into the nearest cabin before shutting the door. 'We're not always going to be this lucky, you know,' she said seriously. 'They're not all going to come at us one by one – and sooner or later one of them will be armed. One loose shot and, storm or not, everyone on the ship will come running.'

Devereau blinked in agreement. From the vague sounds of tinny music and the odd raucous shout he could hear from below, the aforementioned poker game was probably taking place while the crew waited to leave the ship. That meant several of these bastards were grouped together in one area. The trouble was that neither he nor Scarlett knew the ship's layout or what might be waiting for them down the stairs.

He transformed, allowing his fur-covered wolf to become a smooth-skinned man. He straightened up while Scarlett looked him up and down, her eyes lingering on his groin.

'Don't,' he said, the hot glint in her expression more than he could cope with. She smiled slightly but at least she looked up and gazed at his face. 'I'm a big fan of chemistry,' he told her.

She winked. 'So am I. I love biology, too.'

'I'm not talking solely about sexual chemistry.'

Scarlett smirked. 'Go on.'

'Back in the beginnings of my … career, I toyed with the idea of breaking into houses at night time while the people inside were asleep. I was always worried that I might come across the odd insomniac or light sleeper. Or,' he grinned ruefully, 'dog. I looked into ways of getting around such problems.'

Scarlett raised an eyebrow.

'I didn't want to hurt anyone,' he said.

'But?'

'But,' he murmured, 'if you mix rubbing alcohol with bleach, and you're prepared to risk killing yourself in the process, you might be able to create chloroform.'

Scarlett's expression didn't alter. 'You are a scary, scary man, Devereau Webb.'

He shrugged. 'I didn't do it. The potential to cause lethal harm to myself and anyone I used it on put me off.'

She shook her head. 'I'm glad to hear it.'

'If we look around, I'm sure we can find some useful chemicals that might produce enough toxic fumes to serve our purpose.'

'I don't think an indiscriminate attack, which might kill us before it harms the fuckers we're trying to stop, is a good idea.'

He met her eyes. 'You're right.' He shrugged. 'So let's cut to the chase.' He grinned at her then raised his elbow and smashed it into the glass-covered fire alarm set into the wall beside him. Almost instantly, the loud wail of siren rent the air.

'So much for stealth, you fucker,' she muttered.

He gazed at her. 'I won't disagree with that moniker. I'm no saint,' he said. 'And, as I've already told you, I'm not much of a hero either. ' He turned to the staircase, closed his eyes and allowed the wolf inside him to take over once again. Then he waited until he saw the whites of the eyes of the first man to come up the stairs before he attacked.

The Matelot men were expecting fire; they certainly weren't expecting a massive werewolf. With the element of surprise on his side, not to mention a set of gorgeously sharp claws, powerful teeth and a body with more strength behind its muscles than even most supes could ever dream of, Devereau was a whirling dervish of fur and fear.

He smacked into the body of the first man, sending him flying backwards and causing three men behind him to topple as well. The next man reached into the holster at his hip preparing to pull out the gun that was nestled there, but this wasn't the Wild West and he wasn't quick enough on the draw. Before his fingers could curl around the handle, Devereau's teeth were sinking into his arm. The man screamed, clutching at his arm as blood sprayed from the wound.

There were shouts from below and the sound of running feet. More men appeared at the foot of the stairs but Devereau had the higher ground and therefore the advantage. He threw himself down, using the height of the stairs as a springboard to launch himself into the panicked group. From their reactions, not all these men were trained killers but he was in no doubt that they all knew exactly what Matelot was up to. And that meant he owed them no mercy.

The siren continued to scream. One man, with more ill-conceived bravery than others, roared and threw himself from the right-hand side while Devereau was occupied with the others on the left. He landed on Devereau's back, his hands clutching at his fur. A second later, Devereau felt the tip of a knife slide into his skin, but his lupine hide was tougher than the man had reckoned. Before he achieved any real damage, Devereau shook him off with such force that he slammed into the wall, his skull crunching against the hard surface. He slumped to the floor.

Devereau snarled, dipping his head and biting hard into the thigh of a terrified-looking man holding a fire extinguisher. He swung round and threw himself at another man who'd lifted up a chair but, because the guy couldn't decide whether to use the chair to attack or defend himself, Devereau had time to rip it from him with his teeth. The man tripped over his own feet and fell backwards onto a table strewn with coins, notes and playing cards.

Something hit Devereau's side. He couldn't tell what it was, but it was flung with considerable force and made him howl with pain. He turned towards the source and spotted Scarlett out of the corner of his eye. She was tripping down the stairs looking calm and unconcerned. She raised a hand towards him in acknowledgment and spun round to the next set of stairs that led further down into the ship.

A half-empty bottle of vodka smacked Devereau on the head and bounced off his thick skull. He leapt at the man who'd thrown it and cuffed him with one massive paw. It was enough: the man collapsed to the floor and his eyes rolled back.

There was a loud crack. Devereau turned his head just in time to see a dark-haired fellow pointing a gun in his direction. If you're going to shoot me, Devereau thought, you'd better make damned sure you hit me first time. The man fired again but Devereau was ready for the shot. He threw himself to the side as the bullet ripped through the edge of one of his ears. He clenched his jaw against the pain and attacked the gunman, his claws raking across his face. The man dropped the gun immediately. His hands automatically lifted to protect himself so Devereau bit down on them, instantly turning the squat fingers from dexterous instruments of biological wonder to little more than bloody minced meat. The man screamed before passing out.

Devereau moved to meet his next opponent. This time nobody came. He shook himself, his golden-tipped fur bristling as he surveyed the scene. Satisfaction settled deep in his chest.

A sweaty-looking bloke with terrified eyes made a run for the stairs and Devereau watched him escape. Let him run; he wouldn't be stupid enough to come back.

Devereau gazed at the bloodied mess around him and listened to groans of the fallen men who were conscious enough to be aware of their pain. Near his paw was a blood-smeared playing card. With an outstretched claw, he flipped it over. The ace of spades. He grinned. That figured.

A moment later, he turned and padded after Scarlett while the siren continued to bellow out its empty scream.

———

Chapter Twenty-Eight

It wasn't hard to locate her – all he had to do was follow the trail of bodies. There were several of them, some slumped with puncture wounds in their necks, others with bones broken at unnatural angles. Humans, Devereau decided, were very fragile indeed.

How little time it had taken for him to separate himself from his life as a human. For the first time he no longer felt any regret for the actions he'd taken to turn into a wolf. This was what he was meant to be all along. He padded deeper into the bowels of the rolling ship, grim, predatory satisfaction filling his core.

Scarlett was standing at the entrance to another narrow corridor, frowning into the large room beyond. She didn't turn when he approached. 'Wolves,' she muttered. 'Setting off the alarm was a dick move, Devereau. If Dominic Phillips escapes because he knows we're coming for him, the only person to blame will be you.'

Devereau had never spoken to Dominic Phillips but he had seen his turn on the slave-auction stage. He'd learned enough to know that Dom was the kind of man who thought he was invincible. Yes, he'd been trying to flee the dangers posed by the London's supes by coming to this ship and trying to sail away, but Devereau reckoned that Dom didn't really believe that anything untoward would happen. Dominic Phillips thought he was smart, powerful and in control of his own small army of supernatural beings; he wasn't going anywhere.

He lowered his head and nudged Scarlett's hand with his nose as if to say the same to her – and that was when he heard a tiny whine.

Scarlett registered the hackles rising on the back of Devereau's neck and nodded. 'They're in there. Vampires and werewolves. I can't tell how many yet, and I don't know what sort of state they're in.'

Devereau let out a low growl.

Scarlett sighed. 'Go on, then.'

He brushed past her. As soon as he stepped into the room, he saw the cages. They were small and cramped, offering the sort of conditions even an animal shouldn't have to deal with. The scents of blood and faeces combined with anguish and despair were so strong that he felt sick. Nobody should be made to live like this. *Nobody*.

Padding up to the first cage, he peered inside. A man sat huddled in the corner, the very picture of misery. Devereau couldn't see his face but he knew without asking that this was another wolf. The man looked up and Devereau's breath caught; it was Morty, the gunman he'd captured near Lisson Grove and whom he'd interrogated at the playing fields. So he'd found his way back to Dominic Phillips. Unfortunately, he'd been turned into a werewolf for his efforts. No doubt it was some sort of twisted punishment.

Devereau thought of the way Morty had spoken about Martina and his derision for all things supernatural. Perhaps this was poetic justice. Morty whined and dropped his gaze, more terrified of Devereau now than he had been before.

'Isn't that—?' Scarlett came up beside him and stared.

Devereau nodded and looked away. He moved onto the next cage where there was a young male vampire. Thankfully, his fangs appeared to be intact. After that there were two more werewolves, then several more vamps followed by more wolves.

Almost none of the caged supes seemed able to look directly at him. At least four of them were under the influence of heavy drugs and even more displayed evidence of torture. Devereau couldn't prevent the growls deep in his chest. These people had suffered. *All* these people had suffered.

The final cage puzzled him at first because the occupant appeared to be neither wolf nor vampire; he was simply a middle-aged human man wearing a grubby suit and with yellowing bruises on his face. The man groaned and shuddered, then he looked at Devereau. 'Are you here to kill me now?' he asked.

Devereau watched him for one long moment before allowing himself to transform so he could speak. He stood in front of the cage and gazed at the man's familiar face. 'You're Angelica's father,' he said quietly.

There was a sudden flash of stark fear. 'Where is she? Where's my daughter? If you've hurt her…'

Devereau clenched his jaw. 'You worked for Dominic Phillips and Matelot when you must have been aware of what they were doing.' He waved a hand around the room. 'Of *this*.' He glared at the man. 'Your actions led to your own daughter being turned into a wolf. And instead of helping her when she lost control, you ran away.'

The man's head dropped once more. 'I'm sorry. I've failed. I should have done better by her.'

Devereau rolled his eyes. Pathetic. 'Martina deserves better than you.'

Her father gave him a confused frown. 'Who's Martina?'

Devereau slammed his hand against the bars of the cage, making it rattle violently. 'You're her father. You're supposed to protect her!' Blood-red rage filled him. 'You … you…'

'Devereau.' Scarlett spoke quietly. He pulled himself back from the brink and looked at her. 'Not everyone is as strong as you. This isn't the time for recriminations. Let's find a way to open these cages then look for Phillips. We still need to find him and make sure he doesn't escape. He has to pay for what he's done.'

'Actually,' said a loud, chillingly familiar voice from the doorway, 'it is the two of you who need to pay.'

Scarlett and Devereau turned. Without his mask and tailored tuxedo, and without an adoring audience at his feet, Dominic Phillips looked very ordinary. His skin was healthy looking, with enough of an orange tinge to suggest fake tan, and his stubble was definitely of the designer variety, but his body was slight and his face wasn't memorable. Only his eyes gave him away as a sadistic bastard.

Devereau's gaze dropped. Phillips was holding something in his hand. It wasn't a weapon – Devereau wasn't sure what it was, but it worried him, however. Phillips' thumb stroked it possessively.

'You're Dominic Phillips.'

'And you're Devereau Webb. Look at you. Turned yourself into a werewolf and hit the big time. But it doesn't matter how many teeth you grow or how much fur you have, you'll always be a petty criminal.' Phillips gaze dropped and narrowed as he looked at Devereau's naked body. He held up his little finger and waggled it suggestively.

'Are you trying to say I have a small dick?' Devereau questioned. 'Because my fanged friend here seems to think I'm actually a very big dick.'

'I can't deny it,' Scarlett said, nodding. 'He is.'

Phillips looked at her. 'Who are you exactly?'

Scarlett looked at Devereau. 'I should tell him that I'm his worst nightmare.'

'Definitely,' he agreed. 'If I were you, that's what I'd say.'

'True.'

Dominic Phillips stared at them both. 'What are you? Some kind of bizarre comedy act?' He held up his hand. 'Wait. Don't answer that. I've had enough of you. You've done well to find me here, and you've done well to get this far and bring down so many of my men, but it stops here. You're one vampire and one werewolf. I've got thirteen.' He pointed to the cages. 'Never send a human to do a supe's work, right?'

'You can't compel them to do your dirty work,' Scarlett said, her emotion showing for the first time. 'It doesn't matter how they came about. They're supes. They're *us*.'

Phillips threw back his head and laughed. 'They'll do whatever I tell them. They're conditioned to follow my orders. Plus four of them need the drugs I give them and they'll do anything for those little pills. Anything. And those two,' he pointed at a wolf and a vampire who were caged next to each other, 'know that if they don't do as I say, I'll kill their families.'

Devereau looked at Phillips levelly. 'You can't do that if we kill you first.'

'I'd like to see you try.'

Devereau smiled nastily. 'That can be arranged.' He glanced at Scarlett. 'Can you compel him?'

She grimaced. 'It's doubtful. It only works on receptive minds and I'd have to be touching him.'

Oh well, they'd have to do this the hard way. Devereau shrugged and took a step in Phillips' direction. 'You're not going to get away with this. Any of this.'

Dominic Phillips raised his hand with the small object resting inside it. It was a remote control. 'Oh yes I will.' He pointed at them and declared loudly, 'Kill them. Kill them now.' Then he pressed a button on the remote.

The cage doors swung open simultaneously.

'Kill,' Phillips repeated.

Scarlett and Devereau exchanged looks. The caged vamps and werewolves were an unknown factor and neither of them were certain how they would react. Devereau braced himself for the worst but prepared for the best.

As the first werewolf transformed and nosed out of her cage, Devereau also changed. It helped that his wolf was twice the size of hers. He bared his teeth in a silent snarl as she approached. Her pupils flared and her ears flattened. Then a male werewolf stepped out and joined her. He took one look at Devereau and promptly lay down. The female followed his lead and presented her belly in total submission.

Whines could be heard from the other open cages. Devereau breathed out. Dominic Phillips might call himself the Master but he held no sway here, even amongst drugged and conditioned wolves.

'Vampires!' Phillips ordered imperiously. 'Out you come!'

Scarlett straightened her shoulders and raised her chin. 'You can do what he says,' she called confidently in a crystal-clear voice. 'Or you can help us bring him down. Either way, we won't blame you for your choices. With us, you are free.'

'Van Helsing!' Phillips roared. 'Attack her or your children's lives are forfeit.'

Devereau raised an eyebrow. He wasn't a particular fan of fiction but even he knew that Van Helsing was a vampire hunter and not a vampire. Dominic Phillips had clearly been confused when he'd christened the poor bugger.

A thin man with prominent cheekbones and glittering dark eyes came out of one of the cages. He stared at Devereau and Scarlett, then he swung his head and stared at Dominic Phillips.

'I will slit your wife's throat,' Phillips said to the vampire. 'She'll die slowly and in pain.' He stared at him menacingly. 'You are mine to command. Do not forget that.'

Scarlett didn't so much as blink. 'As long as you do what that prick tells you to, your wife will always be in danger. I am a London vampire. I answer to Lord Horvath. He is my Lord but he is not my master, and I have a thousand other vampires who will back me up. This is your chance to join us and break free of *him*.' She gestured derisively at Phillips then dropped her hands to her sides, her gaze still on the vamp. 'If you attack me, I will defend myself. But I am not your enemy and you know it.'

'Van Helsing!' Dominic Phillips snapped. 'Move! Lucifer, Kraken, Medusa! Back him up!'

More vampires emerged. A few of the werewolves growled, indicating that they would join the fight if need be and that they wouldn't be on Phillips' side. They needn't have bothered; each and every vamp simply stood silently. They looked at Scarlett with eerie synchronicity but not with aggression; they looked at her because they were waiting for orders.

A wolfish grin spread across Devereau's face. He licked his lips and faced Phillips. The bastard seemed more irritated than afraid, however.

'You fucking idiots,' he muttered. 'The amount of money I've invested…' He shook his head. 'So be it. You've made your bed, now lie in it.'

Devereau tensed. Hang on a minute. He stared at Phillips as he stepped back out of the room and into the corridor. He held up the remote control again and a chill descended through Devereau's bones.

He sprang forward and the other supes followed his lead, but Phillips was already closing the door. Devereau had just enough time to see his thumb press another button on the remote, then Phillips disappeared from view. The door slammed shut and there was a click as a lock slid into place.

Scarlett sighed. 'We're supes,' she said. 'That door isn't going to hold us for more than a minute or two. We'll break it down. Dominic Phillips won't get far.'

Devereau glanced at Morty and remembered what the gunman had told him on the dark, cold playing field. Contingency plans: Dominic Phillips always had contingency plans.

No sooner had the thought formed than Devereau heard a strange hiss and smelled an acrid scent. He looked up at the vents placed high on the walls and his heart sank as he saw puffs of yellow-tinged smoke appear from them. Apparently he wasn't the only one with a penchant for chemistry and a knowledge of poisonous chemicals.

Chapter Twenty-Nine

The vampire called Medusa reached the door first. She tugged on the handle; when it didn't budge, she started hammering on the steel. 'Hey!' she screamed. 'Hey! Let us out!'

Two of the werewolves threw themselves at it, knocking Medusa out of the way. The door heaved and strained at its hinges but remained closed.

Devereau growled once and they moved obediently to the side. He lunged forward, hitting the door side on. The metal bulged and one of the screws in the lower hinge popped out. Once more, he only needed to hit it once more.

As he backed up, ready to throw himself at it again, he realised that Lucifer and Van Helsing were on their knees, their fingers clawing at their throats. Scarlett was doubled over and the other werewolves looked disorientated.

He tensed. He could do this – he *had* to do this. He bunched up his muscles but, before he could fling himself at the door again, his hind legs gave way. Instead of slamming into the steel door, he found himself falling onto the tiled floor. Shit.

He pulled himself up again, blinking. Whatever that poison was, it was fast acting. His vision swam and he staggered as the ship rolled. The steady stance he'd been so proud of when they'd first boarded the ship had all but abandoned him.

'Help,' someone groaned behind him.

He dimly registered the voice as belonging to Martina's father. He didn't look round; there wasn't time. He had to get to the door. They were so close, so very, very close.

'Devereau,' Scarlett whispered. She fell to the floor with a thump. Everyone else was already down.

He held his breath and shook his head, trying to clear it for one last attempt. The door. Get to the… His legs gave way once again and his head bounced off the tiles.

This was not the ending he would have written for himself, he thought dully. Alice's face flickered in his mind and so did Martina's. He stretched out a paw and touched Scarlett's prone body with the tip of his claws. 'I'm sorry,' he croaked. 'I'm so sorry.'

There was a thud, followed by a loud metallic creak. So that was what death sounded like; he'd been expecting something more melodious. Trumpets perhaps, or at the very least a harp.

Something grabbed him, pulling at his body. He blinked. That hurt. He slid along the floor, jerking as he was yanked over the threshold and out of the poison-filled room. He gasped, his vision still blurry and his lungs burning, but he still caught the scent trail of his saviour. He had just enough energy left to feel disbelief. 'Martina?'

She didn't answer. She was already running back into the room and heading straight for the collapsed body of her father. Devereau pushed himself further back into the clearer air and allowed himself three huge gulps of it. Then he staggered up and transformed into his human body yet again. He needed his hands if he was going to help the others escape.

Martina reappeared, one arm covering her mouth, the other hooked round her father.

'Stay with him,' Devereau grunted, praying she'd listen to his order. Then he dived back inside and headed for Scarlett. She was stronger than the others, she'd recover more quickly and then she'd help with the rescue. But that wasn't why he helped her first.

Scooping her into his arms and feeling the poison burn into his lungs, he jogged out of the room. He gave himself only seconds to recover before he plunged back in to help the others. By the time he'd hauled out three of them, Scarlett had recovered enough to help him.

Martina tried to run back in but he growled at her. She fell back and returned to her father's side.

Devereau was finding it hard to recover from the poison's effects. Although the entire episode probably took less than ten minutes, to him it seemed like an age. Eventually, however, all fourteen of them made it out and stumbled away from the poisoned room with its desperate cages.

As they made their way to the staircase, the ship jerked and there was the sound of a distant rattle. Scarlett looked grimly at Devereau. 'He's raising the anchor,' she croaked. 'Phillips has decided to ignore the harbourmaster's orders and set off.'

Devereau straightened his spine. 'Whether he thinks he's succeeded in killing us or not, he's panicking.' He felt a surge of satisfaction. 'He's got less than half his crew left and that storm might be abating but it's still too rough to set sail. This time,' he said, promising himself as much as her, 'we're going to get him.'

Martina inserted herself between them, her arms folded and her expression set. 'I am coming.'

'No, you are not.' He glared at her. 'And what did you think you were doing coming here? How did you know we were here?'

She returned his glare with a level of derision that only an adolescent girl could master. 'I overheard you speaking on the phone. Besides, if I hadn't come you'd be dead. I saved you.'

'Yes, you did. We owe you our lives and I'll thank you later. After,' Devereau added, 'I make sure you're grounded for life.' He was about to say more but Scarlett was already ahead of him.

'Martina, we still need your help. Make sure that your father and these other people get off this ship before it tries to leave the port. You won't have long – minutes at best.' As she finished speaking, the ship rumbled. Its engines were warming, preparing to depart. 'It won't be easy,' Scarlett continued, 'but their lives are in your hands.'

Martina glanced at Devereau. 'She's right,' he said softly. 'Can you do it?'

The girl sniffed. 'Of course I can.'

'Then go,' he said urgently. 'Now.'

They watched as she took the lead, a tiny figure with her own band of vampires and werewolves trailing after her.

Devereau breathed out. 'That was a good call,' he said to Scarlett. 'It was probably the only way we could make her leave the boat and get to safety.'

A sad smile curved the corner of Scarlett's mouth as she gazed after Martina. 'She's a brave girl,' she murmured. 'She risked everything by coming here. The number of people who know about her existence just multiplied considerably.'

A tightness formed in Devereau's chest that had nothing to do with the effects of the poisoned gas. 'Come on,' he said. 'Let's find Dominic fucking Phillips and finish this.'

***

They returned the way they'd come, weaving through the blood-soaked rooms and up the first staircase. Rather than head out onto the main deck, however, they turned onto the first corridor. Phillips had to be at the helm, directing the ship as it left the wharf.

They lurched from side to side as the ship rolled with the violent wind. The man truly was mad. If this was what things were like here in the Thames, with the relative shelter of the wharf and the city of London around them, Devereau couldn't imagine how bad they would be in the open sea. Maybe Phillips was banking on the storm dying down by the time the ship left the Thames Estuary and headed into the North Sea. Or maybe the man simply had a death wish. If that were the case, Devereau was more than happy to help him with it.

Grabbing Scarlett's hand to keep their balance, they slipped and slid along the corridor. It opened into an empty bar area, which no doubt served the seamen. A door at the far end opened and a man appeared. When he caught sight of them, he stood stock still, his eyes wide and frozen and his legs trembling.

'Where's Phillips?' Devereau demanded.

The man raised a shaky finger beyond the door he'd just come out of.

'How long until we're away from the wharf?'

The seaman swallowed. 'Five minutes maybe.' His voice was barely audible. 'The tide is against us. And the wind … it's too dangerous. We might not make it.'

Scarlett took pity on him. 'You should leave now while you still can.'

All he could manage was a nod. Devereau grunted and pushed past him. A moment later he heard the man's pounding feet as he tried to run in the opposite direction. Not everyone on board this ship was a total idiot, then.

The next corridor was wider but that made it harder to traverse rather than easier. There was more room to be thrown around, and every time the ship jerked he and Scarlett staggered. He lost count of the times he smacked against the walls. Eventually he gave up and transformed into his werewolf body.

Scarlett curled her fingers tightly into his fur. 'Remind me,' she said, 'to get you a saddle for next time.' She managed a brief laugh although there wasn't much humour in it. The movement of the ship and lingering effects of the poison were affecting her badly. Devereau didn't feel much better; it was only sheer adrenalin that was keeping him going.

They heard Phillips long before they saw him. He was bellowing at some poor minion, exhorting him to do more to get the ship underway. 'Why? Why can't you fucking move this boat? What am I paying you for?'

'There's a gale-force wind blowing outside!'

'I don't fucking care. Get us out of here!'

Scarlett and Devereau moved quietly up a flight of stairs to the open door of the drive room. There were four people inside, including Dominic Phillips. The nearest man, who was only about twenty years old, glanced round and caught sight of Devereau. He turned white. 'Sir…'

'I told you!' Phillips snapped. 'I don't want to hear any more damned excuses about the weather! Just get the fucking boat…' His voice faltered when he realised what the others were staring at. 'You,' he said stupidly, staring at Devereau's massive werewolf body. 'How did you get out? How are you still alive?'

One of the men reached across and turned off the ship's engine. It juddered to a stop, although the ship itself continued to sway dangerously. 'He's all yours,' he said simply. 'Come on, boys.'

Devereau and Scarlett let them pass. They were far from innocent but, with the prize of Dominic Phillips so close at hand, Devereau was more than prepared to let them go.

'Come back here!' Phillips screeched. 'Come back here! You can't leave! I'll turn you into fucking vampires if you go! I'll hunt down your families! I'll…'

Scarlett tutted. 'It's time you stopped talking.'

Phillips turned his back, scrabbling around for something. When he faced them again, he was holding a gun but his hands were shaking. He finally seemed to have realised that the game was up. 'I'll give you money,' he said. 'You'll be rich. You can have the ship as well. Just tell me what you want and I'll give it to you.'

Scarlett tilted her head and smiled sweetly. 'All we want, Master Dom, is you.'

Phillips pulled the trigger. Even with a target as large as Devereau, the shot went wide. Dominic Phillips was far too used to getting others to do his dirty work. His pupils flared with undisguised terror and he spun round. He shot again, this time shattering the glass in the window to the right. Then he threw himself through it with a shriek, falling onto the rain-slick deck outside.

Scarlett and Devereau exchanged looks. A split second later, they followed.

Scarlett dived out, rolling as she landed before jumping to her feet. Devereau followed, his large body scraping against the shards of glass that clung to the window's frame. They drew blood but he barely registered the pain. A few scratches weren't important now.

Someone let off a flare at the other end of the boat. Its green glow shot up into the dark sky and lit up the area, then another joined it. The wind caught the ship yet again, this time causing it to crash against the stone wharf. There was a terrible crunching sound as metal ground against stone.

Someone, probably Martina and her band of supe followers, had dropped the gangplank but it was no match for the storm. It jerked and juddered and fought before eventually breaking free. Dominic

Phillips threw back his head and howled then he picked himself up and sprinted down the deck, only just managing to maintain his balance.

The predator inside Devereau Webb roared with delight as he sprang after Phillips, bounding towards him at lightning speed. He jumped at just the right moment. His front paws landed on Phillips' back and sent him sprawling at the very moment a fork of lightning joined the green flares and illuminated the deck.

Phillips twisted his body to face Devereau, the gun still clutched in his shaking hands. 'I won't miss this time!' he shouted.

Devereau dropped his head and sank his teeth into Dominic Phillips' throat. No, he thought, neither will I. Blood filled his mouth and he spat it away.

And then the light in Dominic Phillips' eyes faded away for good.

Chapter Thirty

It took Devereau and Scarlett some time to get off the ship safely. Even after they leapt from its heaving deck onto the wharf, *Monster* continued to slam itself against the stone wall in a strange act of naval self-flagellation. They watched it for a moment or two before turning away and stumbling towards the road which led out of Baron's Wharf.

Devereau knew from the flashing blue lights ahead that they wouldn't get away without another confrontation. Some idiot had caught wind that there was trouble and alerted the authorities – maybe it was one of the escaping sailors. Whatever, it wasn't unexpected given the commotion on the ship.

Devereau told himself he wasn't worried, despite the bloody scene behind him. He was a supe. He'd persuaded the police to let him go before and he could do it again. He was sure they'd want to keep the gruesome truth of *Monster*'s cargo quiet, and that would mean letting Devereau and Scarlett go without too many awkward questions.

When they rounded the corner and he saw who was waiting at the entrance to the wharf, however, his heart sank. 'Shit,' he muttered. 'Oh shit.'

Scarlett followed his gaze and her shoulders slumped. 'Keep a level head, Devereau,' she said in a low, resigned voice. 'It's the only way.'

There was a cluster of police officers with DS Owen Grace at the front. At his side stood Fred Hackert and Emma Bellamy, the latter looking incredibly pissed off. She stalked towards him and handed him a blanket which he wrapped gratefully round his body.

'Did you have a nice holiday?' Devereau asked, doing his best to act nonchalantly.

Bellamy stiffened and didn't answer. She didn't look as if she'd had a particularly restful time and there was certainly no evidence of a sun-kissed tan; quite the opposite, in fact. But despite her angry gaze, it wasn't her presence nor that of the boys in blue that worried Devereau. It was the tall, dark vampire Lord and the collection of stony-faced werewolves who truly concerned him. It didn't particularly help that Lady Sullivan was holding Martina's arm in a vice-like grip and the other escaped vamps and wolves were boxed in by glowering supes.

'Scarlett,' Horvath snapped, 'what the fuck is going on here?'

She blanched. For the first time since Devereau had known her, she actually looked nervous. Before she could answer, he cleared his throat and spoke up. 'This is on me,' he said. 'Scarlett was just making sure I didn't do anything too crazy.' He waved casually back towards *Monster*. 'But you don't have to worry, we've taken care of everything. You can all go home and rest.'

'That might be what you would *like* to happen,' sniffed Lady Sullivan, 'but that is most certainly not what is *going to* happen.' She didn't look at Martina but Devereau knew from the girl's sharp intake of breath that Sullivan had tightened her grip.

He took a step forward, his eyes narrowing. 'Careful.'

Lord McGuigan moved in front of Martina. 'Yes, Mr Webb,' he said icily. 'Be very careful indeed.'

Scarlett's toe nudged his, reminding him of her advice to maintain a level head. He inhaled a lungful of air and forced his shoulders to relax. 'The human who is responsible for all this is dead,' he said. 'You'll find his body on the ship.' He glanced at DS Grace. 'You can arrest me again for his murder, if you wish, but I suspect it won't go well if you do. Dominic Phillips got exactly what he deserved and every supe in this city will know it. Justice has been served to everyone's satisfaction.'

Grace swallowed and looked away. All the fight appeared to have gone out of him.

'We will investigate the scene at the boat, Mr Webb,' DC Bellamy said, speaking up instead of her superior. 'And we'll get to the bottom of what has happened here. However, I suspect from what I've seen and heard so far that there will be no further arrests.' She didn't look at DS Grace and he didn't argue.

Devereau nodded. 'Did you get them all?' he asked. 'Did you get all those bastards who'd bought themselves enslaved supes?'

Once again, it was Bellamy who answered. 'I believe the answer to that is yes.' The gathered supes nodded grudgingly. 'All the humans involved are in custody,' she continued. 'All the vampires and werewolves who were recovered are being taken to supe safe houses to be examined and cared for. We will ensure the same happens to this group that has come off the ship.' She looked at Devereau assessingly. 'You did well to uncover what was going on, Mr Webb, but you should have called for help far sooner.'

Horvath crossed his arms and his black eyes glittered dangerously. 'That's the understatement of the year.'

Devereau met the vampire Lord's eyes. He wasn't going to be

either apologetic or defensive. 'I had my reasons,' he said.

'As we discovered when we arrived here,' Lady Carr said pointedly. She didn't glance in Martina's direction; it was almost as if she were afraid to. 'I know you are not a stupid man, Mr Webb. And I know you remember what happened the last time you wanted a human child transformed into a werewolf.'

'It's not his fault!' Martina's father burst out with a surprising surge of bravery. 'He didn't do this to her! It's not my daughter's fault, either! She didn't ask for this. She didn't want to be a werewolf. That bastard Phillips … that bastard … that…' He choked, unable to finish his sentence.

Devereau saw genuine sympathy in the eyes of the watching supes, including the alpha werewolves and Lord Horvath. Rather than relaxing him, it worried him. 'If it wasn't for Martina,' he said quickly, 'we'd be dead and Dominic Phillips would have escaped.'

Lady Sullivan turned to Martina and gazed down at her. 'You did well, girl, and I'm truly sorry for what is going to happen next. But we cannot allow you to run loose. Things are hard for you now, and you're only just starting puberty. They will get harder as you get older. You won't be able to control yourself and, much as you might not want to, you will kill. Not because you're a bad person but because you can't help yourself. More innocent people will be hurt. We can't let that happen.'

DS Grace finally stirred. 'You can't harm her,' he said. 'It's not fair. None of this is her fault. She's just a child.'

Lord McGuigan gave him a long look. 'It's your law we're adhering to, detective.'

DC Bellamy was pale. 'There must be something we can do.'

Martina's father wrenched free from the vampires. 'You're talking about hurting her! You're talking about my daughter! I know she's a monster but…'

'You're not helping,' Devereau growled.

There was a loud cough from amid the small crowd. A moment later the small figure of Phileas Carmichael appeared, elbowing his way through swarthy werewolves who were three times his size. 'I have to agree, Mr Crystal. You are not helping your daughter's cause in the slightest.' He adjusted his tie. 'I, on the other hand, can offer more effective aid.'

Devereau didn't have the faintest idea how the gremlin lawyer had got here, but the fact that he was dressed in a suit suggested that he'd been waiting for this very opportunity. He was relishing the chance to have an audience hang off his every word.

Devereau was also aware that every single eye had turned hopefully to the gremlin. Nobody wanted to hurt Martina, not the clan alphas, not Lord Horvath, not the police or any of the watching supes. Nobody wanted to kill her, even if her very existence was illegal and she posed a genuine risk. Everyone wanted Phileas Carmichael Esquire to offer a way out.

Devereau glanced at Martina. She looked very pale and very small, as if she couldn't hurt a damned fly.

'I have spent considerable time scanning the law statutes since Mr Webb made me aware of Angelica Crystal's existence,' Carmichael said, indicating Martina with a wave of his hand.

'Martina,' she muttered. 'I want to be called Martina.'

Phileas smiled at her benignly and didn't lose his stride. 'As you wish.' He walked towards her, unafraid of what she was underneath her girlish exterior. He was even smaller than she was. 'It is true,' he said, 'that you should not exist. It is true that the law in its basic form requests that you be … put to sleep for the safety of the public at large. But,' he held up a single, quivering finger, 'there is a way for this not to happen.' He paused and smiled.

'Well?' Lady Sullivan snapped. 'Speak on, man!'

'If it can be proved that the adolescent in question will listen to a responsible adult, who will help her control her wolf and offer her the necessary space away from others during the nights surrounding the full moon, she may be permitted to live.'

Lord McGuigan spat on the ground. 'But when she turns she's not capable of listening to anyone else. That's the entire point.'

'Let's see, shall we?' Phileas turned on his heel and walked over to Martina's father. 'My apologies, Mr Crystal,' he said, then he reached and slapped him across the face.

There were several audible gasps from the crowd.

'Obviously,' Carmichael intoned, with the air of a professor giving a lecture, 'she often won't require any provocation. In this instance, and for these purposes, however…'

Martina snarled. She spun, her clothes bursting off as her werewolf emerged. Lady Sullivan tried to keep hold of her but quickly lost her grip. Within seconds Martina's quivering werewolf was in front of Carmichael, her teeth bared. The gremlin was about to become wolf food.

'Angelica!' her father cried. 'No!' His words fell on deaf ears.

'Back down, girl!' Lady Sullivan ordered. 'Martina Crystal, do as I say!'

Martina took a step closer to Carmichael.

McGuigan added his voice to Sullivan's and his attempt at compulsion reverberated through the night air. 'Halt, Angelica Crystal! Stop what you are doing, Martina Crystal!'

Martina didn't even twitch. Her yellow eyes narrowed and her muscles bunched as she prepared to lunge.

'You will not do this,' Lady Carr said. 'You will…'

Devereau lifted up his chin and interrupted. 'Martina,' he said, without raising his voice, 'stop this nonsense now.'

She dropped to the ground in an instant, her snarl transforming to a whine.

'Come here,' Devereau ordered.

Martina shuffled towards him, her head bowed. Everyone stared at him, their mouths wide open. From the corner of his eye, Devereau saw Cannon Carr nudging the werewolf next to him. 'Told you what he was like, didn't I?'

When Martina reached his feet, she stopped and her body sagged.

Phileas Carmichael withdrew a spotted handkerchief and dabbed his forehead. 'Well,' he said, 'I'm glad that worked.' His eyes met Devereau's. 'It's not just about power, you know. She had to know that she could trust you with her life. That's very rare.'

'I … I…' Her father still couldn't seem to finish a sentence properly. He dropped to the ground in a heap.

'She will be most dangerous around the full moon,' Carmichael said. 'She will need to remain with you for at least a week during that time. *Every* time. Otherwise she can be with her father. It is a large commitment on your part, Mr Webb.'

Devereau didn't take his eyes from Martina. 'That's fine.'

'And it's fortunate, of course,' the lawyer continued, 'that you have exclusive use of Regent's Park during the full moon. Martina can run around to her heart's content without fear of anyone getting hurt, be they werewolf, human or even gremlin.'

'You know what this means,' Lady Carr said in a whispered aside to Lady Sullivan. 'He really was bitten four times. He's more powerful than the rest of us put together.'

For once, Devereau decided to be gracious and not react to her words. Truthfully, he was more relieved than anything. He knew that Martina's wolf would not have listened to him if they hadn't gone through so much together. He'd had to prove his worth to her first.

'Well done,' Scarlett murmured in his ear.

'Carmichael took quite a risk,' Devereau said to her. 'He couldn't have known that Martina was going to be able to trust me.

Not unless…'

Scarlett smiled. 'I made more than one phone call earlier tonight. You're racking up those favours, Devereau Webb. At this rate, you're going to be in debt to me for months.' Her eyes danced, then she withdrew to speak to her Lord.

Devereau reached down and scooped up Martina, holding her furry body in his arms. 'Take her,' he said to her father. 'And for God's sake, man, look after her better than you did before. She needs you as well as me. She's not a monster, she's a brave little girl.'

The man nodded weakly. As Devereau passed her over, his eyes met those of the three clan alphas and he saw their grudging respect. He dipped his head in brief acknowledgment and turned away. Martina was safe and he'd made considerable inroads with the other supes. Today, at least, he'd call that a win.

Chapter Thirty-One

His street was quiet. There were no signs of any passers-by. His old Flock had obviously returned to their own corner of London, and the flotsam and jetsam collection of supes whom Scarlett had pressed into guarding the area had also departed. The weather during the previous night would have sent even the hardiest souls scurrying for cover, and the only scents now were the those of car fumes, blocked drains and the calm, fresh aftermath of the storm.

Devereau picked up several fallen wheelie bins, dragged them to the side of the road so they'd be out of the way of any passing traffic, and scooped up a few fallen roof tiles. He rubbed the back of his neck and sighed. It had taken longer than he'd wanted to extricate himself from Baron's Wharf. Martina had left with her father, although she would return to him in a few days for the full moon. Scarlett had left with Lord Horvath and the other vampires.

DC Bellamy had clearly wanted to question him more thoroughly but she seemed to have her hands full with DS Grace who, by the sounds of things, was trying to tell her that Supe Squad wasn't where he wanted to be. Shocker. Then a werewolf, purportedly from the Fairfax clan, had marched up to Devereau to tell him that he should join them. He knew that he couldn't do it; he couldn't take orders from someone else and pretend to be a loyal soldier. And he didn't know enough about werewolf customs to try and become the Fairfax alpha, even though the position was currently vacant. He wasn't ready and it wouldn't be fair.

Exhaustion hit him all at once and his body screamed with fatigue as he limped down to his house. The bullet holes were still in evidence but, strangely, there seemed to be a light on inside. He peered through one of the cracked windows and smiled when he saw Dr Yara inside making a large pot of tea. He was surprised at how glad the familiar sight of her made him feel, even if he knew she deserved far better than this.

He paused for a moment then, instead of walking to his front door, swivelled round and headed for his immediate neighbour. The lace curtains twitched as he approached so, rather than knock or ring the doorbell, he waited outside. His instinct was correct; after only a few moments, the door opened and the lined face of an elderly pixie peered out. At least he presumed she was a pixie because of her diminutive appearance and brightly coloured hair. He'd never met one before.

'Devereau Webb,' she said in a strong Cockney accent. 'Are you here to borrow a cup of sugar?'

'I'm already sweet enough.' He paused. 'Are you Millicent Thompson?'

She inclined her head, a pleasant smile on her lips. 'I am.'

'You hired Phileas Carmichael for me.'

Her eyes twinkled. 'I did. He's insufferable, of course. All lawyers are. But he's good at his job and, from what I hear, he served you well.'

'He did.' Devereau gazed at her. 'Why? Why did you do that?'

It was clear she'd been expecting the question but she took her time answering. 'We live in troubled times, Mr Webb, and the werewolves need a champion. I saw what you did with the girl – I watched it all from right here. You endangered your own already precarious life by helping her.'

'Some might call me naïve for doing that. Or a fool.' He raised his eyebrows. 'Some might say that by helping her, I was risking the lives of many others.'

'All those people would be right,' Millicent replied. 'But that doesn't mean what you did wasn't right. You're my neighbour now, Mr Webb, and that means it's my duty to look after you as you look after others. I didn't want you to think that you weren't welcome here. You are.' She smiled faintly. 'Though I'd prefer it if you kept the armed men and shoot-outs to a minimum in the future.'

Devereau said quietly, 'I'll do my best. Thank you for your help. If there's ever anything I can do in return, let me know.'

Millicent's gaze was steady. 'Actually, there is something.'

'Name it.'

'Listen to their proposal,' she said. 'Don't dismiss it out of hand until you've considered all the possibilities.'

He frowned. 'Huh?'

She started to close the door. 'Good day, Mr Webb.'

He stood on her doorstep, staring at her closed door. Well, that had been weird. He shrugged and walked the few steps to his house. A coffee first, he decided. Then food. Followed by a long, long sleep.

As soon as he stepped over the threshold, he knew that Dr Yara wasn't alone. He stiffened at the low murmur of voices coming from the dilapidated living room. He was sure it wasn't Rachel Foster who was in there with her. Devereau forced back his exhaustion. If this was someone looking for a confrontation he'd deal with them, no matter who they were. He stalked inside.

Because of the lack of furniture, Dr Yara was seated on a box facing a couple whose scent immediately indicated that they were human. On another box in front of her was the pot of tea she'd just brewed and three cups. There was even a plate of biscuits. Devereau's eyes narrowed.

The two humans were perched on rickety, uncomfortable, high-backed kitchen chairs. When Devereau entered, all three of them sprang up.

'Mr Webb!' Dr Yara beamed. 'You are back. I take Uber from Rachel's house after we find out Martina is okay. I hope is okay I come here. I want to stay.'

He managed a smile in her direction. 'And I want you to stay.' He looked at the two humans; something about them was disturbingly familiar. The man wore a smart blue suit and held himself stiffly. The woman had shiny brown hair tied back in a severe bun and her face was devoid of all but the most basic make-up. Oh yes. Now he remembered where he'd seen them before. They were the journos who'd been following him.

'I leave you to talk with your friends,' Dr Yara said. She smiled at him and went out of the room, taking care to close the door behind her.

The man stuck out his hand. 'It's good to meet you, Mr Webb,' he drawled in a Home Counties accent.

Devereau stared at his hand, making no move to take it. 'I don't talk to journalists.'

'We're not journalists,' the woman said. She had a strange, officious air.

Devereau's lip curled. 'My mistake. You must be police. I've seen you hanging around outside my old block and near here, too. You don't exactly blend in.'

The couple exchanged glances. 'We're not the police either,' the man told him. He withdrew his hand, realising that Devereau was not going to shake it.

'Frankly,' Devereau said, 'I don't care who you are. You're not welcome here.' He pointed to the door. 'Good day.'

They acted like they hadn't heard him. 'My name is Miles DeVant and this is my colleague, Sarah Greensmith,' the man said. 'And you are Devereau Edward Webb, born on the eighth of January 1989. Your parents are deceased but you have one older sister named Natasha, and a niece called Alice who recently recovered from leukaemia, much to the shock of her doctors who had predicted a very different outcome. You have been arrested on several occasions but never convicted of any crimes, although until recently you were the leader of a minor crime organisation named the Flock. Now you are a werewolf without a clan.'

Devereau remained unimpressed. 'Get the fuck out of my house.'

Sarah Greensmith, picked up the thread. 'You voted for the Green Party in the last election and made a sizeable donation to them. Other than a few minor broken bones sustained when you jumped out of a window of a house you were burgling when you were a teenager, and a couple of recent bullet wounds from more recent activities when you were attempting to halt a trafficking ring, you are fit and healthy and all your vaccinations are up to date.'

'What is this?' Devereau growled. 'Who are you people?'

'We are with MI5, Mr Webb.'

Devereau's eyes travelled from the man to the woman and back again. He gave a short, sharp laugh. 'You're spooks? Give me a break.'

'I can assure you it's true. Although we prefer the term intelligence agents.'

The spot between his shoulder blades suddenly spasmed. 'What do you want?'

'You,' the woman said simply. 'For some time now, we have been recruiting supernatural creatures into MI5. We find that they have resources and abilities that humans can't hope to match Unfortunately, despite our best efforts, we've not manage to sway any vampires or werewolves to our side. Both Lord Horvath and the clans make it too difficult for us. But you are not a vampire and you're not in a clan.'

Unbelievable. 'This,' Devereau said, 'is the biggest pile of horse shit I've ever heard – and that's assuming you are who you say you are. You want to make me a spy? My face has been plastered all over the news for weeks. I'm not exactly a low-key figure who can slide by without being noticed.'

'That's exactly what we want,' DeVant said without missing a beat. 'The world knows you're a criminal and a werewolf. You're the last person to work for Her Majesty's Government.'

'You're right,' Devereau shot back. 'I *am* the last person who'd do that. I'm a criminal, remember?'

'Not now you're not. Now you're an upstanding supe. You're also intelligent, empathetic and,' DeVane added, 'you care about your community. And your country.'

Greensmith agreed. 'I had my doubts about you, but your recent actions with Matelot have proved that you are more than capable.'

Devereau's eyes snapped to hers. They knew; they knew about Dominic Phillips and what he'd been up to. 'If you knew about Matelot and Phillips,' he growled, 'why didn't you act against them?'

'We were planning to,' she replied mildly. 'You beat us to it. And with considerable success, I might add.'

It was more likely that they'd seen what he was up to and decided to leave the dirty work for him so they could stay safe. 'I'm not going to work for MI5.' Devereau folded his arms. 'You should leave. Now.'

Miles DeVant smiled. 'We will ensure you are always present in London and free from all duties during every full moon so you can fulfil your lycanthropic obligations. We will not pursue action against Angelica Crystal or her father, and we will permit you to keep the full-moon rights for Regent's Park. We will pay you a decent salary and,' he said, as if it were the cherry on top of the cake, 'if you become a successful MI5 employee, we're prepared to undertake negotiations on the supes' behalf to alter some of the draconian laws that apply to your kind. In time, we might even help you set up your own London-based clan should you wish to do so.'

He reached into his pocket and drew out a business card. There was nothing on it other than a phone number. 'Think about it, Mr Webb. Your country could do with someone like you. And you could do with having us on your side.' He smiled in a perfunctory fashion and headed for the door. 'I'm sure I don't have to say this,' he added over his shoulder, 'but please don't tell anyone about this. We prefer to work anonymously.'

Sarah Greensmith offered a vague smile and they both left. Devereau stared after them. The entire encounter had been stunningly brief and outrageously bizarre. Had it really happened?

He was still standing in the living room, the card in his hand, when there was a knock at the front door. Devereau walked out and opened it, half expecting to see the crazy couple again. Instead it was Scarlett, her head tilted to one side and her lips parted.

She flashed him a slow, sensuous smile. 'I thought it was about time we finally finished what we started. You can start paying me back some of those favours you owe me.'

Delight flickered in the pit of his belly as he stood back and gestured for her to enter.

'Who were the humans?' she asked.

'Pardon?'

'I saw two humans walk out of here as I arrived.'

Devereau slid Miles DeVant's card into his pocket. 'Jehovah's Witnesses,' he lied. 'Dr Yara let them in.' He reached for her, one arm curling round her waist. 'I sent them off with a flea in their ear.'

She smiled up at him then her hand dropped and brushed against his groin. He stiffened and Scarlett's smile widened. 'Good,' she whispered. 'Because I want you to myself for the rest of today. Maybe even the rest of this week. That's a whole lot more commitment than I usually make.'

Devereau gave her a long hard kiss. 'Then what are we waiting for?'

Helen Harper

About the author

After teaching English literature in the UK, Japan and Malaysia, Helen Harper left behind the world of education following the worldwide success of her Blood Destiny series of books. She is a professional member of the Alliance of Independent Authors and writes full time, thanking her lucky stars every day that's she lucky enough to do so!

Helen has always been a book lover, devouring science fiction and fantasy tales when she was a child growing up in Scotland.

She currently lives in Devon in the UK with far too many cats – not to mention the dragons, fairies, demons, wizards and vampires that seem to keep appearing from nowhere.